Praise for

THE MOUNTAINTOP SCHOOL FOR DOGS
AND OTHER SECOND CHANCES

"What Ellen Cooney captures so brilliantly here is the psychological and emotional similarities between dogs and people—the way both respond to trauma and pain, and the way love and kindness can heal even the deepest wounds. *The Mountaintop School for Dogs* is a celebration of the bond that has brought canines and humans together for thousands of years. This book will grab your heart and not let go."

— John Grogan, author of *Marley and Me: Life and Love with the World's Worst Dog*

"Is there such a thing as a Rescue Book? Well, there is now. This is a miracle of a book. It's even a spiritual handbook. And it is for readers young and old and all of the in-between. Cooney is such a wise genius of a writer, and her sentences keep surprising you, but are never the point in themselves. I read with a kind of mental breathlessness. If Cooney needs someone to convince her to write a sequel, I volunteer."

— Gail Godwin, author of *Evensong* and *Unfinished Desires*

"Dogs were bred by us to serve us in practical ways, but then dogs took it on themselves to serve us most profoundly by healing our broken hearts. Ellen Cooney understands this, and is the kind of keenly observational writer who can detail the path to healing only dogs can provide. A delightful read for all of us who can't imagine life without dogs."

— W. Bruce Cameron, author of *A Dog's Purpose* and *A Dog's Journey*

"The real genius of this story is in all the things it doesn't tell you, all the things it assumes you already know—and turns out, you do!—which leaves much more space to be taken up by what really matters: the marvelous canines. Any dog lover—any person lover—will be moved (nearly to the point of slobbering) by this warm, funny, heart-expanding book."

— Pam Houston, author of *Sight Hound* and *Contents May Have Shifted*

"A young woman who knows she's lost, and an older one who doesn't think she is, meet a slew of castaway dogs at a snowy mountaintop sanctuary, and discover what they didn't even know they were looking for. A charming novel about overcoming the past and finding meaning and purpose in the present."

— Susan Richards, author of *Chosen by a Horse*

"A jubilant, wise celebration of love, reciprocal between human and canine, in ways profound, moving, and soul saving. Readers will long remember the central humans in this tale—Evie, Mrs. Auberchon, and Giant George—along with the exquisitely drawn cast of rescued dogs who, in their own delightful, mysterious, and silent ways, heal their rescuers' wounds. Ellen Cooney has written a funny, joyous, and heart-rending book that insists intelligence and kindness must win out over ignorance and cruelty. Exploring the human and canine hearts with equal doses of wisdom and wit, *Mountaintop* is surely a book to be read and reread, preferably with your dog nestled by your side."

— Connie May Fowler, author of *Remembering Blue*

"What if James Herriot had written *The Shining*, but starring Bridget Jones? These pages are that much fun, and that harrowing, and that sweetly tender. Dog by dog by dog by Evie—the star-crossed protagonist, practically a stray herself—we come to understand that we're all a little bit unadoptable, a little bit mis-used, and ready for sure for some loving kindness, the kind that surpasseth understanding, and that only a dog can give."

— Bill Roorbach, author of Life Among Giants
and Writing Life Stories

"Cooney's writing style is lively, inventive, and fun."

— Columbus Dispatch

"From the first pages, the tone is warm and welcoming, drawing you in easily . . . If you've ever loved a dog, this book is a must-read. It's a delightful story with layers of meaning that at times may make you cry, both tears of sadness for the abused animals (and people) and also for the happy endings." — Missourian

"Sure to captivate the reader . . . A charming novel about dam-aged souls looking for a forever home." — Shelf Awareness

"Cooney's writing style is completely her own, lively, inventive, and fun to read. Do not miss this remarkable novel." — Indie Next

"A joyful romp and a thoughtful meditation. The author's deli-cate touch with the pain and trauma endured by abused animals and her sensitive portrayal of dedicated rescuers send a powerful message. Love is a great teacher and we are all a little unadopt-able. Readers of Garth Stein and Carolyn Parkhurst will adore this title." — Library Journal

"Dog lovers rejoice! Cooney has crafted an uncomplicated, feel-good, canine-filled tale of cross-generational friendship, healing, and solidarity." — Publishers Weekly

Also by Ellen Cooney

Small-Town Girl

All the Way Home

The Old Ballerina

The White Palazzo

Gun Ball Hill

A Private Hotel for Gentle Ladies

Lambrusco

Thanksgiving

THE MOUNTAINTOP
SCHOOL FOR DOGS

AND OTHER SECOND CHANCES

Ellen Cooney

MARINER BOOKS

HOUGHTON MIFFLIN HARCOURT

BOSTON ■ NEW YORK

First Mariner Books edition 2015

Copyright © 2014 by Ellen Cooney

For information about permission to reproduce selections from this book, write to Permissions, Houghton Mifflin Harcourt Publishing Company, 215 Park Avenue South, New York, New York 10003.

www.hmhco.com

Library of Congress Cataloging-in-Publication Data
Cooney, Ellen.
The Mountaintop School for Dogs and other second chances /
Ellen Cooney.
pages cm
ISBN 978-0-544-23615-8 (hardcover) — ISBN 978-0-544-48393-4 (pbk.)
I. Title.
PS3553.O5788M78 2014
813'.54 — dc23
2014011211

Book design by Chrissy Kurpeski
Typeset in Minion

Printed in the United States of America
DOC 10 9 8 7 6 5 4 3 2 1

To Joy Harris

THE MOUNTAINTOP SCHOOL FOR DOGS
AND OTHER SECOND CHANCES

One

IT WAS DUSK on a winter day, and from high on the mountain came barking, drifting down above the snow like peals of a bell, one, two, three, four, more, just to say the light was leaving, but that was all right: here I am, I'm a dog, all is well.

At the inn on the flat of the lowland, Mrs. Auberchon made her way upstairs, grumbling to herself. But she paused out of habit to listen. She was a large-frame woman of fifty, with the outer crust of anyone who used to be tender. Her name was Lucille, but no one used it. She was Mrs. Auberchon only: dependable, competent, solitary Mrs. Auberchon, always there, always far away, even if you were standing right in front of her.

Her arms were stacked with bed linens, towels, a six-pack of plastic water bottles, a new bar of soap. The Sanctuary had called only half an hour ago saying that a new trainee was on the way. Usually they gave her plenty of notice. She'd been up to her neck in visitors all week, and she had only just finished cleaning up from them. What she needed was peace, not more chores.

Strangely, they hadn't sent her the application form, or filled her in on any background. She only knew the gender, female, and the age, twenty-four. That wasn't fair. They were busy on the mountain, but they didn't have to treat her like an afterthought, not that she'd say so and be a complainer. It wasn't as if applications were pouring in.

She was liking what she heard. At this time of day the barking up there was usually worried, or even panicked, as in, *oh no, here comes the dark, hurry up, take me in, take me in.* Or it was rough, demanding, obnoxious, only about dinnertime and *hey, don't you know it's time to feed me, feed me, feed me?*

She couldn't tell which dog was barking up there, but the voice was calm, deep, confident. Then came a fade-off and echoes, scattered toward the inn like invisible falling stars. This was maybe a very good sign. Maybe, Mrs. Auberchon was thinking, the new one, female, twenty-four, whoever she was, wherever she came from, wouldn't give her any trouble. That was the most she could hope for: no trouble.

Two

WOULD YOU LIKE TO BECOME A DOG   ?

I clicked on the ad. There was nothing fancy or stand-out grabby about it. It was just a little box of black words, small as a whisper, lost and alone on a sleek professional site. Even without the mistake, I saw that it was a misfit, like in the picture game for children: "Which thing doesn't belong here?"

Somewhere, a human being had made a mistake with an ad. That's what caught my attention: a blank that shouldn't be there. I'd been looking at pages about jobs and careers for I didn't know how many hours — maybe a hundred, maybe more. I didn't even know what I was trying to find. I was getting the feeling that all I'd have for a career was sitting around trying to get one, like my future would be over before I had it. Then suddenly I felt that I stood in the doorway of a crowded, noisy room, picking up the sound of a whisper no one else seemed to hear.

I never had a pet of any kind. I never knew a dog well enough to be friends with. But I couldn't look away from that box. What was the empty space for? Groomer? Breeder? Technician, like in a vet's office?

It was trainer. Trainer! I had never in my life trained anyone or anything, not even a plant. I tried it out. "Hi, I'm Evie. I'm becoming a trainer." Something was so physical about it, so real. A smile. "No, not that kind of trainer. Not like what you do in a gym."

And that was how it started.

Three

It was late when I arrived. The village was deep in snow. The mountain was hidden in misty darkness, without a glimmer of light to show that the Sanctuary was there. But I knew from their website what it was like: a sprawling, rugged, stone and wood lodge built a hundred years ago as a ski resort. In one small photo, my favorite, a flagpole in the front yard had a dark square banner bearing the Sanctuary's logo: an outline in white of a lightly spotted dog. The drawing was roughly done, and the dog was tilted upward, head high, front paw lifted, like he was walking around in just air.

The inn at the foot of the mountain was beaming out lights. It had the frame of a chalet, two stories high and dark brown wooden. Stacks of firewood ran along the front, and to the side I saw a chainlink enclosure, icy and brushed with snow, about five feet high. The space inside was large enough for a toddlers' playground—that's what I thought it was.

I went inside. Welcoming me was a wood stove, huge and black, churning out heat I could almost see in waves.

"Hi. I'm a new trainee in the dog-training school," I said at the lobby desk. "I start up there tomorrow."

The first thing I had to do was find out the schedule for getting to the top. I'd read about the old gondola, still running after all these years, although no one had skied here for ages. I was excited about the ride, being up in the air. For the last ten hours I'd been stuck on things that kept moving too slowly: a taxi in city traffic, an Amtrak that was not an express, a bus to the village, another bus to the end of the lane where the inn was, then my own two feet making sinkholes in deep, thick snow, which felt heavier than it was, because my backpack, brand-new, an enormous one, a real trekker's, was driving me crazy.

It felt light when I put it on my shoulders that morning. I'd sent most of my clothes ahead, care of the Sanctuary, so I'd have room for all my new books, which I needed to keep secret. They were paperbacks, but still, I had to drag the pack the last few yards in the lane, drag it up the steps of the inn, drag it inside, trailing snow. Now it was sitting at my feet, maybe as a dog would, silent and well behaved, indifferent to the snow that was melting and sliding off onto an old, worn carpet. Absurdly, I'd imagined some service. Getting off the bus, I had worried that my hands would be too stiff with cold to finger out a tip for whoever relieved me of that weight.

"There hasn't been a gondola for years. It collapsed. They'll come get you."

"But on the web—"

The sleepy desk clerk interrupted me with a tight little shake of her head. She was a solid-looking woman of late middle age, as pale as if she hadn't been outdoors her whole life. But she seemed to be sturdy and fit, and I had the impression she was stern with all arrivers, and even sterner with herself. Her thick hair was exactly the color of broom straw, with a mix of gray. She wore it pulled back very tightly, and her broad face had a pinch to it, like the knot at the back of her neck caused her pain, but she didn't plan to do anything about it. No one else was in the lobby. The silence all around was another kind of foggy darkness.

"Your room," said the clerk, "is at the top of the stairs."

She wasn't presenting a key, and she shook her head again when I asked for one. "Lock yourself in, if you want to. But it won't be necessary. You're the only one I've got."

She looked at me as if to let me know we'd come to the end of what we needed to say to each other.

I said, "Which room is mine?"

"You'll see it."

"Okay," I said. "I'd like a wake-up call. What time—"

"When they're coming for you, you'll hear them."

"Like with a snowmobile, do you mean?"

"You'll know it when you hear it," the woman said.

"Well, good night then."

This went unacknowledged. I lugged the pack up a narrow flight of steps that led to an open door, and entered a vestibule for outdoor things, where the shelves, wall hooks, and rubber floor mats were empty. Then I felt like Goldilocks, except that the bedroom I stepped into had eight beds, four on each side. They were single futons on top of pine chests of drawers. Each had an overhead wall shelf and a footlocker-type storage box made of pine boards, unpainted, about the size of half a coffin. For light there were no lamps, just ceiling globes. Everything was extremely clean, even the heat vents. No pictures on the walls. No curtains on the windows, just wooden shutters, closed. The floor was pine too, but smooth as a bowling alley, newly oiled.

They made you sleep on a bureau in a bunkroom?

Only one bed was made, in the corner near the doorway. The dark quilt that covered it was goose-feather thick. I cheered up at the thought of my books and emptied my pack. All the titles or subtitles contained the word *training*, along with some form of *dog*.

I'd planned to look at a few of them on my trip, but they were wedged at the bottom. I'd made the mistake of packing them first. But I'd kept out, in my shoulder bag, a handbook on groups and breeds, which I then forgot on the train. I wasn't mad at myself. I'm good with memorization. I'd done a great job of filling my head with types, descriptions, images.

I was too tired for bedtime reading. I found my phone and sat still, looking at it. I'd been out of contact all day. At first I had switched myself off because I was too nervous about traveling; then I'd started to like being all alone, moving through the world.

Sleep was coming at me as naturally as dusk or an incoming tide. I had the sense, in this moment, of all things, strange as it was, I actually felt happy. Report: oh my God, I might really be all right.

Should I call someone? Who would be glad to hear this news, just be glad? An invisible owl was starting to hoot in my ears, who, who, who? I knew I had to contact the world I'd left behind, but all I could manage was a general text. *Got here fine. Here goes the rest of my life, and I'm completely sure it's the best decision I ever made, even though I'm the only one who thinks so!*

I stayed calm. I reminded myself that I had wanted *to be new.* I reminded myself that I was supposed to be learning to be out in the world on my own like a grown-up, as if I'd just hatched out of a big, gooey egg.

As soon as I was under the quilt, I imagined myself back on the train, reading the breed book. To sort the information, I had started with sizes, working up from Chihuahua. I loved what it was like to drift along through this world of new words, my head full of details and dogs, dogs, dogs.

Chihuahua, pug, dachshund, poodle, beagle, schnauzer, collie, shepherd, mastiff.

Boxer, pointer, retriever, setter.

Black and tan, bluetick, redbone.

Clumber, cocker, pinscher, Plott, whippet.

Chow chow, shar-pei, shih tzu.

Jack Russell, King Charles, Parson Russell, St. Bernard.

Short hair, long, straight, curly, hairless. Ears that were floppy, ears sticking up in triangles, ears like a ball of fluff, a circle that was almost round, a flap on a very small envelope. Back-leg fur feathers, manes, whiskers, beards, webbed paws or not. Stumpy tails, curlicues, bushy pompoms, ropey whips. Gray coats, brindle, brown, black, white, yellow, tawny, bronze, rusty, spotted, striped, blotchy.

Bulldog, cattle dog, elkhound, foxhound, otter hound, rat terrier, sheepdog, wolfhound.

Afghan, Australian, Belgian, Black Russian, Boston, English, French, German, Greater Swiss, Irish, Norwegian, Portuguese, Rhodesian, Scottish, Tibetan, Welsh.

I had sorted them by the elements too, as in earth, water, air, fire: field dogs, swimming dogs, dogs that run like wind, dogs with bright eyes like sparks from a flame, and I was telling myself, in my last thought of that day, I had done my homework and I was *ready*.

Seven hours later, I woke sharply, cleanly, and instantly alert, to the sound of dogs on the mountain. They were racing toward the inn with a racket that split the air, the morning, the world, louder than thunder because it sounded so alive.

Four

COMPLETE HETEROCHROMIA, the condition of different irises, is common in sled dogs: one blue and one amber. Some people find it fascinating, not disturbing. But the breed book didn't say the colors would be icily cold when you saw them for real. It didn't say the eyes would be part of the faces of teethy, screaming animals as strong and wild as wolves.

Out back of the inn, every bark, yelp, and howl left echoes that bit the air, as if the echoes had teeth of their own. No, not teeth. They were fangs. Even in the safety of looking down from the window at those dogs, in harnesses that could snap any moment and release them, I was having some trouble containing myself.

I could not go near those dogs. I could not ride up on that sled they were attached to. It looked lighter than a basket.

By now I'd seen the mountain in daylight. It wasn't steep as much as it was vertical. Wind was blowing high up, and in the clouds of swirling snow, I couldn't make out what the height was. It seemed to keep going and going. I had never been anywhere before so full of outdoors, with no buildings, no cars, no anything human at all. Maybe that was helping me feel even more terrified. But I wished that somewhere in my past I'd been traumatized by dogs, so I could blame my escape on a memory, like I was having a flashback.

I washed up quickly in the small bathroom. I saw that I had fooled myself the night before when I thought I was happy. I was supposed to have learned to stop fooling myself.

Loading my pack, I wondered about the bus schedule back to the village, back to the train. I decided to make my way to the main road and flag down a bus while walking briskly, so I didn't die of hypothermia. That was my only plan.

Soon I was quietly descending the stairs, seeing no one. My stay at the inn was part of my Sanctuary tuition, prepaid, so I didn't need to check out, and I didn't want to tangle with that clerk. I stepped outside into a dazzle of whiteness and sun. No dogs had broken free to come lunging around to the front. The barking had stopped.

But a different noise was on the way. I had just set my feet on the ground when a vehicle appeared. It was a Jeep, a Cherokee, thrashing toward the inn through the snow, honking, blowing out exhaust from a broken muffler loud enough to be gunshot.

The thing was souped up on studded tires and fitted with a bar on the grille in the shape of a frown, plus extra, raised headlights, like a second pair of eyes on a clunky, four-footed cyborg. It came to a stop sideways, right by me. On the door was the Sanctuary's name and logo, and I realized, seeing it closely, in actual life, that the picture of the dog, at its airy, sky-walking tilt, was like a drawing on a star chart. It was Canis Major. What I'd thought were spots on its body were *stars*.

At the wheel was a figure wearing sunglasses and a jacket of forest green, like a park ranger's.

The Jeep was in idle, engine throbbing, muffler rumbling in many little explosions. The window on the driver's side was rolled down. There was no way to tell if the driver was a man or a woman, not even when I was greeted by name.

I shouted, "Will you take me to the train?"

"I know you're here to train! We thought you were coming last night!"

"I'm leaving! Leaving!"

"What?"

I started for the passenger's side, but the driver stopped me with a look.

"I came down for the sled puppies! They're too young to go back on their own!"

Puppies? Those animals were *puppies?*

At last the engine was turned off. The driver was a chubby, pink-cheeked boy who looked about twelve. Yet he worked for the Sanctuary. Obviously he could drive. Taking off his sunglasses, he revealed pale, friendly eyes.

"Welcome to the mountain," he said.

"But I'm not on it."

"Welcome anyway. It's great you're in time for breakfast. You look hungry."

I asked him, "How old are you?"

That was when the desk clerk from last night stuck her head out the inn door and yelled two sentences before slamming it shut. She was addressing the driver.

"They're starting her right off! Tell her to get in here and get ready!"

"Uh-oh," said the driver. "I guess they changed the plan. Sorry about this. Mrs. Auberchon will show you where to go. She's the manager."

"Oh, the manager. I guess I'd better meet her."

"You just did. That was her. Listen, you have to hide, but don't be nervous. Just follow instructions and you'll be perfect."

It was cold. My teeth were starting to rattle. I was getting the feeling I should do as I was told.

"The dog who'll try to find you might qualify for SAR," the

driver said. "So we need to practice with a stranger. You have to hide like you're in a building that's on fire, or was bombed, or you were in a plane wreck. You have to pretend you're unconscious."

He gave me a grin, a big one. "By the way," he said, "I'm old enough to figure out you saw those sledders, or at least you heard them, and you didn't get it they're still just pretty much babies. But don't worry. I'm not going to tell on you."

In my application to the Sanctuary, I had sort of suggested I was someone who had actual experience with actual dogs. But still. I'm not going to tell on you? He sounded *four*.

"Get a new muffler!" I cried.

On my way back inside, I thought again of breed names, reciting them as if I'd put them in my head like a drug that's good for you: something to calm you down in moments of trouble.

Airedale, basenji, corgi. Doberman. Entlebucher mountain. Finnish spitz. Glen of Imaal. Havanese. Ibizan. Japanese Chin. Komondor. Lhasa apso. Malamute.

Then I thought of dogs I knew of who are not in the actual world. Lassie, I thought. Sandy in *Annie*. Kep, Pickles, Duchess, and John Joiner of Beatrix Potter. The nanny in *Peter Pan*. Toto. Buck in *The Call of the Wild*. Flush, the dog of Elizabeth Barrett Browning and Virginia Woolf. Crab, the only dog in Shakespeare. Cafall, the dog of King Arthur. Argos, the dog of Odysseus.

And there came back to me the odd contentment I felt when I first looked at the Sanctuary website. I hadn't cared that it looked old and gave few details. I'd read the simple, short description of the training program with the sense that it was saying to me, personally, somehow, *you want to be here*. It hadn't occurred to me to think it strange that there weren't any photos of people, or information about who my teachers would be, or how the program actually worked. I had stared a long time at the photos of the lodge, the evergreens encircling it in a half-moon, the ceiling of mountaintop sky — and then of course the dogs, lots of them, happy, healthy, and friendly, and completely ready to play their parts as perfect students to new trainees. I only now thought to wonder where Sanctuary dogs came from.

I reentered the inn. In my head was the picture of myself I'd imagined, starting with the videos I watched for a whole afternoon of the Westminster Dog Show, the handlers skipping solemnly around the ring holding leashes, the animals gorgeous, flowing in prances, in trots, radiant with well-being, like they were saying, look at me, look at me, look at *me*.

I'd turned on the TV a few times to see *Animal Planet*, but I never timed it when a dog show was on; anyway, there were too many commercials. So I went to YouTube. I watched a few videos from animal shelters and rescue societies, but I didn't give them much attention. They didn't apply to the type of dogs I planned to train.

In a daydreamy way, I had pictured my dogs peering out windows, catching sight of me as I drew near — *the one human in all the world who understands me,* their eyes would be saying, while their owners were somewhere behind them, at the end of their ropes because their dog was mouthy, was obsessive-compulsive, was peeing on carpets, getting into the garbage, shredding upholstery, putting holes in the walls, destroying running shoes, wallets, vacuum cleaner attachments, pot roasts, heirloom Christmas ornaments, everything. And here I would come to save them, competent, confident, maybe carrying some type of satchel like Mary Poppins. Should I call my dogs clients? Or is the client the one who'd be paying my bill?

What I liked best were the videos of military people coming home to their dogs from a war, always taking the dog by surprise, because you can't sit down with an animal and describe an event that hasn't happened yet, which was something I'd never thought about before. I didn't know anyone military, but I wished I did, and that the person had a dog. I would have called to talk about homecomings.

Sometimes when dogs greeted a returning soldier, they'd go over the edge. They would have to take a few moments to run crazily in circles around the human, or around a room or a yard. I'd have to take a break from watching, so my brain had a chance to absorb what I was seeing: that there is such a thing as joy being bigger than the container that holds it.

Maybe I shouldn't think of this as a career. Maybe I should say it's a *calling*.

Back in the lobby, I had to deal with Mrs. Auberchon. She said nothing but motioned for me to leave my shoulder bag and pack by the desk. She pointed the way to a short hallway, where a closet door was ajar. It was a walk-in: shelves full of towels, linens, toilet paper, paper towels. There was plenty of room for me to settle down on the floor in a crouch, sitting back on my heels, my head low. In the dimness, my hearing became acute. So many moments ticked by, I lost count, and I began to feel nothing would happen. Then the waiting suddenly ended. Was that really a dog, that sniffling, that panting, that snorting?

Search-and-rescue dogs *are generally drawn from breeds of a strong work ethic, a high level of trainability, and a high potential for satisfaction and pride at accomplishing a complex, often dangerous task in which the reward is a job well done. German shepherds and Golden retrievers are particular stars of this profession.*

I imagined Rin Tin Tin. I imagined the love-eyed silky goldens in the catalogs from L. L. Bean I'd looked at for new outfits. "Hello and well done!" That's what I thought I'd be saying very soon, while stroking a short-hair, or losing my hands in long, soft fur.

Then I met Shadow.

There were yowly little yips, a paw, a drooly muzzle. It was strange, like meeting an alien. A close, damp, chilly nose was sniffing me, and the paw was pushed into my back. I felt the press of an animal's weight, not too much, not slight.

And then . . . urine. Maybe he was too young and inexperienced to know it's not a good idea to pee on the person you just found? Maybe he was over-excited? Whatever the reason, it happened that the first thing I did with a Sanctuary dog was to let out a yelp of my own.

"Fuck off me!"

The second thing was a threat and also a promise.

"Pee on me again and you will *die*."

He didn't look like he was sorry before he ran away: Shadow, a breed of his own, a puzzle put together with pieces of many different ones that somehow fit together. He was beagle-ish, like a Snoopy mutation, but also basset. There were coonhound or tree hound legs too long for his body, and soft, small envelope flaps for ears. He had the droopy eyes of a bloodhound, a long, dark, skinny tail, and narrow feet like a goat's. His thin body was speckled and spotted: a little white, a little tan, a little black, lots of brown.

Was I supposed to look on the bright side and be glad he only peed on my hand? He'd probably hoped for more. He was probably too stupid to aim.

Mrs. Auberchon must have let him out, but she was nowhere to be seen. The inn was silent. There was only the sound of the Jeep in the distance, driving up, away, sending out its little explosions.

I ran upstairs to wash and found a sheet of paper on the top step. It had someone's careful writing on it, blue, in old-fashioned penmanship. The sheet was standard printer paper, but the writing was so neat it looked like it was done on lined notebook paper.

Shadow. Male. Hound Mix. Age between five and six. Vaccines administered. Heartworm treated. Coat near normal following extensive care. Forty-two pounds, needs to gain. Neutered after arrival, following treatment for severely infected ring of neck skin due to choke collar. Yard dog, rural area, chained to stake, without shelter. Very likely had zero indoor experience. Exhibits qualities of intelligence, concentration, resilience. May be trained for search-and-rescue. Skittish at present, slow to trust. Not yet fully housebroken. Was taken secretly from former situation and transported directly here. Does not vocalize through barking. Almost completely mute.

When I finished reading it, I realized the paper in my hand was shaking. I opened the top drawer of my bunk — mine again, for here I still was — and dropped it in. The drawer smelled like a pinecone. I'd brought up my bag and pack, lugging them with one hand, the one that wasn't wet and stinking. I went into the pack to get out my own soap. The inn soap was Irish Spring, which I refused to use. I didn't want to smell like a guy. I'd almost forgotten to bring my own all that lifetime ago of two days, when I was packing for the Sanctuary. That was something I could say I did right.

I didn't look into the mirror above the bathroom sink as I washed. I didn't want to know what my face was like, now that I knew what I knew about that dog.

Then breaking through to me, floating up from downstairs, was the smell of something that made me forget about everything else, including the fact that, a few months earlier, I became a vegetarian, which I'd meant to stick with for the rest of my life.

I smelled bacon.

Five

————

MRS. AUBERCHON WAS in the kitchen, getting ready to make oatmeal for the guest. She'd sent a message to the Sanctuary asking for information, but so far nothing had come. Maybe they'd predicted among themselves the new girl wouldn't last, which Mrs. Auberchon had told herself one minute after meeting her.

She wouldn't last a week. She might even be gone by tomorrow. She'd almost been gone today!

Mrs. Auberchon's back was to the doorway. The sound of a "hi" made her turn around. She'd forgotten to close the door.

"You're off-limits, miss," she announced. "This is a private area."

But the girl did not apologize and back away like they always did. She leveled her gaze and stayed put. She had a spine to her. If Mrs. Auberchon didn't know how old she was, she'd have taken her, at first glance, for a teenage runaway. They hadn't had one of those for a while: lost souls with that sad way of children pretending to be grown-ups, making their way to the Sanctuary because of some ad they'd sugared in their fantasies to be the answer to a longing, a dream, a prayer. And here they'd be again within days or even hours of starting their training programs. They'd come down off the mountain smelling like dog breath and wet fur, complaining that the work was too hard, the illusion too shattered, like Dorothys who never found Oz and didn't have a Kansas to go back to. They'd disappear when Mrs. Auberchon said no to pleadings for free lodging. She'd point the way to the bus, and they'd tell her she was hard, she was mean, she thought animals were more important than people.

"I smelled the bacon," said the girl.

The bacon was for Mrs. Auberchon's own breakfast. These were the last slices she had until her next shopping day. She was looking forward to a sandwich and the last of the Florida oranges from a box a rescue group sent to the Sanctuary as a gift. The box had mistakenly arrived at the inn; she'd felt she deserved to take a few for herself. She also had the last slice of a coffee cake with walnuts and raisins from Mrs. Walzer, the woman who baked the Sanctuary's treats. Her own meals were never the same as the meals she served to guests.

"I'll bring your tray to the lobby," said Mrs. Auberchon. "You can have it there or take it upstairs. Your choice. We haven't got a dining room, in case you were looking for one."

Still the girl didn't move.

She didn't grow up wanting, observed Mrs. Auberchon. She was city, or maybe city-close suburban. Good teeth, good complexion. Short, thick, light-brown hair. Long neck, high cheekbones, high forehead. She was skinny, but not like one of those anorexics. Her clothes had to be petites. No frills. Mrs. Auberchon never went into the bunkroom when it was occupied, but if she did, she knew she wouldn't find makeup things with this girl. She was not like some of them, who'd spend an hour putting stuff on, then come back all upset to do it over because a dog had licked their faces.

A college girl. Mrs. Auberchon could always tell. They'd had them before, fancy degrees in some subject you can't do anything with except think about it, and then there's nothing to show for it later but unemployment. Was coming here an act of escape? Was she putting something behind her, some tragedy, some heart-break? She wasn't a runaway, although she certainly did seem lost. She was probably often nervous. She was . . .

Sad. But not like depression. She was sad like she didn't know a way to be anything else.

Yes, that was it. Funny how you can tell, when they're still young, if they were children who knew what it was like to be loved, just loved, just taking it for granted that a mother or father or both would of course be always saying, "I completely love it that you're my child." It was the same way with dogs. Everyone connected to the Sanctuary could tell in one minute if a new dog had ever been loved, not that they got many who had. It was something in the way they looked at you, something in their eyes that wasn't blank.

"What's it like up there? At the Sanctuary, I mean."

"Oh, I wouldn't be able to tell you firsthand," said Mrs. Auber-chon. "I've never gone."

"I guess you haven't been here long."

"It's a little over ten years now."

That was as far as Mrs. Auberchon was willing to go with talk-ing about herself. She had a rule of never confiding in guests. She'd already gone too far. Maybe the girl sensed this, maybe not. Her next question was impersonal.

"I was wondering, about the sled puppies, how did the kid with the Jeep get the sled back up the mountain?"

"On the roof rack."

"Oh."

The girl looked mad at herself for failing to notice that the Jeep had a roof rack. Where had Mrs. Auberchon seen that look be-fore? In mirrors.

"I was wondering about Shadow too," said the girl. "Did he come down by himself, like the puppies? Without a human, I mean."

"Oh, the dogs aren't allowed to roam around on their own. The Sanctuary has volunteers."

Again the look, even harsher, sterner. That did it. With a sigh, Mrs. Auberchon pointed to a chair at the small table in the corner. She didn't have it in her to explain that there was no need for this girl to meet anyone from the Sanctuary she didn't have to, seeing as how *she wasn't going to last.*

"I guess you can come in and sit down," said Mrs. Auberchon.

She poured a cup of coffee and put out milk instead of the nondairy creamer she kept for guests. She put her shaker of sugar on the table, not the tiny paper packets.

Then over at the stove, she happened to glance at the girl in time to see her lift the shaker and aim it at her mug. But at the last minute she seemed to change her mind. Sugar spilled out on the flowered oilcloth runner, a little heap of it.

Mrs. Auberchon didn't mention it. She didn't want to be critical. She didn't want to be mean. She apologized for having no eggs, and fixed a bacon sandwich quickly, with deli cheese, not guests-only Kraft slices. The toast was from her good loaf, not the supermarket brand in the freezer. She placed the Florida orange on a dessert plate, with the piece of cake.

The girl was ravenous. There was no further talking. Mrs. Auberchon washed the frying pan, then went out to the back to clean up the poop from the huskies. When she returned to the kitchen to see how the girl was doing, she was good and prepared for the smile she expected — a smile and a thank-you and a warm little glow. Maybe, she was thinking, this would be an all-right time to break her rule of never starting a conversation with a guest. She had realized she didn't know the girl's name. Of course she'd have to ask. Maybe the girl would like another cup of coffee. Maybe . . .

The chair was empty. On the table, the orange peels were tidily stacked on a paper napkin. On the plate were bread crumbs, orange pips, a few fatty bits of bacon, plus raisins picked out of the cake. Mrs. Auberchon had forgotten about the spilled sugar until she saw it again. But this time it was in a line: a white filament, like dry snow, between the daisies of her oilcloth. The line was perfectly straight, as if formed with a sharp, flat tool. Why would that be there? Was the sugar spilled on purpose, arranged this way? Why didn't the girl clean it up?

Well I never, Mrs. Auberchon was thinking. She had a natural dislike of anything that didn't make sense. And look what happens when you're nice to someone! Messes! She had worried this girl was sad! She'd felt bad for her like a dog who never was loved! She rushed for a sponge. That girl didn't thank her for the special breakfast! She would never be invited to this table again!

Six

WHEN WAS I going up the mountain? I couldn't find Mrs. Auberchon to ask. No one else was employed here. No other guests had checked in.

I'd left messages on the Sanctuary's voicemail. I only had one phone number, and it went to an automated message the four times I called. The only way to email them was through their website. My messages had not been answered.

I was starting to feel a little frantic. I had to be careful with myself. I knew what could happen if, suddenly, my new self disappeared, perhaps for forever. I didn't want to be lost. I thought I had already cemented that with myself. I wanted to be the Evie who fell asleep with her head full of dogs, not the Evie who panicked and went for giving up. I wanted to be the Evie who found the Sanctuary's website in the first place, like a dog who's good at searches.

I didn't want to be the Evie who disappeared. In the program I was in, I had told a counselor that I felt I suffered from multiple personality disorder. I'd done some reading on it. I had thought I laid out a good case, like the Evie who'd gotten into what I'd gotten into was not the real me. And what did she tell me? First,

"Sorry, but you're not an MP, Evie." Then she pointed out that I had just described to her the life of a little girl who had parents in different houses because of a split, and the split kept going on and on, and I had given the whole description without using the words *parents, divorce, multiple homes,* and *little girl,* which she thought was pretty clever of me. And I sat there thinking, fuck, she looked in my file. I sort of had poured out an awful lot to the intake worker when I entered that program. I didn't remember most of it.

I never went back to that counselor. She'd also told me to do a certain thing whenever I felt I was on the edge of tipping over into something awful, as if the earth had just wobbled the wrong way and no one but me got thrown off. She told me to go somewhere quiet and be alone with myself and hug myself.

I was stunned. I had just told her what it was like for me to feel I was disappearing. I'd compared it to being alone in the vastness of space, without anyone knowing where I'd gone, and there isn't oxygen and I can't see the light of even one star, and she tells me to hug myself?

But I did it.

It was afternoon at the inn. I was alone and I was doing it again, curled up on my bunk, my right hand on the side of my left shoulder, my left hand on the side of my right. I kept telling myself, I'm a grown-up in the world, I'm a grown-up in the world. I'm a *hatchling.* I just came out of an *egg.*

Then the sound of the Jeep woke me from a nap I had not meant to take.

It was gone by the time I made it downstairs, but I didn't have to worry about my next plan of action. There was nothing for me to do but get into my jacket and boots and hat and gloves and go outdoors to the side yard and look at the dog in the pen. Now I knew it was a pen, not a playground for toddlers.

The dog was a black short-hair with a white chest, white muzzle, and white patch from between his eyes to his nose. He was fairly large, and bull-solid. I found the notes on him propped up by the fence gate, in a paper-size sleeve of clear plastic.

He paced back and forth on one path across the middle of the pen, over and over. Every time he reached a certain section of fencing, he stopped, sat down, raised his right paw, and whacked the fence sideways, with the motion of a tennis player's backhand. The chainlink rattled slightly every time. When the fence didn't fall as he seemed to expect it to, he got up and turned around and started over.

Hank. Male, neutered after arrival. Labrador/Pit. Approximate age of five. Weight is seventy-one. History unknown. No information. Was left anonymously at a shelter which lacked resources for treating/sustaining him. Outlook for adoption: zero. Level of aggression remains high. Do not introduce in his presence until further notice any hand-held wooden object such as fire logs and kindling, including sticks of any length. Do not walk in tree area before checking first for fallen branches. Currently under mild sedation, to be maintained until further notice.

Back and forth he went, back and forth, his feet landing every time in the same paw prints. He kept striking the chainlink with the same amount of force. His expression didn't change, so I couldn't tell what his disappointment was like. He took no notice of me, but when I neared the fence, he growled.

I wished I could have thought of a way to make contact with him. I wished I could have told him, "As you can see, I'm not a dog, but I think I know how you feel."

I hadn't dressed warmly enough. I needed another sweater. I wanted to stay outdoors to wait for the Jeep to appear again, for surely it would. Back inside I went.

In the lobby, Mrs. Auberchon was putting wood in the stove. She looked over her shoulder at me. I asked if I could warm my boots by the heat, and she nodded and said, "I haven't done the shopping. What you had for lunch, you'll be having for supper, just to let you know."

Lunch was awful. I'd found it on a tray outside the bunk door: kidney beans from a can cooked in chicken broth from a can, with corn and peas that also came from cans. But I ate all of it, and the too salty saltines, and the bowl of syrupy peach slices tasting more like a can than like peaches. I decided not to complain.

"I'll probably be leaving for the Sanctuary before supper," I said. "Don't you think so?"

Mrs. Auberchon answered with a shrug. In her hand was a split log. The sight of it made me so nervous, I couldn't say another word. I took off my boots and left my gloves there too. So I was in my socks when I went upstairs, and my hands were bare.

A little dog was on my bunk.

I guessed the gender to be female. She was lying there curled up, eyes closed, ears relaxed, breathing serenely. She was small and white, with light dustings of beige. Her ear flaps were short. She was bigger than a pug, smaller than a spaniel, and thick all over—not plump but small-scale bulky. She had short legs and pointy little feet, and a coat neither long nor short, like a lawn that isn't tidy but could go a while longer without mowing. Her fur looked coarse, but to the touch it was soft, as I discovered when I went to her, to pat her and say hello.

I had noticed the new sheet of notes taped to the wall in the vestibule, eye level above where I would have placed my boots if I hadn't left them downstairs. I had also noticed the yellow sticky on that sheet of paper, with my name on it, plus the command to READ IMMEDIATELY. It was held in place with a small piece of Scotch tape. It didn't come away when I gave the paper a tug. My fingers were white-stiff numb. Whatever was there would have to wait. It had not occurred to me to wonder why the notes would be there. I just wanted to put on another layer and get back outside.

The little dog's name, I'd find out when I looked at the notes, was Josie.

"Josie. Spayed female," I would read.

Small Mix, white, some tan. Age eight. Brought to a shelter by owners several weeks after appearance in household of new baby, their first. House dog, fenced-in yard. Zero prior leash experience. Zero prior contact with other dogs. Zero prior experience riding in vehicles. Zero prior experience with food not cooked in the home. Was cared for by home-visit vet, groomer, and sitter. When questioned at shelter about behavior toward the baby, owners declined to answer. Partial but significant loss of hearing was ascertained at shelter to be recent, and the result of a blow, or several. Up-to-date veterinary records from owners state normal hearing. Head X-rays were not ordered by shelter vet. Recent X-rays and scans inconclusive. Was initially listed as adoptable at shelter. When that status was changed, a person who happened to be there to adopt another dog made contact with us. Was taken from shelter just prior to scheduled euthanasia. Weight loss due to refusal to accept food has been restored. No longer necessary to muzzle for nail clipping, brushing, etc., but necessary to approach patiently. Do not startle. Hearing loss not fully adapted to at this time. Maintain distance until letting her see who you are and what you are doing. May possibly return to the world as a companion animal. Rule of thumb: wait, and let her come to you.

Josie didn't break my skin when she bit the inside of my wrist, in the spot where the sleeve of my jacket slipped up from holding out my hand. But those teeth had come close to making holes.

I reeled back as the dog went into a low stand on the bunk.

Her lips were pulled. Her eyes were narrow. Her ears were back and taut. Her tail was extended, rigid. There was a movement of the fur in her shoulders, and even though I was badly rattled, I remembered the breed book, and I was saying to myself, oh, so that's what they meant about hackles.

I stared down at the dog and felt the rush of my temper warming me. But I didn't raise my voice.

"If you think you're scaring me, you're wrong," I said calmly. "It was just a little nip. You didn't hurt me at all."

The dog kept her stance but tipped her head to one side, as if trying to figure out if I was bluffing.

"Did you hear me say *nip*? In case no one ever told you, you have tiny, tiny teeth. I was insulting you."

I was bluffing about the bite not hurting. The marks were already pinkish red and would soon halo blue in bruises. I moved my other hand to cradle the injured wrist, and suddenly, at that slight gesture, a simple hand in the act of changing position, the eyes of the dog opened wide, and filled with a terrible, instant blankness. She just simply went blank. Her tail dropped like a rope someone had let go loose. Her lips closed. Her body went slack, and she began to tremble — not like shivering from being cold. She was vibrating in her legs, flanks, chest, shoulders. Silently, she turned her head downward. I realized she was waiting for something to be done to her, which she knew she couldn't escape.

I did the first thing I thought of: drop to the floor between my bunk and the next one. I sat still and put my hands behind my back.

"Don't be afraid of me," I whispered. "Please stop shaking. Please . . ."

I hadn't closed the door. I realized too late that all she wanted was to get away from me. She leaped down, yipping madly, and streaked for the stairs as fast as if her tail had caught on fire.

Someone had opened the outside door. She must have felt the new rush of cold air.

Then she was yapping her head off out front. When I got up, forgetting that my feet were in socks on oil-polished wood, I slipped, and went down again on my backside.

I let myself sink, lying flat. Why didn't I leave this place when it was still daylight? Did the kid in the Jeep have a phone? Why didn't I get his number so I could call him for a ride to the train? I could have offered him cash and a new muffler too, from one of the shops I'd noticed on my bus rides. I remembered the names because they all started with the same letter: Meineke, Midas, Monro.

I hadn't noticed a vehicle belonging to the inn. There wasn't a garage. Was there a taxi service out here? A snowmobile for hire? A helicopter?

I was lying with my head near the wall, under a ceiling globe. The light burned and I shifted, putting my hands to my eyes. When I took them away, I saw that a Rottweiler had entered the room.

She was enormous. In her mouth was one of my boots and both of my gloves.

"Hi," I said.

That was how I met Tasha. She was a Rottweiler purely: black with a brown jaw and brown neck. Slightly above each eye, at the ends of invisible eyebrows, were the usual brown spots, almost like polka dots, the size of dimes. Her ears were high up and flap-folded neatly. Her black was like a seal's. Her brown was russet, vivid, rich.

She dropped my boot and gloves, as if commanded to. She was drooly and bright and shiny, and she was smiling at me.

She seemed willing to stick around, but there was the sound of the Jeep, which seemed to call to her — it was getting close to sup-pertime. Off she tore, and when I started to go after her, I tripped on my boot, and found myself distracted by a rolled sheet of paper inside it.

Tasha. Rottweiler. Spayed female. Age between three and four. Weight one hundred twelve. Health very good. No sign of injuries. Was reported to animal officer in urban area by resident who observed a car at a stop sign from which a large dog was released. As the car sped away, the dog disappeared around a corner, chasing it. License plate not recorded. Was found by animal officer the next morning on a nearby block, getting into curb trash. No tags, no collar. Was delivered to humane but crowded shelter. No response to found-dog appeals. Was adopted twice and returned both times due to size issues, difficulty at controlling, intimidation qualities, and destruction of objects. Was brought to obedience class by a shelter volunteer, but attendance had to be terminated due to unfriendly/aggressive behavior toward owners of other dogs. Was then transferred to second shelter with fewer animals. Consistent unruly behavior there, including excessive vocalizing and menacing demeanor. Was nevertheless listed for adoption. Was taken from second shelter in hastily arranged rescue when a staff member received an anonymous tip that persons who arranged to adopt her were in fact involved in dogfighting. Not yet fully leash-trained. Must only be walked by physically strongest. Has demonstrated emotional instability and moderate to extreme depression and anxiety. Receiving medication in gradually lowered dosage. Outlook for place in home as companion animal: fair to low.

I raced downstairs. No one was in the lobby. No one was outside. There was only the Jeep in the distance, going up into the darkness without me.

The room I returned to smelled faintly of dogs. No messages were waiting for me from the Sanctuary. I looked out the window and decided not to close the shutters. It had started to snow, straight down, in light streamers, like trails of falling stars. I thought of the Sanctuary's logo. Then I took a long, hot shower. I could see their faces around me in the steam: Shadow, Hank, Josie, Tasha. It was strange to be alone but not alone.

Seven

WE WERE SNOWBOUND. We were as muffled as if an avalanche had fallen on us in the night, in a silent, wonderful crash. Finally there was a reason for being stuck in the inn. We had electricity but no connections: no phone, no Internet.

Excited with the feel of a holiday, I dressed quickly and followed my nose to the kitchen. I smelled cooking. I smelled baking. I smelled odors that stood alone, and others in strange combinations: roasting chicken, something fishy, something meaty, peanut butter, oats, molasses, vanilla, cinnamon, ginger. Crossing the lobby, I felt waves of heat and food that seemed to be saying, Evie, you know you belong here. Come on in.

But I didn't rush into the kitchen. I paused by the doorway and ducked out of sight, like a shadow no one turned around to see. I peered in silently and felt like an outsider-snoop. I didn't know why I had to do this, but something in my instincts made me feel I should be worried. Something inside my skin was alerting me to trouble.

The table had been moved from against the wall to the center. All four of its extension flaps were raised. Sitting at the table, facing the doorway but with her eyes on her work, was a woman of maybe seventy, maybe older. She looked like anyone's ideal of a warm, kindly, bosomy grandmother. She had the type of old-person face that doesn't wrinkle or toughen, but grows loose, soft, shimmery. She wore a full white apron, streaked and smudged with stains. Her hands were in an enormous bowl of dough.

The windows were so frosted, they looked like oblongs cut out from the moon. On the stove, things in pots were cooking over every burner. I saw that the counters were loaded with cookie sheets cooling on racks, and containers with front openings like in a candy store. Some were filled, some empty.

The cookies were different sizes, as if the woman had placed dough on the sheets without looking or measuring. Some were small as a lozenge, some medium-size, some large and thick. Some were dried strips of . . . chicken! Beef! Salmon!

They were dog biscuits, and kibble, and jerky. I was looking at a production center for treats!

I remembered that the Sanctuary said on its site they believed in positive reinforcement—so of course there would be treats. Right away, I pictured myself as a trainer at the head of a class of dogs, my pockets full. But I'd need to sort the treats. I brainstormed a moment and got lucky. I would get one of those mini-aprons for nails and screws and things, the kind carpenters wear. They probably come with four pouches, which would suit me perfectly, according to the mouths of my pupils: big, medium, small, tiny. My treats would have to be homemade, which meant learning how to bake. This seemed like the right time to start. "I want to learn baking, please," were the words that were forming in my head.

Again, I held back. The woman at the table was not alone. Mrs. Auberchon was out of my sight line, but I realized in a minute that she was working at the counter by the sink. She was grating carrots.

"I swear," came her voice, "if it wasn't for the weather, we'd be seeing the last of that girl today. I give her till the day after tomorrow."

The woman at the table paused in the mixing of her dough. Empty cookie sheets lay on either side of the bowl. She had a warm, liquidy voice. I thought she'd stick up for me, ideal-grandmother-like, even though she didn't know me.

"I'm never one to jump to conclusions, Mrs. Auberchon," she said. "But it doesn't seem to me she's a keeper. I'll give her until the end of the weekend."

"Day after tomorrow," said Mrs. Auberchon. "You didn't see her when she was out at the pen with Hank. And goodness knows what happened with the other three. It was a lot for a first day, giving her the four of them at once, but it showed what's what with her, in my opinion."

"Tell me again about the sugar," said the woman at the table.

"It was a straight line of it, right where you're sitting. I'm telling you, she poured it out on purpose, but I didn't see her make it into the line."

"I wonder why she did that. Do you think she's immature or something, playing with food like a child?"

"I didn't get that feeling, not that I'm saying she's mature. To tell you the truth, I don't think she knows anything about animals. So what do you want to bet?"

"I could put up," said the woman at the table, "doing the laundry once she's gone. I know you could scream sometimes when you've got to do another load."

"It won't be much, with just the one bed and two towels," said Mrs. Auberchon. "How about throwing in you'll clean upstairs too?"

"I could do that, Mrs. Auberchon. How about you take care of the jerky next time? I'd love a break from it. And all the mixing, too."

There was a pause. Mrs. Auberchon was thinking it over. Then she said, "Deal, but I'm sure I'm going to win."

"I don't agree," said the woman at the table. "But what if we're both wrong, and after the weekend, she's still here?"

"Then we'll have to start over," said Mrs. Auberchon. "Wait till you see her clothes. For once I can't complain about the tuition being so much. She'd never miss it. She has a jacket that's got to cost more by itself than everything I own. And she's awful small. You know, one of those petites. I just don't think the small ones should be handling dogs."

"Let's not be prejudicial," said the woman at the table. "But I wonder if she's the kind of small one who looks down on everyone, even if they can't look at you without looking up."

"It's true she has an attitude problem," said Mrs. Auberchon. "Looking down is the right way to put it. Is this enough carrots?"

The woman at the table glanced sideways and said, "Do a few more. I'm almost ready for them here."

"We should put in for a new food processor," said Mrs. Auberchon. "I forgot how long it takes to do grating by hand. I'm getting sore fingers from it, not that I'm being a complainer. That Tasha! You never should've let her in here our last biscuit day, and then you didn't report it that she chewed up the lid and half the bucket."

"She'd be sent to the jail, and you know it," said the woman at the table. "And you know what a soft spot I have for the huge ones. It was a miracle I noticed what she was up to and took it away from her before she started on the blade."

I stopped listening. I did that with sugar? Tasha ate a food processor? The Sanctuary had a jail? I was being accused of looking down on *other people*?

I turned away from the kitchen. I was wearing my new L. L. Bean fleece-lined moccasin slippers, so I was able to slink away

shadow-quiet. My head was low. I didn't know that the boy from
the Jeep was in the lobby until I almost collided with him. He
was dressed for outdoors, in that ranger jacket. On the chest was
the insignia of the Sanctuary. The small white dog made of stars
was eye level with me.

When I'd talked to him before, in the vehicle, I hadn't noticed
how tall and broad he was. I definitely noticed now. I wanted him
to leave me alone.

"I was hoping you'd be up," he said.

"I'm not up. I'm the opposite. I'm going to my room. I don't
want to be—"

He interrupted me in a not unfriendly way. "Wait. Can I ask
you a question?"

Something was sweet about him, I thought, in a *Lord of the
Rings*, hobbity way, regardless of his size. Something about him
felt safe.

"Okay. Ask me a question."

"Can you walk on snowshoes?"

I was quick to answer yes, because what could be hard about
walking on snowshoes? Did I need to pack? Was I finally going
where I was supposed to go, where I'd paid to be?

No, I didn't need to pack. I just needed to dress warmly. I felt
I'd go anywhere with him. Otherwise, I'd be up in the bunkroom
with a phone that didn't work, trying to call the world I'd left behind even though I didn't really want to be there either, and I'd
be crying.

And twenty minutes later I was flat on the ground out in front
of the inn, with my arms out, like I was making a snow angel,
but being unclear on the concept, I was doing it face-down. The
snow was so deep, the walls of it around me began to cave in,
which meant I was getting buried.

The snowshoes the boy lent me had not fallen off. I'd felt so
proud of myself for figuring out how to put them on, and now all

I wanted to do was get rid of them so I could stand up. The boy seemed to read my mind. I was aware of him squatting by my feet, reaching down to undo the clamps. It was complicated. The snowshoes had crisscrossed each other in my fall. I was as good as caught in a snare, and it didn't help that my companion appeared to be happy.

He was saying, "Oh, my God, this is awesomely, stupendously perfect."

In the moment before he got me released, he threw out his voice at full volume, so that even the echoes were loud, and in turn made other echoes, zooming around like invisible pinballs.

"Tasha!" he cried. "Come! Come find!"

He wasn't taking off the snowshoes to be my friend. He was taking them off so there wouldn't be anything poking up telltale in my chamber of all that snow. I heard a deep bark from somewhere nearby, then silence, until he called out again.

"Tasha! Come right now and find! You *come!*"

But nothing was happening except that my face had gone numb, and I'd crossed the line from feeling cold to feeling frozen. I stood up and shook myself off.

"Sorry about this," said the boy.

"That's okay."

"No, I mean I really am sorry."

"And I mean it's really okay."

I hardly knew Tasha, but I could tell she'd never be useful as a search dog. Together, the boy and I turned to look at her in that shine of white and light, so unreal to me, and so beautiful, I felt we were seeing the light of a star that wasn't ours to begin with, like we were astronauts, in our parkas and hoods and boots and thick gloves, and we were standing on a faraway planet that happened to have an old inn with a kitchen, where a snowbank made a window low enough to look inside.

Tasha was up on her back legs, with her paws on the sill. If I didn't know she was a dog, I'd think she was a young, hungry bear. Her face was close to the glass. Her tongue was extended. She was a Rottweiler with a tail, and I remembered, from the breed book: *In order to conform to standards of the American Kennel Club, breeders have the tails of Rottweilers "docked" in the first few days after birth, with variations on size of the stump. Docking has been banned in many countries, but not in the United States. For Rottweilers not intended for show, docking is still advised. These are highly emotional animals and notorious tail-swingers. Owners of undocked "Rotties" frequently cry "ouch!" when being brushed in the legs by their pet, not to mention the pain of losses when objects are swept off a coffee table!*

Docking is a way to say amputate without saying it. I wondered if Tasha's owner pushed her out of that car because she'd knocked a vase off a table. I wondered if, given the choice, Tasha would pick everything that happened to her over being docked.

"I have a tail!" she was saying at the window. It was a black, thick pendulum going back and forth in hyperdrive. She knew it was baking day. The steam of her breath was on the glass, along with rain-like streamers of drool.

They wouldn't be letting her into that kitchen. She didn't know that yet. I wished I could mind-message her. You're on the outs, I wanted to tell her. And believe me, I know how you feel.

Meanwhile, I had to get inside to pee, but I realized I didn't know the boy's name. So I asked him.

"On the mountain they call me Giant George," he answered. "In case you don't know, that's the name of the dog who used to be the biggest one in the world. Somebody else topped him a little while ago, but he used to be *king*. He set a Guinness record. He went on *Oprah*. He's a Newfie and he's totally famous."

"I knew that," I said. "Wait for me here. I'll be right back. I have a ton of questions for you."

I wasn't surprised about the name. Something was Newfie-ish

about him, combined with hobbity. I was feeling a little glow as I plowed my way forward, quoting to myself about Newfies. *Besides their size, Newfoundlands are notable for their loyalty, the value they place on companionship, and their gentle, caring, easy-going natures.*

"Hey, Evie!"

He had waited until I was about to go into the inn before calling to me.

"Giant George is a Great Dane."

I acted like I didn't hear him. When I went back outside, I was returning to emptiness. It had started to snow again, hard and thick and fast. The surface held no sign of tracks: no snowshoes, no paw prints.

There was only me. I reached for a shoulder, cupping my hand around my jacket sleeve at the top of my arm. Then I went for the other one. If anyone happened to be watching me, I wouldn't need to feel ridiculous. I totally looked like I felt like standing there getting snowed on and was keeping myself warm. I made patting motions on my arms, like I was a dog and a person combined. I wasn't mad at Giant George for leaving me. Great Danes have issues with slobbering, I had read in the breed book. They are giants with the mind-set of lap dogs. They're always trying to get onto people's laps, which can *crush* you.

Retracing my steps to the door, I reminded myself of Hank in the pen, the same path over and over.

Suddenly I remembered a counselor in one of my mandatory group talks. I was supposed to say something about *getting over my old self like a mountain I had to climb.* That counselor was forever taking time off to scale peaks somewhere, so everything was compared to mountain climbing. She didn't care that no one else sitting in that circle had a background in large-scale outdoor activities. It was mountain this, mountain that, and I was using up my speaking time by talking about books I'd read containing that word in the title, or if not in the title, then a mountain was somewhere inside. I was doing a good job putting together a list, as a way, I had felt, of showing my group mates the reality that my personal past contained an awful lot of reading. And the counselor stopped me when I'd only got to *H*, for *Heidi*. She had looked at me as if she felt that, if we were on a climbing team together, I would be the one who made sure everyone fell off and perished. So I decided to stop talking at all in that group. I didn't know I had memorized the one thing she said to me when she stopped me at the *H*. Or maybe she had branded me with it.

"Evie," she had said, "I think you should train yourself to pick a different way to do your climbing."

So those were the words that came to me when I was going back inside and thinking of Hank. Well before I reached the door, I found myself sticking one foot in untrodden snow, high as a little mountain. I felt stupid about hacking out a new path. I felt like a little kid doing something a grown-up said to do, which I didn't even have to, because there wasn't a grown-up paying attention to me. I felt like a kid *having to be her own grown-up*.

Inside the doorway, I shook myself off. In the kitchen they were still making biscuits. A table in the lobby held a tray with my breakfast: coffee, packets of nondairy creamer, a bowl of canned peaches, a glass of orange juice, a bowl of crunchy cereal. Under the cereal spoon was a slip of paper. The handwriting, in pencil, was not the same as the writing on the dog notes. The writer was Mrs. Auberchon. The note said, "Sorry to ask you to eat cereal without milk, but I am temporarily out of milk."

I picked up the bowl of cereal, sniffing and looking. It was granola, still warm from the oven: oats, molasses, vanilla, cinnamon, ginger, peanut butter. I meant to just give it a taste, but I ended up wolfing it. The orange juice was from concentrate, but it wasn't overly watered. I downed it, then downed the coffee. I even ate the peaches, slimy and limp as they were. Then I went upstairs to change out of my wet clothes.

The top book on my pile caught my eye. On the cover was a group of dogs, different kinds, purebred and not, sitting pretty on perfect grass in a lush, leafy park. They looked like a bunch of preschoolers who never spent one second being hurt by anyone in any way.

The other covers were pretty much the same. I looked them over with what I felt were brand-new eyes. I opened each one to check the contents, the indexes. Nothing was anywhere about dogs in a shelter being scheduled to no longer be alive, or persons involved in dogfighting, or dogs who were terrified of sticks, or muteness as a result of being chained in a yard night and day with no shelter.

I gathered up the books and went quietly down to the wood stove. In the kitchen they didn't hear me. An almost-spent log was burning in a skimmer of narrow flames. There was plenty of room for the books. I wasn't sure what to do about the controls, so I ignored them. I'd never put anything in a wood stove before. Some smoke escaped, but it wasn't a lot, and set off no alarm.

I crept upstairs and looked outside. It was snowing even harder. I didn't feel wasteful or destructive or anti-printed-matter, strange as it was to be someone who thought it was a good idea to burn books. Soon, I felt, I'd have new ones from the Sanctuary — or at least one, perhaps as thick as the Bible. Nothing was on the website about a training manual, but surely there'd be some sort of text. Maybe there'd be blank pages for notes, maybe not.

I wondered what Shadow was doing. I wondered what Hank was doing. I wondered what Josie was doing. I wondered if Tasha, paws on the kitchen window, had thought about smashing that glass to give herself a better chance at insideness. I told myself I needed to remember always what her face was like, and her drool as well, in those moments when she was purely, blissfully hopeful.

Then I found myself with the urge to start setting things down. It wasn't okay with me to have loose sheets of dog notes just lying around. I couldn't let another minute go by without doing something about getting organized.

It occurred to me that I should keep some kind of personal log about what I was learning, with entries, of course, in alphabetical order, like in a dictionary or maybe an encyclopedia. I opened my laptop. I made a list of vocabulary words — basic words I had to learn all over again, now that I could connect them with my first four dogs.

I felt as if I'd landed here from another planet and had to get to work right away on my language skills. I was sort of on automatic. I didn't know what the first word would be until I typed it.

Eight

ABANDON. TO TURN away on purpose from someone you were supposed to never turn away from. Bad verb. Bad word. Bad everything.

Aggression. I think Hank growled at me when I came a little close to the pen because I wasn't approaching him the right way. I mean, dogs are *animals.* Probably in his position I'd have done the same thing, like, get away from me or you'll really be sorry. Probably he thought the one with the aggression was me, just simply for being a human. I think he picked up on how I was watching him like, oh, God, this creature is a total obsessive-compulsive, and that is *terrible.* I should have let him know I admired him for being up on his feet and not curled in a ball of himself in a corner like a quitter who gave up on his life. But it's a good thing I backed off. I might not be typing this because of missing some fingers. It wouldn't have been like a nip from Josie.

Note to self: aggression in small dogs is totally different from aggression in big ones. It's like the difference between, say, getting into a substance you don't put into yourself with a needle and getting into needles, *which no one ever gave me one tiny bit of credit for never doing.*

Anxiety. The state of expecting the wrong things to happen to you, based on previous learning and experience. Probably, all dogs who came out of a household that went through a divorce are automatically anxious about pretty much everything, if the divorce just kept going on and on, and the two people doing the divorcing were so busy with the divorce, they basically forgot they even had a dog in the first place. Or, if not "forgot," they thought all they had to do was provide things like healthy food and somewhere nice to go to the bathroom, and also good grooming.

Baby (new in a household). Someone brought home a new baby to a home a little dog thought was totally her own, where she was totally the center of attention, and all of a sudden there's this whole other thing, and all of a sudden she's deaf and homeless?

I don't care that it didn't say in the notes what Josie did to that baby. I care that it didn't say what was done to the side of her head. Was she hit with a hand? With an object?

Note to self: remember, me getting nipped by Josie was not her fault.

Bark. Shadow is mute, but nothing is wrong with the parts of his body that are there for making sounds. He could bark. Would changing his name help?

No, that's stupid. A dog doesn't know which human words have silence built into them and which don't. But he should have looked sorry for peeing on me.

Car. So Tasha was riding in a car, until she wasn't.

I wonder, how long did she run after the car before she had to give up? How close did she come to being hit by other cars? This was in a city. This was somewhere with serious traffic. Were horns blown at her? Were steering wheels turned, brakes stepped on? Where did she spend her city night? Did she sleep at all? Did she jump to her feet, her heart leaping, every time a car went by that was the same sort of model as hers? Should I even be asking questions like this, when they can't be answered?

Yes, I should. Yes.

Chain, collar. I wish I knew the length of the chain Shadow was attached to in his yard. I wish I knew exactly what he had to deal with. Also, there is no way to know what type of metal collar infected his neck. I looked at some online. I learned there's such a thing as a "choke collar," with spikes around the inside rim, like little nails. Some types of this collar have spikes with rubber tips. Some don't.

Companion. Shadow was never anyone's companion. What's worse, to never be one, or to be a companion to a human who threw you out of a car, made you homeless and deaf, hit you with hand-held things of wood? (To be continued, because I think the whole be-a-companion thing is actually a big deal.)

Answer: stupid question. There's no "worse." It's all equal.

Depression. When being sad for a very good reason goes too far. Basically, the same as *anxiety*, but the other side of a coin.

Hackles. The fur on the back of the neck, which rises in certain situations. An act of communication where fear plus ready-to-attack can make for complications. Best to consider this a system of Warning. Best to consider it's always done for a very good reason.

Home. You can have one, or even two, but at the same time, even though you're fed well, and groomed well, and all the rest of it, you can be someone who doesn't have anywhere to apply the word to, that is, if you're willing to be honest when someone asks you, "Where are you when you're at home?"

In. There must be a dog-language version of this word, and not only for every dog chained for life in someone's yard. Note to self: do you really think that learning to talk to dogs is going to be easy?

Also note to self: stop thinking so much and maybe just do it.

Kill. What the notes on Josie were talking about when they were talking about euthanize.

Out. What Shadow knew in his soul about where he was, on

his chain. But probably, as with *in,* everyone here is on the same wavelength about it.

Rescue. Best. Verb. Ever.

Shelter. A place where you're glad to be. Unless you're a dog in one, with the feeling that this is where you have to be for the rest of your life, because you haven't got a home.

Wag. Dogs can talk with their tails? Okay, I just got here and I don't know anything about dogs, but I know that if a tail of a dog is going side to side, either quickly or slowly, *it's a very positive sign.*

Nine

———

TREATS-MAKING TIME was over. Mrs. Auberchon stood by a window in the lobby, waving goodbye to Mrs. Walzer, riding passenger on the Polaris of a Sanctuary volunteer who brings the treats up the mountain and returns Mrs. Walzer to her house in the village.

It used to be that Mrs. Walzer made the treats at home, but several years earlier her quality went into decline. Maybe it was age creeping up on her; maybe it was carelessness. A human hair was found dangling from the mouth of a dog who'd eaten a large biscuit, and once you're alerted to something like that, you have to pay attention. The offenses began to pile up, such as undercooked jerky and chunks of brown sugar. Sugar was forbidden to the dogs. Finally the worst happened when someone at the Sanctuary broke apart a biscuit and found shards of chicken bones, one of them quite long.

Mrs. Auberchon was supposed to fire Mrs. Walzer, and never mind that making treats was her one activity, since the day she retired from a whole adult lifetime of baking, first in the little shop that used to be part of the village, then at the supermarket. And never mind that Mrs. Walzer wasn't paid. Or that the slipping of the quality took place just shortly after she became a widow.

The snowmobile chugged off in splashes of snow that looked like sea foam. You had to admire her, Mrs. Auberchon felt, for riding that thing at her age, and also for going along with the new plan about where to make the treats. She never knew of the almost-firing, or the charges against her. When Mrs. Auberchon put it to her that the baking would have to be done at the inn, she had said it was the Sanctuary's idea: a new rule, not to be argued with. This way she could take over ordering the ingredients and doing some supervising. She never had to talk about standards. She never had to say, "I'd welcome the companionship once a week."

It was a good companionship because it had formalities. Unlike Mrs. Auberchon, Mrs. Walzer hadn't grown up in the village. She'd come to work in the bakery when she was barely out of her teenage years. Mrs. Auberchon hadn't met her until after she'd married a local. They fell into the habit right away of never calling each other by their first names. They were friends but not *friends*.

Mrs. Auberchon went to the wood stove. In the urgency of the baking, she'd let it go. She looked at the red beads of embers and wondered why there was so much ash. Why did it look so powdery, compared with the regular stuff of the hardwoods? She reached for the ash bucket and the little iron shovel. Was something burned that she didn't know about? Impossible. She must have put in rotten wood without realizing it. She scolded herself as she shoveled out the extra ashes, careful not to scoop up any embers. When the new fire was going, she found herself wondering about the guest. All was silent upstairs, but that didn't tell her a thing. Was the girl being a slob and a pig? Probably yes, and yes. She was probably used to hired help. You could tell. Mrs.

Auberchon provided meals for the duration of a stay, and she'd launder the towels and bed linens if a stay lasted longer than a week, provided the guest brought the towels and linens down. She did not provide daily cleaning — this wasn't a hotel.

She looked at the remains of the girl's breakfast on the tray and brought it to the kitchen to take care of it. There wouldn't be grocery shopping today, which was just as well, because more and more, lately, she'd been feeling herself putting up resistance to going out; but she had set aside a chicken from the treats. Well, she'd ordered one extra, on that budget. It was on the counter, cooling in its roasting pan. There'd be enough for dinner, then sandwiches for tomorrow's lunch, dinner tomorrow evening, then soup.

It was making her restless that there wasn't any Internet, so she bundled up for outdoors, craving activity. She found the long-handled brush and went out to clear snow off the roof of the rickety, slumping back porch. The roof itself was in good shape, but she'd decided the buildup might any minute make it collapse. Standing on a snowbank, she rained down sprays on herself with every stroke of the brush, so she was constantly spitting out snow. She could not decide what made her madder — her Internet connection or the Sanctuary, because they still hadn't told her anything about the girl. All she could do was be equally angry at both.

When the roof was as clear as she could get it, she returned to the kitchen, stomping and aching and breathing hard. The guest was sitting at the table. In front of her was the roasting pan containing the chicken. She was hunched over it. The silverware drawer had not been gone into for a fork, a knife. The cabinet had not been gone into for a plate. The rack of paper napkins on the counter had not been disturbed for a napkin. There was just the food and herself.

Two flaps of breast skin, each of them removed in one piece, were looped on a side of the pan, like miniature, brown-yellow rags hung to dry. A great deal of the chicken, Mrs. Auberchon saw, had been consumed.

The girl looked up at Mrs. Auberchon. She hadn't touched the wings or drumsticks. Bits of white chicken were in her teeth and in a corner of her mouth.

"Hi!" said the girl. "You didn't fix lunch. I was *starving*."

Then she got up from the table as normally as anything and went to the counter where Mrs. Auberchon kept the rack of paper napkins. She took one and wiped her mouth, took a second napkin for her hands, and balled the the two together when she was finished. She turned to face the trash pail in the corner. It was a plastic one with a center push-slot in the lid. She gave a throw to the napkin ball, holding up her arm, flicking her wrist just so. The thing landed perfectly. It dropped the lid on its hinges and disappeared.

The girl's face lit up with a grin.

"Oh," she said, "I didn't think you'd want me going through your drawers and cabinets for silverware and things."

Mrs. Auberchon had left the snow brush on the porch, but the kindling hatchet was in her hand. She was dripping melting snow. She couldn't blink right; snow had crusted her eyes. Her skin was tingling with cold, but she was sweaty and hot, head to foot. She loosened her grip on the hatchet because the way she squeezed the handle was suddenly alarming to her. She set it down, propping it against the wall. Then she changed her mind about having it close at hand. She put it into the broom closet.

"By the way, it's weird we never introduced ourselves. I'm Evie," said the girl. "I know you're Mrs. Auberchon, but I don't know your first name."

Mrs. Auberchon unzipped her parka and reached down to undo her boots. She stepped out of them. She placed them on the little rug by the electric wall heater.

"I'll be in my room, off-limits to guests," she said. "I wish to be undisturbed."

"No problem. I totally respect your privacy."

Evie. Mrs. Auberchon willed the name to delete itself from her mind, like letters typed on a screen, then backspaced into a vanishing. As soon as she was in her room, she bolted the door. She peeled off her outer clothes and turned up the heat on her stove, a smaller, gas version of the lobby one. She went to the work table, to her computer.

There was a knocking at her door.

"Mrs. Auberchon? I found a plate for the chicken. I put it away in the fridge. I hated to think what could happen to it if a dog showed up."

"Thank you," Mrs. Auberchon managed to say.

"But I couldn't find aluminum foil to cover it with."

"That's all right. This is my private time."

Mrs. Auberchon turned on the computer. She had Internet.

But the girl wasn't going away. Mrs. Auberchon could almost hear her breathing on the other side of the door.

"Will a dog show up again, Mrs. Auberchon?"

"Not today."

"Can I ask you one more question? Then I'll go upstairs."

"All right."

"Do you work for the Sanctuary?"

"I do," answered Mrs. Auberchon.

Silence. Good. Mrs. Auberchon put on her fuzzy slippers, towel-dried her face and hair, filled her electric kettle from her bathroom sink, plugged it in, dropped a tea bag into the mug by her computer, and sat down. Her room closed around her like a shell. It was a large one, with doors for a closet, the bathroom, and access to the porch. It held a single bed, an armchair by the biggest window, a couple of bureaus, and this table and chair. She waited until her tea was ready before putting on her headset and crossing the mental line that separated "Mrs. Auberchon the inn-keeper" from "Mrs. Auberchon the Sanctuary Warden."

A moment later she was in. As usual, she started with a sweep of her three locations.

On the screen appeared the large outer room near Solitary. The holding room, it was called. It was the first stop for a newly arriving dog, but for now it was an isolation unit for six juvenile huskies. They needed to be apart from the others as a preface to training for work. They didn't need her. They'd be leaving soon. All were asleep, sprawled and well fed.

Next, she looked at the infirmary. No one was there. Then she keyed into Solitary.

The little room was once a storeroom for the old ski resort. It was large enough for even the biggest dogs to walk around. A pair of ventilation windows were set high up, to be unreachable. The heat vent in the floor was heavily grated. Dogs who were jailed in winter tended to stay close to it, hunkering like lost, worried hikers in the wilderness, terrified that flames of a camp-fire might go out.

A dog was there. Mrs. Auberchon saw black, solidness, mus-cularity. She saw a white chest, a black face with a white muzzle. But she knew by the pacing who it was: Hank, partly black Lab, partly pit bull. This was his first time in Solitary.

She brought up a second screen to remind herself of his bio. Age about five. Adoption possibility zero. *Do not introduce in his presence until further notice any hand-held natural wood object such as fire kindling, including sticks of any length.*

Back and forth he went, back and forth, his feet going in the same steps every time. When he reached the door, he raised a paw and struck at it, sideways, like a punch thrown out from an arm that was crossed at a chest. When the door didn't open as he seemed to expect it to, he turned around and started over.

He'd been sentenced for an hour, and longer if he didn't calm down, she learned, reading the most recent entry. He was there because a new volunteer failed to put away the broom being used in an area Hank had entered.

"Bite sustained on hand which was holding the broom. Injury far from serious, but volunteer will not be returning," Mrs. Auberchon read in the report. "The broomstick was also attacked. Wood splinters were removed from his teeth."

Mrs. Auberchon took a sip of her tea. When she first started with this, it was an experiment she'd agreed to try. She was the only Warden the Sanctuary ever had. In the early days they used long-range walkie-talkies, which were trouble, because sooner or later there'd be static to hurt the dogs' ears, as if the noise were part of a punishment. But then came computers, cameras, speakers, mikes, magic.

She said, "Hello there, Hank."

He paused, but only for a second. He didn't look up at the shelf her voice was coming from. Sometimes they did. It was always easier when they did, especially when they knew her. But she and Hank had never met.

"Hank," she said, "I'm here to tell you, you're not alone. I'm sorry I'm late, but it couldn't be helped."

Hank took a swipe at the door, and Mrs. Auberchon said, "Cut it out. That door's not doing anything but staying closed, at least for now. It's time to be quiet. I want you to sit. Sit, Hank."

He took two steps and stopped abruptly when she repeated the command in a much firmer way. He dropped to the floor to lie down. Close enough.

"Good," said Mrs. Auberchon. "Good dog. Good strong dog."

He was panting hard with anxiety. She often sang with the radio while doing chores, as long as no one else was around, but she'd never worked up the nerve to sing to a dog. She didn't know if anyone might be listening in, which meant the fear that some-one—a human—could make fun of her for having no pitch, or no sense of melody, or whatever people said of people who were awful at singing. But she had a pile of books, stacked like a tower beside the tower of her desktop. Some she'd bought herself, some were left by guests, some were brought down from the mountain. What they had in common was that they didn't have people in them, except now and then as minor characters.

The one she wanted was near the bottom of the pile, after *Black Beauty, Watership Down, The Story of Ferdinand, Charlotte's Web, Animal Farm*. It was *The Hobbit*.

"I'm going to read to you, Hank," said Mrs. Auberchon, opening the book.

"'In a hole in the ground,'" she read, getting right to it, "'there lived a hobbit. Not a nasty, dirty, wet hole, filled with the ends of worms and an oozy smell, nor yet a dry, bare, sandy hole with nothing in it to sit on or to eat: it was a hobbit-hole, and that means comfort.

"'It had a perfectly round door like a porthole . . .'"

A pop-up box in the corner of the screen startled Mrs. Auberchon. It came with an icon. Only one person messaged her this way. The icon was a Great Dane.

AWESOME CHOICE, MRS. AUBERCHON. PLS. READ THE WHOLE THING. I'M ON DUTY TILL MIDNIGHT.

That boy!

"George, don't interrupt me again, or I'll pick a different book and make sure it's one you don't like, thank you very much," said Mrs. Auberchon, without changing the tone of her voice, like she was reading the next sentence of the story.

He's the one who gave her the hobbit books. He didn't like it when anyone called him George and left out the Giant, but honestly, a Great Dane? A Great Dane my foot, she was always telling him. If he had to have a dog for a symbol, he'd be better off picking something big and shaggy, like a Newfoundland. She had no idea what his name really was, but that wasn't unusual. So many of them chose new ones, just as the rescues without a past were given names when they arrived. What was Hank's name in his old life? It wasn't as if he could tell her. It wasn't as if he'd choose to remember.

There was nothing more from that boy. Hank turned to his side. He was closer to the heat vent. Mrs. Auberchon's eyes went back to the page, and she took up where she'd left off, all voice, talking and talking and talking.

Ten

I LEFT ANOTHER voice message for the Sanctuary. This time I stuck up for myself. I was forceful. I said I *wasn't having a good time down here.* I said I expected a reply *momentarily,* with information about going up the mountain to take *the training course I had paid for in full.*

I sat on my bunk to wait for the call back. I kept the door open in case someone from the Sanctuary came looking for me in person. I sat cross-legged, my back straight, my hands on my thighs, as I'd learned to do in a yoga class at the program I used to be in.

The yoga was supposed to be a break from spending all my time on those websites about careers, but I didn't last with it, although I'd done a lot of reading to prepare. After the first class I was asked to never return. I was a failure at following directions about the right way to breathe and how to be quiet and still. And people around me complained that they didn't like how I watched them, which wasn't fair, when I was only trying to follow examples. No one had told me you're not supposed to look at anyone in a roomful of people doing yoga.

My problem with quiet and still, I was told, was that I wasn't being quiet and still from the inside out.

But I didn't want to waste what I knew. I kept my position on the bunk for maybe five minutes, which was five minutes too long, and also boring. I couldn't add to my new log because I didn't know anything new. I couldn't get in touch with anyone from my life of before, because, if I called my former program, all I'd need to say would be "Hi, it's Evie," and before those words were out of my mouth, any one of those counselors would know from the tone of my voice, like in an auditory X-ray, that I was feeling a little agitated, like I was calling for help, not just to say hi and also talk about abused rescued dogs and how I was stuck in the inn, which I couldn't remember even telling anyone about, because of being so excited and nervous when I was leaving. If I tried to explain my situation, what would it sound like to a counselor? It would sound like, shit, Evie's *back to her previous self.* I couldn't call home because which one should I call first? Who wouldn't ask me first thing if I'd already called the other one? And then my little agitation would change like a washing machine from wash on gentle to a spin so fast, you could pull out the plug and the whole thing would keep shaking.

So I went online to look at dog training websites.

I kept clicking until I hit one that felt like a good place to settle in. It featured a trainer who was about to retire. In his photo he wore a suit and a tie, but he reminded me of the grandfather in *Heidi.*

If my counselor hadn't stopped me when I reached the letter *H,* I would have told my group something personal and very specific. I would have confided that, when I was five years old, *Heidi* was the best book ever written. I was certain of that, even though it was the first book I read on my own that contained more words than pictures. If anyone in the group thought I was mistaken about how old I'd been, like five is automatically too young for all those pages, I wouldn't have gotten mad. I wouldn't have been surprised. I'd just say I could never be confused about something

as important as my first book, which had *thrilled* me. Maybe I
would have talked about what it was like when I didn't know
how to stick up for myself when my parents and also steppar-
ents got together with me, like a court of four judges, to discuss
how wrong it was for someone in kindergarten to say a book had
been read when the book, objectively, was on a whole other level.
Maybe I had looked at the words, they said, but looking at words
wasn't reading. Did I understand the difference between pretend
and real? Did I understand that if I seemed to have a problem
with pretend and real, they would call in a child psychologist?
They loved me, they said, and I must promise I'd never pretend
I'd done something I wasn't able to do. I must promise to never
tell another lie. I must wait until I was nine or ten to read things
like *Heidi.*

It wasn't as if I had a lawyer. All those evenings, I'd been turning the pages of *Heidi,* rapt and excited, and no one noticed? I
hadn't read that book in only rooms where I was alone. I hadn't
been quiet about it. I'd sounded out words aloud. I'd exclaimed
things like *oh no* and *oh yay* at the top of my lungs. I couldn't figure it out. How could they say, "We love you, Evie," and not know
such an important thing about me?

If I'd known ahead of time that you're supposed to be, like,
nine or ten to read that book, I never would have told anyone I'd
read it. But I think I'll always remember how it felt to fall asleep
calmly, happily, my head full of goats and a girl who fit in somewhere, and also the Alps.

I was happy to find the old trainer. I wanted to connect with
him through an email, to thank him, and let him know I was putting him in my log. But at the end of his last posting was a black-
bordered box containing his obituary.

He had posted data he collected through his long career in dog
classes. He'd also been trained as a statistician. His specialty was

teaching the type of classes where you actually train the humans, not the animals. Maybe, like the grandfather in *Heidi*, he was inclined to be pessimistic about people, not that I had the feeling his data was skewed by emotions. The last thing he wrote was a question. He asked, *Please can more people be nicer to dogs?*

Eleven

DATA, PEOPLE, *in training classes with their dogs.* I learned that 31 percent of people in training with their dogs were observed in the act of punishing them, either during the class or afterward, for failing to meet their expectations. Forms of punishment included shouting at close range, slaps of varying force, and surprise yanks on collars or leashes. There was no difference in the number of these episodes in classes where the trainer spoke out against physical punishment, or outright forbade it. But people who brought electronic devices to administer shocks as training enhancements were never allowed to use those devices. They had to be left at the door, like guns at a security check.

I learned that 38 percent of dog owners in training classes felt anger, frustration, or bitterness toward the breeder, pet store, or shelter the animal was acquired from, as in, "What I received for a pet is not what I had in mind." The most common complaints were (1) the animal's bad behaviors, such as chewing and leash pulling, had not been disclosed; (2) the owner had been conned into believing the animal would arrive in the home housebroken; and (3) the owner had not been warned (when the dog was acquired as a puppy) what the size of the grown dog would be.

I learned that 40 percent of dog owners who described themselves as "happier in my life in general, due to having a dog," nevertheless felt strongly that the dog was not a member of his or her family, because families are people and a dog is not a person.

I learned that 52 percent of dog owners admitted to feelings of disappointment and hopelessness due to observations that other people's dogs were doing better than theirs. Of this group, slightly less than half admitted to having these feelings frequently. Of the "frequently" group, more than half answered no to the question "Do you think you could adjust your needs and expectations about your dog?"

I learned that 56 percent of owners in first-time training had to be instructed/reminded to smile at their dogs, especially when their dog felt awful about screwing up some command or routine.

I learned that 88 percent of owners in all levels of training, including puppy classes, answered no to the question "Would you be inclined to turn in your dog to a shelter if you felt your dog hadn't met your expectations?"

And I ended this lesson by wondering, what about that other 12 percent?

Devices, electronic. Of course I had to look these up. It led me right away to "invisible fences" and "shock collars."

I watched a few videos of people putting on a shock collar to see what it felt like. I saw that they were shocked by the shock, and they were shocked even more that *it really did hurt, and in a really bad way.*

I learned that representatives of dog-shocking companies who go out to the home of new shockers don't like to let the dog owners see them at work, training the animal to get used to the invisible fence, because sometimes it takes an awful lot of zaps before the animal figures out what's going on. I discovered that people whose dogs have shock devices, who did not observe the dog being zapped by a company rep, were far more likely to have positive feelings about the whole thing than people who watched, or people who did the conditioning themselves.

After that, I watched a video about a Weimaraner whose owners bought a house in a new development where invisible fences were already installed, as part of the package. The device collar was waiting for the dog on the kitchen counter, with a brochure explaining "the answer to all your worries about safe, humane containment." The owners didn't know anything about invisible fences. They'd always lived in buildings in a city. The look of the prongs on the collar made them nervous, but they were willing to give it a try.

They were a middle-aged husband and wife, a little smaller than average, both of them, sort of like my parents. The first thing I thought of when they appeared on my screen was, if they split up, and both remarried soon afterward, would they become the husband and wife of people who were taller and bigger than their original spouses? And if they did, would their dog be in the same position I was, always looking up baffled, because the new wife was such a tower, and the new husband was twice the size of the original one? And the original couple would seem to *shrink?*

But I could see a moment later that this was a couple their dog could count on to never split up. They sat in their living room in front of their videocam and described how, after their dog was shocked once, he would not go out of the house. Together, they had to carry him out to do his business. The husband finally threw the collar in the wastebasket, but even then the Weimaraner waited to go out on his own until after that trash bag was brought to the curb for the regular pickup. He scratched at the door to go out and peed on the bag as the trash truck was approaching.

In the video, he lay at his owners' feet. He was sleek and gorgeous. His coat was gray-pearl. The couple said he didn't make eye contact with either of them for days and days after the shocking. They wanted to put up a real fence, but the owners' association wouldn't let them. It was an open-land development. You couldn't even have an outdoor clothesline or put drying racks on your patio.

They didn't feel comfortable anymore walking their dog in the neighborhood, because dogs would come running across lawns, then stop short to avoid being zapped. They didn't like looking at the faces of those dogs. They knew now that invisible fences are based on the memory of administered pain. And meanwhile, as the dogs were wondering why they were the only ones around with a device on their necks, squirrels would be entering and leaving those yards, and cats and chipmunks, and the occasional fox, wild turkey, woodchuck, and also birds and windblown leaves, and toy airplanes, balls, shadows, rays of sunlight, butterflies, children, the whole family.

The couple planned to move away. Just before they made their video, they said, their computer was infected by a virus. They had a hard time getting it off, but the experience had made them realize their dog's memory of shocking was the same thing: a virus in the hard drive of his brain.

Their video was on a blog they'd started, with lots of links about not only invisible fencing but all kinds of *training devices administering pain or acute discomfort*. I clicked on them all, even as I wished I wasn't finding out what I was finding out. And all along, I kept asking myself, could it be true? Can you really get rid of bad memories?

I ended up seeing famous photos by William Wegman, because you can't look up Weimaraners without finding him. I lucked out. I hit upon a YouTube clip where two of his dogs are on *Sesame Street,* baking bread. It's called *Sesame Street—Dogs Bake Homemade Bread.*

I watched it six times. I loved their ears. I loved their eyes, their faces, their dresses, their aprons. And then I could go to bed. I was feeling a little better about the things I might see in my dreams.

Twelve

I HATE OATMEAL, but that's what was on my breakfast tray in the lobby. Mixed into it was syrup from a can of peaches and also slices cut up into little bits. As I ate it fast to get it over with, I realized that a portion of the wall I faced was in fact a sliding door, made of the same dark paneling. I should have known that the lobby didn't take up all the space of this floor, the way the bunkroom did upstairs, with the sharp angles of its rafters. I should have known there had to be another room.

I hadn't noticed before that there was a metal grab handle. I went over to it. I slid the door open just enough to squeeze through sideways.

The room I entered was an indoor porch or sunroom for guests of the inn. Against the wall it shared with the lobby were armchairs and tables, pushed to the side, for the place had been pressed into service as a training room. In one corner was the only piece of furniture that mattered now, if you can call a large metal dog cage a piece of furniture. This, I would learn, was the time-out crate. In the opposite corner was a stack of heavy-duty plastic storage containers atop a square table used for people playing card games, chess, whatever. The other three walls were mostly windows, long and wide, unshaded, with glass so clean I almost thought no glass was there. I was blasted with white sunlight coming in from a world of snow, and the dogs were nice enough to let my eyes get adjusted before they went crazy that I was there.

Oh my God, here were my dogs!

What I didn't know at once was that Giant George was in there too. I didn't turn around to check for the presence of another human. In his hand was his phone, and he was catching me on video as I was mobbed.

The pattern of being knocked off my feet held true. But I shouldn't have thrown out my arms and waved them about. That was a mistake of enthusiasm and a lack of self-control. And I shouldn't have let my next move be an attempt at a crouch, in the start of going down to their level, like to hug them all at once — well, three of them. Hank was too busy pacing.

I should have remembered I'd just eaten oatmeal, and oatmeal reminded them of their treats. So my mouth was of interest, especially to Josie, who slipped through the bigger two and went for my lips. The nipping she gave me was maybe accidental and maybe not.

There was growling. There was friction, jostling. There was an awful lot of barking. I panicked. They were all over me. I had to get away from them. When I licked my lips, I tasted blood. I managed to get myself back to the lobby, and when Giant George stepped out after me, I nearly jumped out of my skin.

"Everyone freaks out when stuff like that happens," he said. "I hope you don't think you flunked a test of being around dogs."

The Sanctuary never said anything about testing. I'd made a vow to myself I'd never agree to be tested for anything again, even though all the tests in my recent past had involved my bodily fluids. I turned away from Giant George and rushed upstairs, holding back crying until I made it to my bunk, my face in the pillow so no one could hear me.

When I ran out of tears, I felt it was time to call my former program. I was willing to admit I needed some help. But as soon as I turned on my phone, a text was coming in. The sender was Giant George.

"Evie! Come back down & I swear I'll delete what I video'd & no one will see it not even me. Please come back PLEASE."

Then came a second one.

"I'm 16," it said. "In case you care, the sled pups left the mountain. I almost went with them."

I returned downstairs. I knocked on the sliding door.

"Hi," said Giant George, closing it behind me. "I deleted it."

"Honest?"

"Honest."

"Okay," I said. I looked around. Hank was still pacing, but the other three were quiet in the center of the room. Tasha appeared to be sulking.

"What's the matter with Tasha?"

Giant George pointed to the time-out crate. "I just let her out of there. She tried to knock over the bins to get at the treats. She wants you to feel sorry for her."

"I don't feel sorry for her," I said. "Is your name really George?"

"It is now," he answered.

"Are you really sixteen?"

"Almost. Well, kind of."

"How long have you been here?"

"A few years," he said.

"Is your family here?"

"No."

I saw his unease. He didn't want to be questioned, at least not about himself. That was something we had in common.

I said, "Did the sled puppies leave for sled-dog school?"

He nodded.

"Is it in Alaska?"

"Yeah. Good guess."

"Why were they here? What happened to them?"

"We had them since their rescue," he said. "They came when they were tiny. They were taken from a place that, they needed not to be there. It was bad. I'd rather not go into it, now that it's over."

"Okay. Why didn't you go with them?"

"No reason. Welcome to your first day of school."

"But I'm supposed to be up on the mountain," I reminded him.

"Welcome anyway."

It occurred to me that there wasn't going to be a grown-up professional from the Sanctuary sweeping in to run the show and start training me. This was it.

"Hank needs to get out of the pacing. He needs to learn to look up on command," said Giant George. "In fact, they all do."

"Look up on command?"

"Yeah."

"Can I try it myself?"

"Go for it," he answered.

How was I supposed to know that if you hold up your hand, index finger pointing upward, like the number one, and a big wide smile is on your face, and you're gazing up at a ceiling, you're inviting your dogs to jump you? I deliberately didn't say anything, such as "Look up, guys," because of Josie's deafness. I wanted the playing ground to be level. I felt smart for thinking of that.

"Uh-oh," I heard from Giant George, the instant my arm went up.

Only Hank didn't rush me, and I was down on the floor and three dogs were all over me *again*. Josie was trying to lick the blood on my lip. Tasha nosed me roughly to see if treats were in my pockets. Shadow plopped down across my outstretched legs and made the weak little whine sounds of dogs who want to bark but don't. I looked over at Giant George to see if he was getting this on video. He wasn't. He was strolling to the bins. Hank took no notice, due to his feeling that nothing was more important than pacing. But the rest of them forgot about me and took off for Giant George. They were all looking up at the treats he held in his hand. He lavished them with *Good looking up, guys,* and *Way to go with learning looking up.* All I could do was listen to the clicking of Hank's nails on the floor as he paced, and the peacefulness of three dogs eating biscuits.

Giant George took hold of Hank and snapped on a leash. While he was doing this, Tasha jumped him, as if he had a treat in a pocket, just for her. He pushed her away and told her, *Bad move.* She didn't seem sorry. Shadow and Josie looked at her like they were proud of her, like she was the coolest one in the room. Hank tried to start pacing again. But the leash was too short. And that was how it went with my first class.

I watched from a lobby window as Giant George set off in his snowshoes, away from the inn, holding the leashes of Hank and Shadow and Tasha. Josie was in a pack on his back, her little white head sticking up like the head of a toy. Giant George had left the Jeep on the mountain road, so he and the three bigger dogs could get some exercise. I wondered how high up the mountain it was, but I couldn't go after them, not in all that snow.

When they were out of sight, I knocked on the kitchen door. Mrs. Auberchon came to see what I wanted. I was not invited in. I asked her, were there snowshoes anywhere around the inn I could borrow, to go out and practice on? She said there weren't. Would anyone else be checking in? No. No one else was coming. Would I be going up the mountain soon? She didn't know, and would I please excuse her, she had lots to do?

Back I went upstairs. Nothing had come in for me from the

Sanctuary. Back I went online. I found myself starting a search for "trainers talking about abused rescued dogs." I didn't know why I put it that way. It just came to me.

"Trainers talk about abused rescued dogs" brought up one hundred ten million results. So I knew what I'd be doing for a while, which was better than sitting there thinking about what it felt like when Giant George and the dogs left the inn. They didn't look behind to see if I was in the window. It was the same as if I'd turned into a memory, incredibly easy to erase. It was just like I wasn't there. I saw how wrong that was. I *wanted to be there.*

Thirteen

AGILITY TRAINING. Many dogs in recovery from abusive situations, including dogs who are broken in spirit, do well with the goal-oriented challenges of an agility course, which may be considered "track and field for dogs." For some, it's one more thing to be stressed about, while others simply don't see the point.

I could see Shadow doing agility. Josie would be stressed, but she might be good at it. Hank might do well if nothing on the course was wooden. Tasha would look around and say, "You have got to be kidding."

Alpha. Another way to say "bully."

Alpha, belief in. Some trainers say dogs are happiest if everyone understands that, basically, a dog is a domesticated wolf, and so there has to be a system of Order, and everyone does better when it's dominance and submission all the time, absolutely, one dominant and everyone else not so much. Meanwhile, if someone is in a corner quivering, afraid of doing something wrong, or afraid they're not submitting the right way, well, they have to learn the alpha knows best, although it's sometimes distressing to see the alpha in action, doing what the alpha's got to do, and that is *fascist.*

Clicker training. There is such a thing as "clicker training," where you hold a plastic clicker between the forefinger and thumb, in order to condition the dog's behavior by means of clicks. At first I thought this was a joke, like an insider-trainer sort of thing. But it's for real. It reminded me of the TV commercial I saw late one night, when I was clicking through four hundred channels like I was the only person in America who couldn't fall asleep. It was an infomercial for an electronic foot-massage device, where a husband and wife of late middle age sat on a sofa watching TV, in their pajamas, while their feet were massaged by a pair of devices, one for him and one for her, on the floor. I wondered, why aren't they rubbing each other's feet? Why would anyone rather have a foot massage from a gadget than from a person? Why aren't they divorcing each other and finding people who'd like to rub them and get rubbed?

Using clicks on abused rescued dogs isn't widely recommended. Many people say their dogs become obsessed with the clicker, as in, excuse me while I try to grab that thing from your hand, and destroy it.

Conditioning and teaching, differences between. If you want a dog to look up on command, why not take hold of the chin and give it an upward push? And repeat and repeat and repeat? The dog will get it, and it doesn't take long. But if I were a dog and someone did this to me, I'd begin to learn that being touched by a human isn't all that great of a thing. I'd want to be in charge of my own head and my own eyes. I'd be conditioned to obey a command because I wanted a human to stop touching me, which is *heartbreaking,* which also goes for trainers who don't believe in treats you can eat.

Treats you can eat, some trainers say, is an awful way to teach, because (1) dogs should be conditioned to have meals in bowls and nothing in between, and (2) even if the treats are healthy, homemade, and non-fattening, food treats only condition the dog to attach behavior to food.

That is all just mean. It's not as if a dog would feel rewarded if you gave it, say, a star, like the sticky stars I used to get all the time, which I really like remembering. There are probably teachers of little kids who say it's a terrible practice, since it only conditions the kid to go for stars. If someone came into my classroom when I was little and told my teacher to stop giving stars, I would have decided to quit school. Failing that, I would have stopped being interested in learning. What would be the point of learning if there were no stars?

Dealing with menacing behavior. One thing you have to figure out early is, what are the warning signs in a dog's face, tail, posture? Dogs are animals. Remember this. Just because they're not wolves doesn't mean they're not animals.

Establishing trust. If you don't know how much it matters, get another career. Get a career that doesn't have animals.

Fear. The major factor in alpha-ness and certain types of training.

Hope. Can I have it? Can I actually figure out what it actually is?

Humping. Dogs hump dogs in order to (1) literally be "top dog," or (2) have fun. Be able to tell the difference. (This is humping in the non-reproductive sense.) Do not be surprised to see a neutered male hump a male. Common thing! Probably they miss their balls, even if they lost them when they were babies.

Jumping. Don't allow! Say NO JUMP. Or you can say DOWN.

Leash training. Some trainers continue using the old method of leash learning in which a dog is yanked suddenly and hard, in a way that cuts off its air. The dog is conditioned to know that if correct leash walking doesn't happen, strangulation will take place. Trainers who use this method say it's quick and effective. Some say it's part of following what God said to do in Genesis about who gets to be the ruler of animals.

Maybe trainers who quote Genesis to explain their techniques would say that the part in the Bible about "do to others what you'd like to have done to yourself" does not include dogs. But what about the act of yanking when the one being yanked is you? Do you want to have your shoulder dislocated? Do you want to have injuries to your hand? Do you want to hit the ground head-first, and there goes your brain?

Dogs on leashes are going to try to chase things. Plus, sooner or later, a dog on a leash will be attracted to something dead, like a rotting fish on a beach, or roadkill. The dog will think there's something wrong with you because you don't agree that a stinking, guts-exposed, maggoty corpse is thrilling. The dog will want to roll around in the dead thing. The dog will want to smell just like it. The dog will want to *exult* in it.

So you have to deal with how disgusting dogs are. You have to hang on to the leash. You have to say, "Walk with me nicely, dog." You have to be a good manager, which is different from being, say, a fascist.

Loneliness. There is no worse loneliness than the loneliness of a dog who never was anything but lonely, because the loneliness is normal, like a heartbeat. Do you think it's easy to go to the place inside a dog where the loneliness is, when you can't even do it with yourself?

Obedience, types of. I'm thinking trainers are right when they say it's possible to teach a dog to make good decisions because making good decisions is cool, and there are always rewards of treats. (To be continued.)

Pack. A pack without the fear thing is dogs being okay while being together.

Patience. Have it. If you don't have it already, get it. If you get it, keep it.

Sit, come, stay, lie down, drop it. The basic commands. The starter stuff, best learned young. Five like the fingers of a hand. You can pretty much take it for granted that abused rescued dogs don't have a certificate from Puppy Class saying they've got the basics, from back when their minds were open and new.

I learned "five like the fingers of a hand" from my boyfriend in college. I'll call him Made Me Happy. He was a transfer, and almost completely alien to me because he was in science. His major was chemistry. He'd come in with a grade average of close to perfect. I thought it was funny that he believed the alien was *me*. He called my major "sitting around reading stuff dead people made up a long time ago."

We met on his first day. One afternoon, a few weeks later, I went to his room as we'd planned and found him worried and upset, when his usual way was a calmness I envied, and counted on. He showed me a paper he did for a class in I don't remember what — some requirement that wasn't science or math. It was so marked up with corrections and negative comments, I almost couldn't see what he'd written. I looked it over. I was ready to take his side. I was thinking his professor was maybe an alpha, or a hostile-to-transfers snob.

But Made Me Happy had problems. Many of his sentences were like listening to someone speak whose mouth is full of food. He thought papers had to always be done in five paragraphs, the way a hand has five fingers, with the pinkie as the introduction, the thumb as the conclusion, and the middle three as the place where you work out the stuff you promised to do in the pinkie. He told me "like a hand" was how he'd been conditioned to put down his thoughts, not that he said *conditioned*. He said *taught*.

And he didn't know he didn't know the basics. He didn't have a learning disability; he just really didn't know. His commas, for example, turned up in weird places, like shoes on the wrong feet. He'd never received a grade of less than B+ on anything, and now he was looking at an F.

I wish I could say I became his tutor, not the person who corrected his assignments before he handed them in.

I also got him to take a creative-writing class in poetry, with an elderly professor who loved, absolutely loved, poems in forms. I didn't take it, because I couldn't, because, as in all the creative courses, you couldn't just show what you'd written to the prof. You had to show everything to everyone. But I was proud of myself for predicting that Made Me Happy would be brilliant in there. He didn't say *form*. He said *formula*. His specialty became the haiku, because, he said, by the time you realized if it was good or bad, it was over. He wrote tons of them.

One was about me. The prof gave him an assignment, special for him, to write one that had, for a change, (1) a human being, (2) an emotion, and (3) something green, from the actual world of nature. He wrote it in about two minutes, like it was waiting in the tips of his fingers. He did the title in seventeen syllables too; that's where he put the emotion. He called it "The Moment I Fell for Evie, and She Thinks It Wasn't on Purpose." It went like this:

> *Outdoors on green grass,*
> *Evie lay reading, alone.*
> *I tripped on her feet.*

We didn't last as boyfriend and girlfriend. In one of the last conversations we had, while we still were okay with each other, he asked me to promise him I'd try a poem of my own, and of course it had to be seventeen syllables. He used to nag me all the time to stop just writing things about things other people had written. So I promised I'd try. I said I'd write a haiku if something came up that could only be said in haiku. I'd know it when I met it, he told me.

I liked correcting his papers, even though it meant staying up later at night than I was already doing with my own classes. And that was how I started to give myself little treats now and then of cocaine.

Trouble. Do you think that being around rescued dogs is sunshine and blue skies? It's not. It's really, really not. Rescued dogs are dogs in *rehab.*

Victories. They happen. But most of them happen very slowly, like evolution.

Wolves. Who doesn't have ancestors? We used to be Cro-Magnons. Birds used to be *dinosaurs.*

Worst things to do. Never believe the whole point of education is to help a dog think about things and make intelligent decisions. Train their bodies and not their minds, which you don't even think they have. Yell at a dog you are training. Physically punish. Lose your cool if a dog gets menacing. Feel good about getting pleasure from someone's submission to you. Only have one way of doing things. Always think you're more important than the dog. Never be generous with praise and rewards. Never smile. Get into cocaine way too much, then say it's not your own fault, and you did it for a really good reason.

Fourteen

MRS. AUBERCHON LEFT her room to start lunch and check on Evie, who was outdoors with Hank. She'd been reading Evie's Sanctuary application. Finally, it had arrived in her email.

Her brain was spinning. There was a shortage of recruits this year, but what was wrong with them? Yes, they were idealistic, and yes, Mrs. Auberchon was thinking, as if debating herself, they were living in a sort of bubble up there, in a very unworldly way, with their heads full of dogs, dogs, dogs, and their eyes always looking for brightness and silver linings, and never mind the fact that reality keeps bringing messy, dark, sometimes awful complications.

They never learned! Just because the Sanctuary staffers were nuns was no reason why they couldn't do a simple thing like refuse an application that so obviously needed to be refused. They weren't even nuns *really*. They never mentioned a single religious-type thing. The lodge was not a convent. They wore clothes they bought from catalogs or the Internet, all casual; often they were dressed in sweatpants, sweatshirts, jerseys made purely for comfort and durability. "Ex-nuns" might be a more accurate description, but they were so private, they made you feel their own pasts were nothing to know about, or even ask about, just like dogs who came to the mountain with zero paperwork or information. How long had they been up there? A long time. Certainly longer than Evie had been alive. All right, they were aging, and it was possible one or two of them might be losing some eyesight, but that was no excuse.

Evie's application was *alarming*. There was not a single detail, not even in the section for the bio. All she'd put was this: "I went to school for what felt like forever, then I felt I was through with it, but here I am, ready for more school."

Had she ever worked with dogs?

Yes, she had answered.

Would she describe her personal history with dogs?

She'd left that blank. She'd left all the other questions blank too, except the last one. She wanted to talk to aliens?

The last question was, "What would you choose for a career if you lived in a world that had no animals?" Mrs. Auberchon thought of it as a throwaway, although it was asked on purpose so the nuns could get a feel for an applicant's talents and interests. Before Evie, everyone answered that question by saying they'd be teachers of children, or they'd undertake some sort of work to bring animals back into the world somehow. Or they'd be something in a helping profession, such as social worker, nurse, counselor, or occupational therapist.

"If the world had no animals and I couldn't be a dog trainer, I'd become someone who talks to aliens professionally."

This wasn't something to look on the bright side about. Mrs. Auberchon could not get Evie's words out of her head. Instead of just answering the question, she'd gone on and on about it.

It was hard to get through all those sentences, but one thing was clear. All along, the one thing Mrs. Auberchon hadn't considered was that *Evie was mentally ill*. Naturally she'd be vague about her past in the application! She must have been in some kind of treatment place. What about her family? Did her family encourage her to apply to the Sanctuary because she embarrassed them, because they wanted her out of their hair? What about her mother? Mrs. Auberchon was not a mother, but she felt that if Evie were her daughter, she would never . . .

She forced herself to stifle that thought as she entered the kitchen. She looked out at the radiant, white-sun clarity that only came on certain winter mornings, like a holiday. But it didn't feel like a holiday now. Mentally ill! In the past, when new trainees had to leave for mental health reasons, they'd been more or less all right to begin with, and Sanctuary dogs were involved in their breakdowns. There'd been people who came from sheltered lives and couldn't take being face-to-face with broken dogs, when all the damage was done on purpose, by a human. There'd been people who wept and couldn't stop, and people who shut down, just shut down, and people so overwhelmed they couldn't sleep. It wasn't as if the Sanctuary was up front about the condition of their animals. Did they say on their website or in their advertising that their rescues were hard-core cases? That it was a place where dogs came when other places despaired of them? They did not. Always it was, oh, all we care about is the future. Oh, all we care about is what our dogs are going to be, not what they were.

But this was different. New trainees who fell apart because of broken dogs did not say they wanted to talk to aliens.

Hank was in the pen, pacing, tail down. His agitation was intense. He was trodding the same path over and over, his tracks two furrows in the snow. Where was Evie? She was supposed to be outside the fence, working on getting him to interrupt the pacing with commands to *look up*, and maybe try for eye contact with a human.

Then Mrs. Auberchon spotted her. Evie was coming from the back of the inn, trudging in snow past her knees, and she was carrying something, large and heavy — she was dragging and carrying it, combined. It was one of the big metal trash barrels, minus its lid. The trash had been taken a few hours ago. The barrel now contained snow.

Why Mrs. Auberchon didn't rush out there and find out what was going on, and put a stop to it, she didn't know. All she could do was stand there and look, like watching a movie she could not turn away from. It couldn't be possible that Evie planned to go into the pen with that barrel.

But there was her gloved hand on the latch. She waited to step inside until Hank was at the opposite end, and then inside she went, dragging the barrel at a tilt, her face straining with the effort. When she reached the halfway point of Hank's path, she placed the barrel on its side and pressed down on it, so that it lay in Hank's way like a roadblock. She placed herself at the mouth of it, and suddenly, as Hank neared it, she lifted her arms and swayed them in the air like a pair of waves cresting and falling.

Up went Hank's head. His eyes went wider. His lips were pulled back—a grimace? A warning sign? Should Mrs. Auberchon do something?

But Evie's voice boomed out like the burst of a bell.

"Jump, Hank! You can do it! Forget the pacing and JUMP!"

Hank's tail went up like an exclamation point. He stopped in his tracks for the first time ever. He looked up at Evie. He seemed to realize the barrel was too heavy for him to push out of his way. Going around it would have meant leaving his path. His body tensed up. What to do? What to do?

"You can do it! Do it now! It'll feel real good!" screamed Evie, and the next thing Mrs. Auberchon knew, Hank was leaping.

It wasn't merely that he went over that thing. He had made the decision to go airborne, and it seemed that he'd been waiting all his life for this moment to arrive. His body left the ground in a liftoff that took Mrs. Auberchon's breath away, and when he landed softly on all his paws in the snow, and turned around and *did it again,* even higher, Mrs. Auberchon found herself laughing a laugh that was sobbing too.

There were several more jumps before Evie calmly reached for the leash that was draped on the fence by the gate. She went over to him and snapped it on him. He let her. He let her pat his head. He let her bend toward his face, nuzzling him. Then he pulled hard, wanting to get back to it, and she held on, shaking her head. Mrs. Auberchon raised the window, mindless of the cold air rushing in. She wanted to know what Evie was saying to him. It didn't sound crazy. It sounded the opposite.

"That's enough for today," she was saying. "If I let you keep doing that, you'll just get addicted. Believe me, the last thing you need is another thing to be obsessed about. Let's go for a walk where there aren't any trees, and you can jump again tomorrow."

He pulled again, so forcefully that Evie tottered and nearly went down face first. But somehow she was holding on. The leash was a long one. She knew to wrap the end around her hand for a better grip. Strong girl, Mrs. Auberchon was thinking. Who knew?

Mrs. Auberchon watched them leave the pen, Hank resisting, Evie pulling. He was quite a strong dog. It didn't look like they'd get far.

Evie reached into her jacket pocket and pulled out a biscuit. But when she held it out, Hank bumped her hand with his head, and it fell to the snow. He didn't try getting it. He wanted only to keep jumping.

And down to the ground went Evie. She still had the leash in her hand. She was flat on her back, same as the morning she lied about being able to snowshoe.

Mrs. Auberchon remembered that she was crazy. Should she put on her coat before she went out there to help, or should she just rush out there?

Then she heard Evie yelling again.

"Jump, Hank!"

Hank understood. He had plenty of room on the leash to make this new leap. Evie got up, walked him a few yards, and dropped down again.

"Jump, Hank!"

And where was George? He was supposed to be here to take Hank up the mountain, and leave Josie for an hour with Evie in the training room. George was assigned to Evie. He was expected to be responsible. Oh, he was young, but he knew the rules as well as Mrs. Auberchon did — when the Sanctuary took you in, you couldn't be some kind of freeloader.

Evie was on the ground again, shouting at Hank to jump over her. And there was George! If there were such a thing as creeping while being upright on your feet, he was doing it. He had a back-pack strapped snugly on his shoulders. Poking up from the open top was Josie, completely quiet, in cahoots with the human she was riding. Her little white head and dark eyes were toylike, as if a manufacturer of stuffed dogs had created one in her image. In George's hands was a video camera. Evie and Hank didn't know they were being recorded.

When they passed out of sight, Mrs. Auberchon looked at white sunlight glinting on the barrel in the pen. She looked at the snow prints of Hank's paws. She looked at the snow angels Evie had made in the clearing, and the paw prints there, too.

The sound of deep barking in the distance startled her, followed by the yapping of Josie, which in turn was followed by the shouting voice of Evie. She was telling George that if he taped her one more time without her permission, she was going to take that phone of his and break it and also cause him serious bodily harm, because she was a whole lot stronger than she looked; and also, in case he didn't know what she thought of him in general, she thought he was *an asshole.*

Well, they'd found each other.

Mrs. Auberchon closed the window. She wasn't willing to call herself hasty or mistaken for maybe jumping to a wrong conclusion about "If the world had no animals and I couldn't be a dog trainer, I'd become someone who talks to aliens professionally." But she was willing to give that thing another look, one of these days. She would have to read it again with new eyes.

Fifteen

THIS WAS THE first time I was naked in front of a dog.

I had closed the bunkroom door before my shower, and I'd locked it. Where the little white dog had been hiding, I'd never know. She was sitting on the bunk closest to the bathroom when I came out, trailing steam and the smells of my soap and shampoo and bareness. Her head was tipped to one side. Her eyes were wide open and her lips were a little bit parted, like she'd caught me doing something not allowed, which surprised her, and which she very much disapproved of. I had to remind myself that animals and people don't feel the same way about clothing.

"Hi, Josie," I said. "I know you're kind of deaf, but how about you and I starting over with each other?"

In answer, she pulled back her lips to show me her teeth, in case I'd forgotten she had them, as sharp as little knife points. Why didn't I have treats with me? Why wasn't I a person who never went anywhere, even in and out of a bathroom, without dog treats? Then I felt stupid and way too self-conscious about grabbing a towel and wrapping it around me, modest-like. I was hoping she'd look at me in a friendlier way.

She didn't. She looked at me like we were enemies. I remembered, *baby*. I remembered, *hit on the head and in a shelter, refusing to eat, scheduled to be euthanized*. I remembered what it was like the day we met, when she thought I was going to hurt her. She had lowered her head to me — a sad dog trembling all over, small and alone, getting ready for the shock and the pain of a blow from the hand of a human, as if all she expected, for the rest of her life, was getting hurt.

"I'm not going to hurt you," I said. "I don't care if you're saying you hate me. I totally do not hate you back, not that you're making it easy for me to say so."

I took a step toward her. That was a mistake. She raised her hackles and let out a hissy little growl, showing her teeth even more. I was only trying to pretend I was a fully trained trainer with a lesson in mind for my pupil. The lesson involved letting me pat her. One pat! It seemed reasonable. It seemed like a thing we could get to. I was starting to think that if she bit me, which obviously she extremely much wanted to do, I wouldn't care. I'd call it an occupational hazard and go for the pat.

But I remembered, yoga.

"Okay," I said, backing off. "I'll wait."

I sat down on the floor at the foot of the bunk she was on. I told myself I was Buddha-like with my stillness. I listened to her short, nervous breaths, and found out about her anxiety in those rhythms, the same as if she'd been running around the room and collapsed exhausted, panting. I wondered about the force of will it had taken her to turn her face away from food bowls. Maybe, when she refused to eat, people tried to feed her by hand. Did she bite the hands that were trying to feed her? She would have been terribly hungry. She would have been terribly weak. I had the feeling she remembered that.

"Josie," I said. "You would not believe how much I get it that your will is a whole lot bigger than your body. I'm in *awe* of you. I mean, I know about things like that."

She let herself go out of a crouch into a lie-down. I could feel her unhappiness and confusion like a message being broadcast somehow to a part of my brain I didn't even know I had. I wished I could tell her she wasn't the only one in this room with memories that needed erasing. I wished she'd look warmly at all this *me*.

I was careful not to look into her eyes too long, which I somehow knew would set off new alarms in her. I stared at my own feet, then my legs, which I saw were in need of a shaving. I was usually so fussy about that. I could not believe I'd just showered without noticing I was growing leg hair. Or maybe I'd noticed, and thought, so what?

It was late afternoon. I had the window shutters open. Evening was beginning to slide to us from the mountain, gray and soft like fur. I was chilly in my towel. I was only human, only skin, hair. How was I supposed to get through to this dog? What did I know about life anyway, except that, against incredible odds, even when it's been really hurt, it can still keep going, ticking along, heartbeat to heartbeat? Why couldn't I think of a way to let this dog know she might like it if I patted her in the spot where her heart was?

All I was getting was tired. I told her that.

"I'm wiped out, Josie," I whispered. "I know you can't hear me, but I just feel like telling someone I'm pretty wiped."

Sometimes in my body I still didn't know the difference between sleep need and dangling at the edge of coming down from a high, especially a high I'd forgotten to cushion with a pill or something to drink. Sometimes I'd really been careless with that. So instead of being okay with dropping into slumber like a normal person, I could sort of panic.

I was sitting there. I couldn't know what sort of look came into my eyes and over my face, what sort of vibrations started passing from me upward, invisibly, to that little white dog. It wasn't as if I was shaking.

I had the towel tucked in so I didn't have to hold on to it. I crisscrossed my arms at my chest, and suddenly Josie's expression changed. First it seemed to me that she was telling me she knew the meaning of *scared*. Then it seemed she'd just learned the meaning of *hold on*. I looked into her eyes. She let me. And then she rose and jumped down to the floor, landing lightly at my side.

I was so busy with my own self, I couldn't reach out a hand to pat her. So we didn't have to go through the whole reach-out-and-get-bitten thing, even though patting her was my goal. What are goals anyway? Goals are for fields where people play games. Goals are totally overrated. In fact, over the last couple of years, whenever anyone started nagging me again about my goals, I'd say, "Hello? Am I supposed to think life is a game? Do I look like someone who's into *sports?*"

Josie stared at me as if reading my thoughts and finding herself in complete agreement with me. She came closer, closer. She acted as though she'd just been swimming, or she'd been out in snow or rain getting drenched. She rubbed herself against my towel, left side and back. Then she hunkered down flat at my right, pressing herself against me, her head in the curve above my hip. Her body was relaxed. Her tail wagged from side to side, very slowly. I could feel her weight as she leaned into me. I felt she was letting me hold her, sort of.

I became so all right, I nearly dozed off upright, as if I were slipping out of being awake as sweetly and softly as a baby. But she felt she'd had enough. She went to the door and positioned herself in front of it, looking at me over her shoulder. I saw how polite she was about asking me to open it for her.

I got up. I wanted to dress in a hurry and follow her downstairs, but it took everything I had just to get myself to my bunk for a nap. I didn't care that the towel was damp. It smelled good. It smelled like a dog.

Sixteen

"LET'S START A conversation, Shadow."

He looked up at me: the puzzle, speckled, spotted, tan, brown, black, as quiet as snow with his droopy eyes, with his face so narrow and haunted. He and I were in the lobby. Mrs. Auberchon had promised she'd signal from the kitchen when she was ready to hide in the broom closet and scream for help, so I could see what Shadow would do. While I waited for the scream, I chose the beagle aspect of his heritage for our first try at one-on-one.

"When I was a kid," I told him, "I was the only one I knew who hated *Peanuts*. Every holiday there was a special — Christmas, Halloween, Thanksgiving, everything. I had a teacher who made us say who your favorite character was, and everyone else was saying, Charlie Brown! Snoopy! Or whoever else they picked. I stayed out of it. I couldn't pick a character because I thought they all were morons. I thought Snoopy was a smug little jerk. I thought he was an insult to beagles, not that I knew any beagles."

I was sitting in the heavily upholstered armchair not far from the wood stove. It looked like it was placed there maybe fifty years ago and never moved. It was so high, my feet weren't touching the floor. Shadow was sitting in front of me. I held a tennis ball in my hand. He wanted it. But he didn't know how to ask for it.

"I know you agree with me about Snoopy," I said.

I was really only letting him get used to my voice. I thought it would be fair to give him a chance to see that he was an insider with me. I wanted him to know I was imagining him outside a house where people were moving about, passing by windows, making noise.

Maybe he knew that not all dogs in the world are attached to a chain. Or maybe he thought he was the same as everyone else. Maybe, even at the height of being hopeful, he knew he was never going to be inside that house. At night, he probably saw the weird glow of a television throbbing in a window, whites and grays and pale blues. If he were a little kid, he might have fantasized those lights turning into a vehicle—a spaceship, say. There it would come, hovering above him, opening a hatch. Friendly aliens would use unearthly powers to get him out of there, off the chain, away from his own shit and piss. It must have shamed him to live every day in his own mess.

I wondered, how can anyone go to a place inside someone where the loneliness is, when the someone was never anything but lonely?

And I wondered if, at sunrise, Shadow lifted his head to see light coming into the sky. Maybe he did for a while, but then he stopped bothering. Maybe he was twilight and darkness inside himself and that was all there was.

I thought about what it's like to give up on looking at light.

"Scooby-Doo," I said. "That's another example of famous dogs in cartoons for kids. Trust me, they're all idiots."

He stared at the ball. I tried another approach.

"If you were a kid in school with me," I said, "I'd want you near me all the time. I could have used the support. You wouldn't believe what it was like to keep trying to figure out why everyone loved things I thought were stupid."

He backed away a little and lay down. One day, or perhaps it was night, in a secret operation, someone showed up. A stranger? A neighbor? Someone who lived in the house? I wondered what it was like for him when the hand of a human took hold of the chain where it was attached to him, to a choke collar. A choke collar is metal. When he came to the Sanctuary, he had to be treated for a ring of infection, like a necklace. How many times did he pull at that chain with the collar digging into him? How many times did he bark before he stopped barking?

A hand of a human undid the chain. Somewhere in the world a person went to bed with this thought: I saved a dog today.

Mute Shadow. Maybe he fell in love with his silence, like a monk in the vault of a cloister, softly padding through the hours. I wondered if he barked in his dreams.

I had looked at his neck. There wasn't a scar from the infection. His collar now was a loose, fabric one. Nothing was wrong with his vocal cords. But if he went into search-and-rescue, he needed to first have some rehab. I pictured him finding a hiker in an avalanche. He'd be standing there proud of himself, licking the face of the person. The person could be dying, and he'd keep the news to himself.

Then the person would be dead before humans arrived with life-saving things, and they'd throw him off the rescue team and there would go his pride. He would sink to new levels of silence, and feel worse about himself, like he was back on the chain, but this time his chain was invisible.

"Ask me for the ball," I told him.

That was when Mrs. Auberchon walked in. She was wearing her coat and boots. A purse was on her arm. She seemed anxious. For once, she wasn't looking at me as if she'd call that treats woman and say, *I can't believe this girl is still here.*

"You'll never guess what happened. The Jeep has to go to Midas Muffler."

Shadow looked up at her with interest. Like Tasha, he connected her with the kitchen. A little drool was slopping out of him. Maybe he thought drooling was a form of talking.

I said, "I guess that can only mean one thing."

"It does," said Mrs. Auberchon. "Someone donated the money for a muffler, directly to the shop. It's a gift certificate. From an anonymous donor."

"Wow," I said. "That's so cool."

"I don't like the change in my plans, but George is in charge of it, and he can't drive into town. I don't like driving. I like the bus. I like taxis."

I was sure she'd only confided in me because of her agitation. She liked her routine.

"I'm taking George with me," she said. "You'll be keeping Shadow here with you."

I waited for her to give me a list of things not to do, like I was a babysitter she'd hired. But she just gave me a distracted little wave of goodbye before she hurried outside. Shadow pricked his ears at the noise of the Jeep. It was entering the lane.

"It's not coming here to pick you up. You're stuck with me," I said.

Suddenly, in the absence of Mrs. Auberchon, I felt the inn around me in a big, expansive, comfortable, familiar way. The stove was radiating heat. The sun was shining. The temperature outdoors had risen to double digits for the first time since I'd arrived. I realized I wasn't sure what the day was. I also realized it wasn't important to me to know, or to care, as if I'd lost the ability to measure time by what it said on a calendar, or even a clock.

But Shadow and I were not to be on our own. A whining was coming in from just outside the front door, like the sound of a broken heart. It was a whimper and a moan, combined. I knew right away who it was.

Shadow stayed put while I opened the door. Tasha was splayed in her Rottweiler self on the ground, as if someone turned her into a rug.

She raised her eyes but not her head. I guessed what had happened. My first reaction was all softness and sympathy, but I decided I'd better be tough.

"Get in here, Tasha," I said. "Stop with the misery and come in."

She sighed so deeply, it was almost the sound of wind.

I said, "You came down in the Jeep with Giant George, right? And then you got thrown out because they wouldn't take you to Midas Muffler, right?"

She started whining again, but softly, mixed in with her normal breathing.

"Did you chase the Jeep down the lane? And then you gave up?"

I'd guessed right. Tasha entered the soprano range of the whine, letting out long, reedy notes. She sounded like an oboe in the opening lines of something so melancholy and wrenching, you'd want to start crying right away.

"This is not like how it was like before," I told her. "Do you have any idea how fucked up it is to live over and over the worst thing that ever happened to you? It's pretty fucked up, Tasha. Come on. Get up and come inside *now*."

There was no reaction. I felt Shadow brushing up against me. I couldn't tell from his expression if he felt sorry for Tasha, or worried, or nothing at all.

"Tasha got dumped from a vehicle again," I told Shadow. "She's having a flashback, and she can't make it go away."

Then Shadow was pushing past me, bounding out the doorway. When he reached Tasha, he placed himself in a stand in front of her. He lowered his head as far as he could, and looked into her eyes, and started barking at her.

At first it was weak, almost like the squeak of a puppy, but then he got the hang of it. He was a tenor. He was a trumpet. He was . . . a siren! After several big barks with little pauses between them, he lifted his head and howled, like an ambulance, like a fire engine, like a hound. So that's what people mean when they say dogs like to howl at the moon, I was thinking, even though the moon was in a phase of being invisible in daylight.

Tasha's eyes opened wide, but not in amazement, not like mine. She could not have cared less if Shadow found his bark or stayed mute forever. She was irritated. She looked at him like he was hurting her ears. She didn't get hostile to him, or casually lift a paw to smack him away, but maybe she would have done so if I weren't there.

She heaved herself up and walked around him. I stepped back from the doorway so she could come in. She wouldn't look at me, but she let out one bark, which was more like a Rottweiler-grunt of information, in case no one had figured out that she was having a terrible day.

Shadow had turned around so he could bay at her bum and her tail. I threw him the tennis ball. I was shaky with too many feelings at once, so my aim was off, and he didn't catch it. But that meant he had to search for it. He had to rescue it. He came up from the depths with a beard of snow and a snowy ball in his mouth, and I threw back my head and laughed at him. I didn't try to remember the last time such sounds came out of me. But I felt it might have been never.

Shadow stared at me proudly, like I'd done a copycat thing, like I'd learned from him to make a good noise, even though it wasn't on a level with barking and howling. I had to ask myself, who *are* you?

I looked at who I was: *new Evie.* I was someone holding out a hand to pat a dog in front of me, while my other hand was reaching to grab the collar of the huge dog behind me, who very much wanted to get into my pockets to see if I had treats. I was some-one with echoes ringing in my ears, both human and dog, and I wanted them never to stop. I was someone waiting for a cranky middle-aged woman who didn't like me to come back in a Jeep with a big teenage boy who was a total mystery and also a pain in the ass, and the Jeep would have a muffler that didn't sound like gunshot. And as soon as they returned, I'd be telling them, "Shadow barked and howled."

I was someone outside the world. I was someone with a phone turned on briefly to make a call. I was someone with a credit card taken out of a wallet. I was someone who remembered three muffler shops starting with M: Meineke, Midas, Monro. I was someone who picked Midas because the Meineke customer ser-vice phone went to voicemail, and a person answered at Midas, because of course I had to go in alphabetic order. I was someone who said to Midas, "Put down my name as Anonymous."

That was all I could think of, plus the fact that I knew I didn't want anything bad to happen to any dog ever.

I motioned for Shadow to follow me inside. He was barely through the doorway when Tasha saw the ball in his mouth and decided it ought to be hers. I was still holding her by the collar. She was pulling like crazy. She'd opened her jaws to try to go for a grab, and I saw that most of Shadow's head could fit between her teeth. But he was smart. He rushed to the armchair, slid under it, and curled himself up, his chin on top of his front paws, his front paws on top of the ball. I was proud of him all over again.

"Tasha, sit," I said. "I'll get you a treat when you *sit*."

That was a mistake. I should have known not to say ahead of time the only word in human language she cared about. She pre-tended to do what I commanded, but one second after I let go of her collar, she jumped me. She got her paws on my shoulders. We were nearly the same height, body to body, like we were dancing partners. Her tongue slobbered on my cheeks.

Then the phone was ringing in Mrs. Auberchon's kitchen, where no one was.

"Down, Tasha," I said.

She made me push her off. It wasn't easy. I was busy with that as the answering machine kicked in. The kitchen door was open, so I heard the message being left.

The voice was a woman's, strong and clear. The caller was addressing Mrs. Auberchon.

Tasha recognized the voice. She sat at once, tilting back her head, with her tongue lolling and her eyes full of calmness. Under the chair, Shadow stuck out his head. His ears perked up. Yes, I know the voice, he was saying to me, with a look. That was how I knew the call was coming from the Sanctuary.

"You can send Evie up today, Mrs. Auberchon," the voice said.

And suddenly I was someone who was going up the mountain. Going up the mountain!

But first, I had to deal with Tasha, whose day was getting worse. Her calmness was over when the voice from the Sanctuary stopped. She jumped again, a little rougher this time, not like play, but I remembered *don't allow*. I whirled around, so Tasha thudded off my back and bounced down.

"No jumping, Tasha," I said.

Her look was pure innocence. Her eyes were saying, jumping on humans is a thrill. I looked over at Shadow. His eyes were closing. He'd exhausted himself. He needed to stay in his safe place, dreaming of barking and howling and finding something hidden in snow.

I was full of new confidence. I made up my mind to teach Tasha the basic commands—well, maybe one or two. I slid open the door to the other room, and she bounded in.

"Tasha, listen," I said. "You have to learn the five basics. Five like fingers. On a human."

Again, a jump. Again I spun around. Again a thudding.

Then I faced her, arms folded across my chest. I refused to turn into a softie from being melted inside by the sweetness of her face, especially with those polka dots above her eyes, bronze-brown like new pennies, but soft and smooth. How could anyone resist the urge to stroke each one?

I resisted. I walked backward toward the storage containers and took a biscuit. I almost held it up in the air to show it to her, but I figured out quickly it would have been stupid, as if I'd brought this dog here to give meaning and purpose to jumping.

"Sit, Tasha. You know what that means. *Sit*."

I grabbed her collar as she started going into another jump. But I didn't hang on to the biscuit. It fell to the floor. Tasha started going for it as if she hadn't eaten anything for days and might die of starvation. I heard a sound of gasping. I will never forget that sound. I realized she was panicking, as if I'd cut off her air, on purpose.

The power of her pulling sent hot shocks of pain up my arm and into my shoulder. But still, I didn't agree with her that what I was doing was choking her. I didn't think I was yanking on the collar too hard because I'd gone out of control with trying to control this animal—this animal I was suddenly not allowing to breathe.

I was a blank to myself in the long time of that moment before I let go of the collar.

Tasha sat. The biscuit was just a couple of inches away. She did not make a move to get it. She didn't look at me. She panted heavily. When she was finally okay again about her air, she furrowed her brow. I saw the dots above her eyes go narrow, in a terrible diminishing. I saw her bowing her head to me, her beautiful Rottweiler head. She was looking at the floor and the biscuit, and I knew she wasn't saying, I'm sorry for the jumping. I knew she was saying, you're my alpha, you've terrified me, and please, I'll do anything you want, just please don't strangle me again.

Now I was the one who couldn't breathe right. I picked up the biscuit. I held it to Tasha's mouth. She accepted it but did not look up.

"Good dog, Tasha," I said.

Still she hung her head, sitting on her haunches, subdued. It was clear to me that, if I wanted to, I could get her through the basic commands. She'd learn them because she'd be saying to herself, what else will this human do to me if I don't obey?

"Tasha," I whispered. "I don't want to be a fascist. I'm sorry. I need a time-out."

She knew right away who'd be going into the crate. It felt good to see her polka dots come back to being round.

"I want you to erase the memory of what I did to you," I said.

She looked like she was willing to think about it. She followed me to the cage. Her tail was wagging as I went down on my hands and knees and crawled in. The floor smelled like dog. Every atom of every piece of metal smelled like dog.

The cage was high enough for me to sit. I decided the best way to handle this was in a yoga position. I crossed my legs before reaching to close the door, because it's not really a time-out if the door stays open.

But here was Tasha, head-butting the door to stop it from shutting.

There wasn't enough room for both of us. Tasha's bum was sticking out, following her command to herself to lie down. Much of the front of her came into my lap, as if the true purpose of the lotus position is to better receive a Rottweiler. She let out her tongue to lick my chin, in a huge amount of slobber. I didn't tell her that her weight would cramp me in about one minute. I told her I thought she was wonderful. I told her many other adjectives that mean the same thing, and I told her I was mad at myself, not at her, although it really did suck of her to jump humans, and then I started humming to her.

It popped into my head as the right thing to do. I didn't hum an actual tune. I was just making sounds up and down. When I was sick of having no words, I sang the words of the basic commands, over and over, mixing them up so they weren't always in the same order. Then the tune became a combination of the opening of *The Simpsons,* because of talking to Shadow, and *Sesame Street,* because of the Weimaraners. She tucked into me. I patted and patted her. I had no way of knowing if this was the first time a human ever sang to her. When I interrupted myself to say again that I was sorry for what I did to her breath, she raised a paw and thumped me. Stop talking and get back to the song, she was saying.

And so I felt what it's like to be forgiven by a dog.

The time-out was over when I had to make her get off me before I was paralyzed forever from the crush of her. She followed me around for the next few hours, until we heard Shadow barking at the Jeep coming into the yard. He thought it was a stranger, because of the noise it wasn't making.

Seventeen

A NEW DOG WAS in Solitary. Mrs. Auberchon only knew a name, an age, a gender.

Alfie. Male. Age approximately three.

He was facing away from the camera, and he was absolutely still. She saw a tan coat, a thin, curled tail, long and skinny legs. The coat was smooth as suede. The body was lean, angular. He was bred to be sleek as a bullet. He was a greyhound. His silence filled her with an awful aching — only that, the silence of the dog on her screen, not the strange new quiet of the inn.

Evie was just a guest. Guests left the inn all the time. That's what guests did.

And the newly quiet Jeep was on its way up the mountain road, George at the wheel, Evie beside him, the two dogs in the back, Tasha and Shadow. They left with the windows rolled down so the dogs could stick their heads out and bark and howl. It was a victory that Shadow found his voice, but enough was enough.

"Bye, Mrs. Auberchon!" Evie had yelled.

She'd run out to the Jeep like a dog breaking into a leap, like she was Hank. Slung by one strap on her shoulder was her pack, so heavy on the night she arrived, she couldn't carry it and had to drag it. Why was it so light now? Had she left things behind? Would she be phoning Mrs. Auberchon to ask her to come up to the top with her forgotten things, like Mrs. Auberchon was her servant?

Evie. Selfish girl. Twenty-four. Why couldn't she have cared a tiny bit that maybe her innkeeper deserved a nice thank-you and a nice farewell?

Mrs. Auberchon began to look forward to finishing her session as Warden and going upstairs to find out what sort of a mess that girl had left behind. It might take the whole evening to clean up. She knew Evie had been down in the laundry room, without permission, while she was away.

"I hope you don't mind I did my laundry, Mrs. Auberchon!"

That's what she sang out in a yippy voice, when she was upstairs packing. She had Tasha and Shadow in the bunkroom with her. What damage had Tasha done? Had Shadow peed on a mattress? Mrs. Auberchon would see; she would see. She had already checked the laundry room. Evie left lint in the dryer screen, but that wasn't enough to get upset about.

Mrs. Auberchon remembered the chicken in the roasting pan, the strange spilled sugar, and how she'd imagined herself as Evie's mother, back when she thought Evie was crazy. She drew herself together. She had to do her job. Greyhound. Three. Alfie.

"Hello there, Alfie," she said. "What's it all about?"

Turning at her greeting, he looked up. He was all tan, with a patch of white in the narrow place from between his eyes to his nose. His beauty was strange and a little unnerving. His big round eyes were empty of expression, like dark, shiny marbles. They looked too big for that triangle of a face. They looked like the eyes of a wild animal, or maybe an alien.

Where was that piece of paper from Evie's application? Mrs. Auberchon knew she'd printed it. She just couldn't remember where she'd put it. Here on the shelf? In a drawer? She found it folded in half, inside the cover of a Beatrix Potter. She had thought the little white dog, Josie, with her biting and snapping and outbursts of chaos, might go too far one day and get herself confined. Beatrix Potter had seemed the best choice for her. But her behavior was improving. Mrs. Auberchon didn't know why, although she suspected it had something to do with Evie. Not that Mrs. Auberchon was missing Evie.

"Bye, Mrs. Auberchon!"

She had raced down the stairs with her backpack. Tasha and Shadow were in a frenzy of barking and baying, and the Jeep horn was blowing, and George was calling to her to hurry, we're going up the mountain, hurry up! In Mrs. Auberchon's hand was a log. She had to put it down. She didn't need to keep the stove going, because no one would be upstairs. What had possessed her to step toward the door as Evie approached it? Still she could feel the motion of her arms going up and out in half circles. She could feel the joke — yes, the joke — of the position she'd put herself in. She never gave departing guests a hug!

There wasn't even a backward glance, and then the door closed.

"I asked you what it's all about, Alfie," said Mrs. Auberchon, "because that's a famous song. It's an oldie. I won't sing it to you, though. What I'm going to do is read to you."

She put on her reading glasses. The font was small. She'd pushed the whole thing together in one paragraph so she could get it all on one sheet; she hated wasting paper. She unfolded it. She read straight through, without pausing or looking up.

"If the world had no animals and I couldn't be a dog trainer, I'd become someone who talks to aliens professionally. Basically, all I've done with my life so far is read, which I feel is a good background. I mean, I've been on the receiving end of massive amounts of written communication. It's only a matter of time before I get around to doing some output. I wouldn't expect my new career to be lucrative, so I'm not talking about a goal of financial bliss. I'd have to be freelance about it. And how will I know an alien when I find one? I just will. I'd start with the reality that, from the alien's point of view, the one who's the alien is *me*. And what makes me know I can communicate, somehow, with a non-human? I just know. The real question is, would I want to communicate my experiences to other people? Or would I keep what I know a secret, just for me? I might be tempted to go with "just for me," but it happened that, in preparing for a yoga class I ended up not taking, I read about a monk somewhere in Asia who climbed a mountain every day to have the sky really close to his head. He'd sit at the top and wait for enlightenment. Every twilight, when he passed through the village at the bottom of the mountain to return to his monastery, people stopped him to ask if he'd been lucky that day. Then one day, Buddha appeared to him. When the visit was over, down went the monk toward the village. Again came people and the question, and he shook his head, same as always, and followed his regular path to his evening tea, his bowl of rice, his bedroll. He didn't even tell his fellow monks what happened to him, and it wasn't a monastery where you took a vow of silence. After his death, it was discovered he'd written a memoir. He admitted he'd seen Buddha, and it was amazing, like coming face-to-face with an extraterrestrial, combined with the thing of being holy, but he couldn't say anything more, because (1) he was the one Buddha chose to appear to, so it wasn't anyone else's business, and (2) he didn't want to wreck his experience by putting it into mere stupid human words, and do you know what that is? That is pathetic. That is *selfish*. That's all I need to say, except that, although many people in my life have told me they think I'm selfish, I don't think I am, not absolutely totally. One thing I'm sure of is that I'd never be selfish about anything concerning an alien, or, actually, a dog."

Having reached the end, Mrs. Auberchon paused for breath,

then looked at the greyhound. He was stretched out on the floor, lying on his side, legs tucked in. His eyes were closed.

There was a movement. A tautness came over him, like an all-body spasm. His front legs became unfolded, extended, and Mrs. Auberchon saw them twitch, then sweep in small arcs against the floor. She knew what was happening. He was back on a track. He was running a race, the only thing waiting for him in his dreamland.

"It's all right," she said softly into the microphone. "Everything that happened to you before is over. Believe me, I know what I'm talking about. Good dog. Sleep well. You need it. I won't be far away."

The inn was in the hush of twilight as she made her way upstairs. She thought of the narrow mountain road, which she'd only ever seen from the bottom. The snowbanks were tall as walls—an upward tunnel with a ceiling of sky. Evie had wanted to be up in the air. She had wanted to be high. She'd been so disappointed about the gondola.

Mrs. Auberchon reminded herself to get back to the pleasure of looking forward to being angry. She pictured the bunkroom as if a tornado went through it. She was ready for smells of dog pee, of a dirty bathroom, of every leftover scent of a guest there could be.

In the doorway she gasped. The room was as clean and pristine as if no one had been there. Evie had laundered her sheets, had folded them, had left them on the edge of her bunk. Mrs. Auberchon looked at the folding and knew she couldn't do better herself.

Evie had done her towels too. There they were on the bathroom rack, smelling clean, fresh from the dryer. She had washed down the bathroom like a maid. Nothing had been left behind. The wastebasket was empty. The toilet had been scrubbed. The floor was still damp from being washed. The bar of soap on its chrome wall holder had not been used; it was as dry as a stone.

The toilet brush was as clean as if newly bought. The fleecy rug by the shower stall had also been laundered. The tiles in the stall were shiny clean.

Mrs. Auberchon picked up the bed linen and went back downstairs. She put the linen away in the closet. She told herself it was wonderful that she didn't have to bother with laundry or a cleanup after a guest.

Back at her screen, she remembered for the first time that day to check her email. She found a message from the Sanctuary, hours and hours old. Before Evie left the inn, would Mrs. Auberchon speak to her about being in touch with people who expected her to be in touch with them? There'd been phone calls. It seemed she had not been in touch. Would Mrs. Auberchon take care of this? It was perfectly reasonable for people in her life to be upset about not hearing from her. But the calls were very distracting.

Mrs. Auberchon saw no need to respond. They could speak to her themselves. She checked the greyhound, all right for now in his sleep. She did a scan of the holding area and wondered how the sled pups were doing—the last time she'd looked around there, they were almost ready to leave, and blissfully at rest, with full bellies. The door stood ajar, which meant a new one was on the way. And when she switched to the infirmary, she saw a new one flat out in a post-surgery cage: a small-to-medium terrier, Scottish, with a coat the color of pepper mixed here and there with salt. The dog was deep in sedation and had no need of her, not yet.

She returned to look at sleeping Alfie, then back to Holding. The new arrival was entering on long, skittish legs, like a newborn colt, head down, and she thought it might be another greyhound. It *was* a hound, but a too skinny one, a mix of maybe three or four breeds. Large, light brown spots, cowlike, showed here and there on a creamy white coat. The too thin face was white, with a patch of the brown around one eye, in an oval that began right under the eye and extended to the forehead.

Three of them! She would have to eat supper in her room, something light, a can of soup. She didn't care what she ate.

She went back to her email and deleted the Sanctuary's message so she wouldn't be tempted to read it again and wonder about it. She hoped that removing it from her computer would be the same as removing it from her mind. Then she listened to what it was like without Evie overhead, Evie coming down the stairs, Evie running water through the pipes. She told herself how good it was to be here, alone in this quiet, doing her job, in her own private Solitary, just the way she wanted it, just the way she liked it.

Eighteen

It was almost night when I arrived at the top of the mountain.

The stone and timber lodge looked older than it did in the photos I'd stared at so hopefully. But there it was, solid and broad, three stories tall, with a wide front porch and a background of pines, hemlocks, oaks, birches. All around in the dusk were sprays of powdery, swirling, windy snow.

Tasha and Shadow leaped out of the Jeep before Giant George got hold of their leashes. He ran after them as they tore around to the back, to the door leading into the kennels. They knew what time it was: dinnertime.

On the path to the lodge, I paused to look up at the Sanctuary's banner, flapping and dipping as the cold wind rose and fell.

I didn't mind being left to climb the wide stone steps to the front door alone. I knew from Giant George that I'd be greeted by a staffer who'd show me my room and bring me to supper, where I'd meet everyone I was about to be with for the rest of the winter and well into spring.

I'd expected to be nervous. The stonework and rough-hewn logs of the lodge should have made it intimidating, but the opposite was true. The chimneys on either side were like bookends pressed up to the walls. The smell of their smoke, scattered by wind like the snow, was woody and rich and warm. Nothing was harsh or lonely about this place. The front steps were lit by round solar bulbs on slender rods poking up from the snow along the risers. The lights in the windows had the mellow glow of candle-light, and for a few moments I was enchanted, as if I'd entered a Christmas card or a carol.

Then the nervousness kicked in. Playing back to me was the voice on Mrs. Auberchon's answering machine. I thought about how strange it was that I didn't know anything about who was running the Sanctuary, or who was there. Their website gave no information in terms of names or photos of people. There were only the photos of the happy, healthy dogs, plus a long page of testimonials from people who had gone through training, and what jobs they'd secured later, and how their lives had been changed for the better, for the best.

I had loved that page. Those statements had the feel of some-thing true. They were signed with nicknames, or first names and a last initial, and a place they were from, such as "Buzzy the Big-Dog Whisperer in Wisconsin," "Julie A., Topeka," "Mrs. L., proud to be a K-9 kindergarten lady in Delaware." I remembered what it was like to want to be one of them. But what about the person the voice belonged to?

I felt it was the voice of an alpha. The Sanctuary was based on positive reinforcement, but what about the one at the top? How long would it take her to disapprove of me and wish I'd never been accepted? Did this alpha get reports on me from Mrs. Au-berchon and Giant George, none of which put me in a positive light? Would I be back at the inn for another baking day, with an ear to the kitchen, agreeing with everything being said about me, all of it negative?

I gulped mountain air. All the questions I'd planned to ask Giant George on the way up had disappeared from my mind. It was too wonderful to be moving. My head was still throbbing from the rush of the ascent, because of course I'd gone up with my window open — up along the road that was an almost vertical tunnel, with walls of snow and a ceiling of sky. Did it make up for not getting a ride in a gondola, which I knew from the photo wasn't glassed-in, but open? It did. I had stepped on the snow at the top of the mountain with the feeling that I'd arrived in the car of a roller coaster, up, up, up.

Now was the plunge. I had nowhere else to go. I pushed open the front door and stepped inside. No one was there to meet me.

It was a wide, open room filled with dog cages of different sizes, and dog beds, and stacked storage bins, lots of them, same as in the training room at the inn, but on a much grander scale. The floor was made of pine boards, and in the big area away from the bins and beds and cages it was covered by a huge mat of thin, tough-looking rubber, in a chessboard pattern of squares in all the primary colors, but mostly greens and yellows.

I called out a hello, and another, with question marks at the ends.

There was a movement in a corner. One of the cages, door open, had an occupant. This cage was different from the others. It had a large, round cushion and, on the side, hanging from little hooks, a laminated pinewood sign with a name that someone carved into it in balloonish letters painted in a tawny shade of gold. The name was Boomer. What I'd thought was a heaped-up fleecy blanket or rug, thrown onto the cushion, was a dog, stirring, rising.

He was a golden retriever, old, old, old, coming toward me on legs that were obviously arthritic. His muzzle was gray and white, and his tongue was unfurled, like a damp little banner he carried in front of himself. His coat was thick and healthy, and curly here and there, in combinations of tawny and yellow. The flaps of his ears were dark gold velvet. He was large in a lionlike way, and a little overweight. His mane was white and flowing. At his other end, his plush, feathery tail was going back and forth gently, swishing, almost in slow motion. But maybe in his own mind he was swinging it as vigorously as a puppy.

Boomer. Welcome to the mountain, he was saying.

On duty as he was, he allowed me to scruff my fingers behind his ears. Then he opened his jaws and soft-mouthed my wrist, tugging at me to follow him. I shouldered my pack and obeyed.

The staircase to the second floor was down a hallway off that huge front room. I hadn't known how weary I was until I had to wait behind Boomer as he climbed up ahead of me. At every step, he had to pause to catch his breath, then look back to make sure I was doing what I was supposed to.

I was ready for another bunkroom, but here was a corridor of old, highly polished, knotty-pine doors, three on each side. One door was open, in the middle.

Lamplight gleamed out with a friendly warmth, and Boomer took up a position in the hall, a few feet away, facing it. I knew I was meant to leave my things and follow the dog back downstairs, but it seemed a good idea to try out the bed, just for a second, to see how it felt. It was a twin: narrow, sturdy, a good mattress.

Boomer came in. He seemed concerned. I told him not to worry.

The air was unusually heavy, I thought, as if that's why my eyes were closing. I was aware of comfort, in a small space that didn't bother me for being so narrow. I saw pale blue walls, a bronze lamp with a yellow shade on a square wood table, timber rafters over my head with white lanes of ceiling between them, and a big window where the drapes were undrawn. Darkness pressed up outside the glass. I heard the wind, whistling faintly, light as breath. I noticed, too, on the floor beside the table, the cardboard packing box of the rest of my clothes. So it had arrived. The tape was still in place, but it was looking beat up, as if it had been kicked and mangled — then I saw the rips, the bite marks.

Tasha, I was saying to myself, I hope that wasn't you. But I knew it was.

I tumbled into sleep with my jacket and boots still on, and woke by being licked on the hand by Boomer.

He was too arthritic to get up onto the bed. When I opened my eyes, he was impatient about pulling at me. I felt I'd slept a whole night, but it was only a nap, a short one. I was glad about that. It meant I wouldn't be late by much for my first supper on the mountain and the warm welcome from humans I felt I deserved.

Down we went, slowly, across that open front area toward the back. But halfway down the hall to the dining room, Boomer caught the food smells ahead. He decided to take himself off duty. He went into denial about his bad joints and oldness and extra weight. He hurried away from me almost in a prance, head high, nose up, as if he hoped to find a place at a Sanctuary table, set for him without silverware.

I was counting on him to stick with me. I didn't think it was too much to ask for. Golden retrievers, I'd read in the breed book, *are profoundly responsible and selfless. Their greatest instincts are for human approval and love.*

I came to a halt. I felt frozen, like I was getting hypothermia without being cold or outdoors. This was not the first time I wasn't okay with myself because of someone I thought would stand by me and then he didn't.

They had warned me about this sort of thing in my former program. I'd been warned, "Evie, back in the day, when you were so busy with your D of C, you totally didn't tune in to, like, reality, which sooner or later in some form is going to catch up with you, somehow, especially if a big-deal thing took place."

D of C means "drug of choice." It hadn't sounded like something I should worry about. I understood the point of, oh, I might have feelings about things retroactively, because you can't have feelings while you're deep in a relationship with your drug of choice. You can only have feelings the choice will let you have.

And what feelings will the choice let you have?

The choice will only let you have feelings about the choice, plain and simple, like it's your *alpha.*

And all along I hadn't worried. I listened to the warning and said, "Do I look like someone who'd be afraid of having feelings?" I even looked forward to having some, like flashbacks of things I didn't get to experience the first time around. So I wasn't prepared at all for this freeze.

He had promised he'd stand by me. It was: program, great. It was: pass the first stage and then the principal person gets to visit all the time, completely unrestricted.

He had graduated before I did. He was a year ahead of me. He went off to graduate school, and then I did too. That was the plan. Same place, different planets.

I hated graduate school. I knew I needed not to be there practically my first day. But both our planets were always having parties, not that I'm saying I became more involved with my D of C because of parties. I became more involved because I didn't want to go to sleep. I didn't want to go to sleep because all that would happen was waking up to wonder even harder why everyone else liked something I hated, and what was I going to do when I *dropped out to wander around in my life like a stray,* not that I'd put it to myself that way at the time. In my former life, I never compared anything to dogs.

I was glad they let you have a principal person and it was him.

And then it wasn't. But he stayed on my intake form. They wouldn't let you cross out your principal unless you gave them a new name. They wouldn't let you fill in that blank with "Myself."

I looked at where I was. Evie, I was saying to myself. This is now. The walls on the way to the Sanctuary dining room were pale with old paint, like cream that's gone by. I saw different-tone squares and rectangles where pictures used to hang. Of course they would have been photos of long-ago skiers, of this place as a resort, and the gondola too. I thought of people passing this way toward dinner, in sexy after-ski outfits, probably coming from a cocktail hour, smelling of liquor, wool, leather, perfume and cologne, pleasure, desire, calm nerves, jumpy nerves, plus liniment for where they'd fallen and it hurt.

It felt good to look at blank spaces and fill them in.

He said he was sorry he never came. This was in a letter. He'd said he was embarrassed about how he kept planning to, but then something would always come up he couldn't get away from, because that was how it was in the field of chemical engineering, with labs and things. He was so busy, he'd given up parties. He said he wished he could be there for me. I'd probably be amazed, he said, if I had any idea how awful he felt about not being able to get away. I didn't know it was a breakup letter until after I'd memorized it and played it back to myself maybe one hundred times.

This wasn't the program I was in when I found the Sanctuary website. This was the one I was in near our graduate school. The number of minutes it took to drive there from the chemistry planet was twenty-one. I had checked it on a map, back when I was looking out windows over the parking lot and saying to myself, he must be stuck in traffic.

My real program came after the letter and also after I went back to graduate school to see if I'd been wrong about it, which I wasn't. I didn't see him again. He hadn't lied about no longer going to parties.

I'm not going to call him Made Me Happy again. He only made me happy for a little while. Also in the letter, he told me he was never going to stop being sorry, ever. He said that, for the rest of his life, whenever he was in his car with the radio on scan, which was his favorite way to listen to the radio while driving, he would hit Play if that song "Stand By Me" came on, so he could really rub it in with himself how, when it came to me, he didn't.

That was when I started to unfreeze in the hallway. I'd started thinking about "Stand By Me." I started hearing it in my head. It's a good song. But rub it in with? With a tune on a radio in a car?

That is pathetic. That is shallow. That is selfish. That is the act of a *coward*. And his poetry *sucked*, except for the seventeen syllables about me.

I was okay. I remembered how he wanted me to write a haiku. I had promised I would. I remembered I wanted to be someone who keeps promises. I'd never said in the promise that it would be about him, which of course was what he'd meant. This *freed* me. I thought about how good it might feel someday to be taken over by the craving to write a haiku. Probably it would have to be about a dog. Probably I wouldn't be able to write just one, once I got going.

So I had something to look forward to, besides putting one foot in front of the other and entering the Sanctuary dining room by myself because Boomer *abandoned* me.

I went in. The doorway had wooden swing doors like a saloon in a western. Boomer was able to duck and go in at a crawl. That was the reason I couldn't see what I was about to walk into, before I did. I should have known it was strange that I wasn't hearing sounds of people together at a meal.

But first, the dining room: shabby-rustic, plain, warm, smells of burning wood, ashes, barbecue, meat, people, dog fur, furniture oil.

Something about it made me feel it had aged like anyone who hates being old but can't do anything about it except hang on to a personal dignity, the kind that only comes from inside out. It was smaller than I expected. There were exposed ceiling beams and bare floorboards so worn, they almost looked bleached. A fireplace with a floor skirt of flagstones took up most of one wall. Set above the logs was a shelf of an iron grill, where meat juices had dripped, so it smelled like the cooking was still going on.

Quilted shades, as dark brown as mud, were drawn as insulation on all the windows, so that the room had the feel of being sealed. The tables, four of them, left over from the resort, were oak and round, with high-backed chairs that looked like armless thrones. They were arranged to be close to the fire flaming low and bright in that hearth, but not one of them was set.

Two long tables stood parallel to each other just beyond them. These were conference-type, on folding legs. One was the buffet, although that's not the right word for it: a platter of brisket in strips, charred-attractive, enough for two sandwiches; a basket of homemade bread in crusty slices; a plate of lettuce, iceberg, just outer leaves sitting there limply; a plate of yellow squash slices lined with scars from the grill and looking rubbery; little bowls of mayo and a red-brown barbecue sauce; one plate, one fork, one butter knife, one napkin, one glass, and a pitcher of tea, cold, chamomile, the only tea I hate (I sniffed it), with lemon wedges tipping this way and that, as if they'd drowned and popped back to the surface, bloated.

It was a very depressing spread, except for the meat and the bread. Under it all was an old linen tablecloth, like a magnified lady's handkerchief from a couple of centuries ago. It dangled low, almost touching the floor, and I saw that, in the middle of it, two blond paws were sticking out, just by a few inches. The black nails were trimly clipped. Boomer. The spot where his face was hiding wafted in and out with his breath. I could see the shape of the end of his muzzle, pressed against the cloth like he was veiled. Of course he thought he was invisible. I guessed he was supposed to go back to his own area, after he delivered me. I won't tell on you, I messaged him.

The humans in the room who weren't me were at the other long table, without a cloth. Plates of partially eaten meals were strewn about. A giant-screen laptop sat on it like a centerpiece. Something was playing on the screen.

They were clustered around it: four women, one man, and Giant George. I tried to catch his eye, but he was riveted on whatever it was. He stood behind the woman at the keyboard. He looked older and almost a stranger, as if he changed into a man while I was upstairs having my nap. He was sandwiched between an almost old man and an elderly woman who reminded me of Mrs. Treats, in that ideal-grandmother way, but not so cushiony-looking. The man was soft in the face, his hair sparse and pale. He wore a jacket that was herringbone and very old-time English countryside, so I thought of the senior guy vet in that James Herriot series that's always turning up on PBS. I had tried to watch it one evening when I was waiting for the Sanctuary to let me know if they'd accepted me. But I had to turn it off because the episode only had cows and pigs.

And in fact this man was a vet. I had *nailed* that. He'd come up from the village hours earlier for a surgery.

I didn't know that yet. I only knew that three people were standing around a computer, and three were sitting. Giant George was in the same baggy, grubby jeans he always had on, although his sweater was a different one, clean, a pullover, baggy too, hanging on him like a cable-knit woolen bag. The Mrs. Treats–like woman wore a fleecy outfit of sweats with a zippered top, but it wasn't a hoodie. A white L. L. Bean–type turtleneck jersey was under it. Her outfit was dark gray. She wore no makeup, no jewelry, and neither did the other three women, who were dressed exactly like her but in other colors of fleece: forest green, a lighter gray, navy blue. If I had to arrange us all by age, I wouldn't do it one by one. I'd start at the bottom with Giant George, then me, then jump ahead by forty years or more for everyone else, like a group picture of young people and old, or grandchildren and grandmas and a grandpa, missing anyone in between.

Yet these old women looked rugged and strong and also sharp in the eyes, probably as a result of mountain air. And which one was the alpha?

The standing one, in the dark gray! The Mrs. Treats one! I recognized her, just as the dogs had, Tasha and Shadow, when they heard her voice on the answering machine. She lifted a finger to her lips to signal *keep quiet please and do as you're told*, before she told me I was late for dinner by twenty-five minutes, and please would I fix myself a plate and go back to my room with it, and stay there until morning?

There was no harshness. I had the feeling that any one of those women would have said the same thing to me, the same way. The word *please* was definitely involved. Alphas don't say *please*.

Everyone, even Giant George, turned their heads to look at me in a not completely hostile way. But I felt like I was *five*.

At last I paid attention to the laptop. I thought for a moment they'd tuned in to a movie, or a news report, with the sound off, for some reason. But then I noticed that the woman at the keyboard, the navy blue one, had a headset on, and the two at her sides, green and light gray, were whispering into cellphones.

I looked at the screen. I'd walked into the control center for a rescue, somewhere in the outside world, where dogs were in a place they needed very much to get out of. I saw the gleam of a flashlight or headlamp on rough terrain—a road or driveway, dirt, stony, like a NASA video of Mars. The gleam moved forward: a shaft of thin light in foggy darkness, revealing up ahead the glint of a metal fence, then a section of what seemed to be a run-down wooden shed. My heart started feeling squeezed, as if grabbed by a powerful hand. I could sense the tautness of the anxiety around me through my skin, as if my whole body was prickling from burrs. I smelled sweat as it was happening, male, female, dampening the underarms of the turtlenecks, the fleece zip-ups, the baggy sweater, the tweed of the vet.

"Please point to the fence so we can make sure they're in the building," whispered the woman in forest green into her phone.

"No one's coming out of the house. Roger that, I heard you," whispered the woman in light gray into hers. "But keep someone posted."

The light cut away. I saw weeds poking thickly and tall between links of the fence. I did not see a dog from my angle, but the woman in navy blue in front of the keyboard gave a little gasp, and the green one whispered, "We see him too. Yes, they've got him muzzled. No barking."

"Tell them to get that one first, please," said the dark gray one.

"He's going to need triage," whispered the vet.

"Fuck," whispered Giant George, then, "Sorry, I couldn't help it," and the dark gray one turned to me, tipping her head to mean *go*.

I don't know how I brought off giving in, not that I was meek about it. I kept thinking how I didn't want them sending me back to Mrs. Auberchon, where it could happen that no one came to rescue me ever. But I had a question. It occurred to me that I could put myself in a good light by being eager to get to work studying. Everything that happened at the inn with Giant George and my four dogs, it seemed to me now, was a combination of practice and testing for my actual course of training.

I said to the dark-gray one, "How about my training books? Or one, if you've only got one? I'm thinking I could do some reading. You know, like homework, even though my course hasn't started."

"Evie," she responded, "it's been started."

She was completely matter-of-fact about it, and also: no more questions; you are dismissed. At the buffet, I placed myself by invisible Boomer, my feet near his paws. I made like I needed to reach down and scratch my ankle. Lifting the cloth, I fed him the chunkiest strip of the brisket, which of course he was dog-praying for. He followed me out of the dining room of his own free will. He stayed behind me closely, and I thought, oh, that's what they meant in the breed book about dogs doing *heeling*.

No one said good night to me. I ate in the hall while Boomer looked up at me with eyes of absolute trust—I mean, he totally trusted me to cut him in on my supper. I ended up giving him about a quarter of a sandwich. I tried to hear what was going on behind those saloon doors, but I didn't hear a thing. I left my empty plate and glass and napkin on the floor. Boomer licked my hands extremely intensively, partly to praise me for doing the right thing by him. But mostly he was looking for traces of food, and then we parted ways—he to his crate, me to my room.

I was ready to toss and turn in bed, but the same thing happened to me that had happened my first night at the inn, only faster. It was a total, instant pull of gravity into sleep. The only thing I was aware of during the night was the knocking on my door, muffled, persistent, entering whatever dream I was having, probably about dogs. I roused a little, wanting it to go away. The door was cracking open. In the shadows appeared a figure. Giant George. He was back to being a boy, hobbity, Newfie-like. If he thought I'd let him crawl in with me, he had another thing coming, not that I was planning to actually bite him.

He was excited but spoke softly. "Evie," he said. "They've got the dogs. Every one of them is a pittie. They got them all out, half a dozen, all alive. No one was shot at. I mean, no one got hit. I'm sorry they didn't let you watch. Good night."

All of that went into my dreaming, although I heard the word *pittie* as *pity*.

And then it was the next morning and *oh my God I'm going to a class.*

Nineteen

ALLIANCES. WHAT DOGS will form in a basic obedience class, often against one another, as in cliques, but always together against the boring, horrible teacher.

Class. I don't get an orientation? What about giving me advice? It's my first mountain morning, and I'm supposed to pretend I'm the teacher?

Family. Abused rescued dogs don't get to be in training with a member or members of their human family. They have no principal person or persons. They are orphans.

Well, I'd wondered already if I wanted to be a trainer in classes without humans, not that this was what I'd had in mind.

I looked around at my orphans and saw the blanks in the air where members of families should be. I tried to take care of the blanks by imagining that family members were waiting nearby out of sight, like parents of kids in school on teacher-conference days, or parents of someone who was living, say, in a treatment or rehab program not far from their homes, and the program had regular things of, oh, let's get the family in here, because if one member has a problem, it's everyone's problem too, automatically, because that's what a family _is._

Is it too idealistic of me to agree with that definition of a family? Maybe. But maybe not.

Gains. Better word than *goals.* I was saying, "So, dogs, what are we working on gaining here today?" I thought that appropriate answers would be things like self-esteem, or learning how to stop being sad about previous-life experiences with humans they had belonged to, as in, I need to stop wishing the humans I belonged to didn't make me so sad.

But it can be a gain to not have any biting, and not have any raised hackles.

Gentle. Good adjective. Good non-alpha thing to be. Good thing to aspire to, but not until you're ready to stop being a softie, desperate to be liked and admired.

Housebreaking. Trainers have to deal with bodily functions. I hadn't thought about this. The only toilet training experience I was ever involved in was my own. Why couldn't I remember my own toilet training and apply it, not that a toilet would be involved? Why isn't there such a thing as litter boxes for dogs? (To be continued.)

Learning. Dogs don't want you to teach them. They feel they know everything already. Sit? Stay? Come? Down? Drop it? They're saying, you can't possibly think we'd listen to you. They're saying, didn't anyone tell you we're basically wolves? They're saying, teacher! Leave us dogs alone!

A new male, a greyhound called Alfie, feels that coming to class means curling up in a corner and being still. When I explained that this wasn't allowed, he bristled and showed me his teeth. I don't have notes on him yet, but I know he was a racer. He thought he had the right to never move again. Also, he was not interested in learning this thing called housebreaking. Did I know where he used to live? He used to live in a *stable.* I hated it there, he was telling me, but that's who I am.

A new hound mix, female, white with large brown spots, and

tall and fearful and constantly cowering, let me know that if I tried to speak to her, never mind teach her, she'd become so upset, her heart would stop, and she'd be dead. No notes on her either, but I think she had it bad, maybe even worse than all the others. Her name is Dapple, for her coat.

Josie was yap, yap, yapping like a wind-up toy with a battery that would never wear down. She was telling me she didn't want to come close to me. She felt that all she needed to learn was how to look even cuter, so her photo could go on Internet adoption sites, and she could stop being miserable like an orphan in a novel by Dickens. Why wasn't anyone teaching her to be cuter? Why wasn't she getting lessons in how to pose for photo shoots? And oh, one more thing: she felt she'd already taught me what would happen to me if I tried to pat her, so let's not even discuss it.

Hank had expanded his pacing technique to include loops, which meant circling whatever he planned to clear. For now, he only wanted to learn a good way of getting the other dogs to like it when he jumped over them. He was saying, is there such a thing as an Olympics for dogs? If there is, don't think I'm training for anything but hurdles.

Tasha was telling me she was impressed I'd made it to the top of the mountain, but in case I'd forgotten, she was still a Rottweiler, which meant she could do whatever she wanted. Would I never mind all this stuff about learning? However, she loved it when I sang to her at the inn. That was a memory she'd decided to keep. So please, would I stroke her polka dots, and make like Julie Andrews in *The Sound of Music*, and just sing to her?

Shadow was depressed. He was telling me he didn't want anyone to send out applications for him to SAR programs, because he was sure he'd never get accepted, and anyway, he'd probably flunk the requirement of basic obedience. He would never overcome having spent his childhood outdoors on a chain. Yes, he'd been able to learn that he couldn't pee or poop indoors. Yes, he was using his voice again. Yes, those were victories, but he was sure there could never be more. He felt he was too disadvantaged to keep learning. And, sorry about this, but following the example of Josie, he wanted nothing to do with me, as if we'd never known each other at all.

Obedience. I do not agree that a trainee should have to obey any old thing the runners of the program insist on, due to their feeling that Evie, you can't teach obedience to a dog unless you know what it feels like yourself. (To be continued.)

Patience. Working on it.

Pity. Never have. Not for abused rescued dogs, if you're the one who has to train them. Totally say no to it, *no matter what happened to them.* Pity's too easy. It rushes all through you like a drug, and then you don't feel anything but the rush. This is easier than sitting down with the dog and wondering, like an actual question you would like to have answered: so, what's it really like inside that fur?

Probation. What I was on in the inn, not that I knew it.

Real. You cannot be fake with dogs. They watch you. They X-ray you. They scan you. They try to smell your bum and your crotch. They stick their noses in your ears. One minute after they meet you, they know things about you that you don't know yourself. On a website I didn't spend time on, just before I found the one with the Heidi's-grandfather trainer, I saw a banner with a slogan urging people to have dogs. It said, "Get real. Get a dog." I didn't know then that I needed to take that literally.

Sayings. You can't rely on just words with a dog. You can't just let out a saying that, to a human, represents an important or hoped-for thing, such as "I love you." A human who is hearing those words might be okay with just having the words, because maybe the human thinks the only thing love is, is when someone says so. But maybe the human — for example, me — is not so okay with that anymore.

You can tell a dog "I love you" over and over, every single day, and absolutely, 100 percent of the time, the dog isn't going to look at you with the eyes of someone who feels loved by you, just because you said so, even if you said so in a very nice way. The dog is going to look at you like, what the fuck? What is this person talking about? What do I have to do to get this person to love me?

Seven. They're making me start my training with three new dogs on top of my starter four? Me and seven dogs? And I'm the only trainee they have?

Terrier, Scottish. The seventh, last dog on my roster. Female, age approximately nine, which makes her the eldest. Her name is Dora. She'll join later, when she's out of the infirmary. I don't know anything about the surgery she had.

Zip it! A good thing to say to a noisy, disruptive dog. Much better than, "Shut up! Or I'll take you outside and push you off this mountain!"

Twenty

DAPPLE, THE NEW spotted hound, was a local, from the village. I'd seen the notes on her. I'd thought from the notes that she was an ordinary mixed breed, not that I'm saying there's anything ordinary about dogs made of mixes — or in fact, any dog at all. "Dapple. Female," said the notes.

Treeing Walker Coonhound/Hound Mix. Age approximately three. Was delivered without collar or identification by anonymous person who left quickly, providing zero information. Underweight. Sensitive to light; may have vision issues. Highly nervous. Unsocialized. Fearful. Passive. Withdrawn. Not on medication. Will be monitored closely. Decision was made not to crate or confine. Showed zero prior experience with collar and leash, but after several attempts, became willing. Shows delight in outdoors and snow.

On the afternoon Dapple was kidnapped from the Sanctuary grounds, I was telling Boomer my troubles in the front room.

That's where Giant George found me. I was sort of in Boomer's crate with him. Mostly I was lying curled up on the floor at his open door, his paws on my shoulders, his golden mane all over my face, his big old shaggy head on top of mine. He was totally there for me. I felt partly like a scullery maid in a British import on PBS, bringing my woes to the butler, and partly like the cub of a lion.

It was my first time finding out what it's like to be held in the arms of someone who has no arms. I felt his breath in my hair, along with some drool. I felt his sleepy, Zen-like quiet, his jaw against my skull, his paw pads on the other side of my bones and skin and sweatshirt. He was good at holding. He was doing a better job with me than I'd ever done with myself.

What was I telling him? I was telling him about my classroom failures, and how maybe I could switch to washing pots and pans for the Sanctuary staffers, and spend the rest of my time picking up poop and cleaning crates and kennels, things like that, because I didn't want to leave, but obviously, as probably everyone else knew already, I wasn't going to make it as a trainer. Plus I was telling him how weird it felt to be a student in a training program where no one was actually teaching me — at least, not in an organized, normal way. I didn't even have a textbook! The only stuff I had in writing was the stuff I composed on my own!

I decided to put a positive spin on my entire situation. I found myself describing to Boomer something I'd read in my yoga period, about a young monk-in-training in a Buddhist monastery, maybe eight or nine centuries ago. The student monk was mystified about the way he was left on his own so much. The only instructions he received were given to him in questions, like "Why aren't you glad to be washing the rice pots today?" The student monk became despondent. He wondered if his teachers, who weren't acting like teachers, had despaired of him, finding him unworthy, inadequate, stupid, a loser. Then one day, after an elderly big-deal monk asked him to sweep fallen leaves off one of their outdoor meditation patios, he spoke up. What, the student wondered, would that teach him? What did dead leaves have to do with his program of training? Shouldn't he at least have something in mind while his hands did the sweeping? Some Zen thing to ponder? Something profound and also practical, in terms of his future? And the teacher-monk answered him, of course, with a question, a long one: "Why would anyone want to think of anything except fallen leaves while sweeping fallen leaves, and why would anyone think fallen leaves are not profound, and why would anyone need a teacher for anything that needs to be discovered from fallen leaves?"

I explained to Boomer that in order to feel a little calmer about the reality of my own training and future, I was mentally changing "fallen leaves" to "Sanctuary dogs." It was a leap of imagination, I explained. He seemed proud of me, although I had the feeling I'd lost him when I mentioned rice pots. He probably took it literally. He was such a food guy, he was probably imagining I'd magically produce one, so he could lick it.

"Evie, you have to get up."

I hadn't heard Giant George come in. He was geared for outside, in his Sanctuary ranger jacket. He looked down at me with a solemn, worried expression. I thought he felt sorry for me for hanging around Boomer and acting like such a baby.

"We have to re-kidnap Dapple," he said.

"What?"

"We have to go to town and rescue Dapple."

Boomer's ears went right up. I could feel the little buzz from his brain-jolt of recognition. He knew what the look on Giant George's face was saying, and why that somber, edgy tone was in his voice. He knew the word *rescue*. I could tell it was high on his personal vocabulary list, along with his words about eating, being comfortable, being a golden, doing his job.

Rescue. It had happened to Boomer, or he wouldn't be here. The only thing known about his old life was that he'd been found as a stray when he was still a very young guy. There weren't any notes on him. But I'd picked up the awareness that he wasn't the type of stray who gets accidentally lost one day and no one could be found to reclaim him. He was the type of stray who escaped a bad home. He had waited for a chance to break free, having figured out that whatever was being done to him was just plain wrong. I don't know how I knew this about him. I just knew it.

Maybe he had ESP with Dapple. Maybe he knew she didn't have a chance to turn herself into a stray.

I felt Boomer nudging me away from him, like a lion telling his cub to grow the hell up. The other crates in the room were empty except for one, open-doored, where Alfie the greyhound had curled himself up in the shape of a crescent moon. He was ignoring us. I looked at the suede of his fur, his skinny triangle of a face, his big eyes like a drawing of an alien by a child, maybe a drawing I'd done myself. I was always drawing aliens, and all of them were supposed to come to life and hang around with me. I used to think the reason they didn't was that I hadn't figured out the right words to say to them.

No eye contact, Alfie was telling me, turning his head. If he sensed the vibrations of the alarm Giant George had brought in, he kept it to himself. But being near Boomer made me feel confident.

I'll get to you later, Alfie, I messaged him. If you think you're not coming to life, you are *wrong*.

Now I was up on my feet. About an hour before, I'd seen one of the staffers pass by a window with Dapple on a leash, headed through deep snow for the easier walking on the road. I'd only looked long enough to see which of the four women she was. I'd stopped thinking of them as four strangers, but I was still in the process of undoing the way I was branded with them from my first Sanctuary supper: the Dark Gray One, the Forest Green One, the Light Gray One, the Navy Blue One. Unfortunately for me, they didn't wear the same colors all the time.

I'd seen that the one walking Dapple was Light Gray, and now she was surrounded by the other three in her room. She had walked much farther down the road than they usually did.

Giant George was told she'd broken no bones when she fell. She was a little deaf, and wasn't wearing her hearing aid. She had not heard the approaching car until it was nearly upon her. She didn't recognize the driver, a woman, or the passenger, a man. She wouldn't have connected them to Dapple. But when Dapple dropped her tail and went limp and shaky on her leash, she understood, too late, who they were.

The leash was a long one. She didn't have time to pull Dapple toward her. The man had jumped out of the car, had taken hold of Dapple by the collar, yanking the leash from her hand. Giant George was calling her Margaret. So I could change her name from Light Gray. She had lost her balance and fallen sideways. She was seventy-six. It was lucky the road was snowy.

Margaret. Staffer, female. Seventy-six. Hard of hearing. In her room, distraught, angry, frantic, blaming herself, refusing comfort, *and what was happening to Dapple right now?*

The car with Dapple had gone down the hill in reverse. The walls of snowbanks were too high for a turnaround. Dapple hadn't wanted to get into that car. You can't call police or the sheriff on a case of having dog owners take back their dog from the place the dog was brought from being kidnapped from home.

Rescue. Flashing in me was the thought of Dalmatians and Cruella De Vil. But that was all right. It took off the edge. It made me feel brave, like maybe I could actually do this.

"We have a description of the car and the guy," said Giant George. "The driver, not so much. It only took a call to Mrs. Auberchon to find out where we're going."

Boomer came out of his crate. He licked Giant George's hand, then mine, like he was wishing us good luck. I went over to Alfie to say bye, hoping maybe he'd do the same. He had closed his eyes. He wasn't asleep. I knew he was faking. I squatted and reached in the crate to pat him. He pretended he didn't feel it, and I wondered if he was afraid someone would show up to grab him and put him back on a track. Maybe he thought being rescued was a temporary thing, like being brought outdoors to do his business.

I said to Giant George, "The first thing you did was call Mrs. Auberchon?"

"She knows everyone. Get your coat, and hurry."

"Wait. Is Mrs. Auberchon coming with us?"

"Evie, no," he said, looking at me the same way the dogs looked at me in class, as if mystified about why I kept saying things that were stupid. "Mrs. Auberchon's busy with Dora in the infirmary."

"Wait. She came up? I thought she never does."

"She didn't. She doesn't. Oh, never mind. Get your *coat*."

I gave no further thought to Mrs. Auberchon. Five minutes later when I went down the front steps, I found the Jeep warming in neutral, Giant George at the wheel. I remembered he couldn't drive in the outside world. I mentioned this as soon as I was in.

"Here's what we're doing," he told me. "We have to be obsessed, completely obsessed, with being worried a cop will pull us over and ask me for a license. That way we don't have to worry about anything else."

"You're planning to speed, you mean."

"Yeah."

"I can obsess," I said.

We went down the hill fast and smoothly, as if we were on a toboggan, my ears full of engine and heater and the purring, still-new muffler, plus bits of Walt Disney tunes popping up from the memory vat of my childhood, all from *101 Dalmatians*. It never occurred to me to ask Giant George what the plan was, or if he had one. I just stayed tense and watched for a cruiser or sheriff's car. But hardly anyone else was out.

We didn't speak until we approached the village.

"I want you to tell me your real name," I said.

He must have had a soundtrack of his own going on in his head, probably something all-guy: electronic, boomy, screechy. It took him a moment to answer me. His real name was Giant George, he told me, and would I please not ask him any questions, and would I please promise him right now I'd follow his lead and do what he told me to do? I promised, but I needed to know a vital piece of information.

"Just tell me if this is your first rescue, not counting watching one on a laptop," I said.

"It's not my first one. Remember the sled pups?"

"You were in on that?"

"I ran it. That wasn't my first one either."

"Was your first one, like, on yourself?"

"Stop talking, Evie."

The change in his manner wasn't the same as the brief time before, in the dining room my first night, in front of the screen where the rescue I was banished from took place. It seemed to me then that he had changed himself magically from a big teenage boy to a man, not that it lasted. I remembered how he'd tricked me the morning I lied about walking on snowshoes. I saw, and felt in all my senses, that the change in him now wasn't only from being a kid to being a grown-up. It was the change of a kid playing soldiers or cops to actually being a cop or a soldier. It was the change of a hobbit to a human, a shaggy, bulky, drooly, awkward young Newfie to, yes, Giant George, a Great Dane.

"I'm stopping talking now," I said. "But first, if I was a dog, what kind do you think I would be? Don't say a mix. I'm just curious."

He didn't hesitate. "You're totally, totally Tasha," he said. "I mean, not counting, like, in size."

He thought I was a Rottweiler!

And suddenly he was saying, "We're almost here," and he was

turning the Jeep into a postcard of a neighborhood just beyond the supermarket and a row of shops. Or maybe not a postcard, but a came-to-life picture of a perfect place in America to live, from the days when the president was Eisenhower. It was a short street of six or seven houses on each side, all Capes with a couple of ranches, tidy and friendly and solid in the sunlight and snow. Towers of maples and oaks were everywhere. The front yards were squared by shoveled sidewalks and cleared, paved drive-ways. The backs were white carpets at the edge of woodsy pines, towers too, green and snow-fleeced and gorgeous. Most drive-ways held cars or pickup trucks, or both. It was a Saturday. No one was outside, but people were home.

The house Giant George stopped in front of was a dark brown ranch. In the windows were lacy curves of tied-back drapes and hanging plants looking happy from light and water and love. The shrubs along the foundation were covered by wooden tepees of winter protection. Absolutely everything was saying, "Decent, normal people live inside these walls."

We pulled parallel to the sidewalk. We couldn't enter the drive-way. A big heavy Buick was there, its fender just a couple of feet from the road.

"That's the car," said Giant George, turning off the Jeep. "Come on."

"Come *on*? Like we're just walking in?"

"They're not here. See that house?" He pointed down the road to a Cape, where chimney smoke chugged upward in wide, thick streamers.

"The husband and wife who live here," said Giant George, turning sideways to face me, "got invited to that house to watch a movie."

"How do you know that?"

"Because, Evie, Mrs. Auberchon knows them from, like, for-ever. She got them to do the inviting. They have a new TV. It's a huge one, the biggest one there is. And they pulled down their shades, and they're ordering pizza. And they've got a bar, like in a real bar."

I noticed that smoke wasn't coming from the chimney of the ranch. But I was getting scared, and I was doubtful.

"How do you know the husband and wife went over there?"

"Well, if they didn't, they'd be rushing out here to get rid of us. But I really know they went because, that was the first time anyone invited them to something. Mrs. Auberchon said they're kind of unpopular around here. Are you ready?"

"Just tell me if the people in the house with the new TV were the ones who delivered Dapple."

"No. They didn't know there was a dog here. Mrs. Auberchon thinks the one who delivered her was one of their kids. They've got grown-up kids who moved away. But one of them came for a visit. Seems they don't do that very much. Take a deep breath, okay?"

I took a deep breath and thought, Rottweiler, and we got out of the Jeep. I followed Giant George past the Buick and up the driveway to the side door. He'd say later the door was unlocked, but his broad back was in front of me before we entered, and I was aware that it took him at least a minute, maybe longer, to get the door open. It also seemed to me that he'd taken out, and put back into his jacket pocket, something I couldn't see, which could have been a tool for a break-in.

We were in the kitchen of these strangers. I was looking at brightness, coziness, a teakettle with daisies, more potted plants, everything impressively clean. Giant George tried a door that turned out to be a broom closet, another that was a bathroom, then a third that was the cellar.

"Dapple," he called softly down the dark stairs. "Dapple, Dapple."

I heard her whimpering. She hadn't had her new name for long. But she knew it.

Giant George found the light switch. Down we went, landing in a section of what seemed a normal basement: a laundry area, patio furniture in storage, rakes, a leaf blower, gardening tools on a shelf. This area was separated from the other half by a wall of plywood, with a door in the center, and that was where the basement stopped being normal. Giant George pushed the door open and stepped inside ahead of me. A moment later he said over his shoulder, "I don't know if you want to see this. I won't think you're a coward or something, if you'd rather not."

I went in. There was no ventilation. The glass of the narrow cellar window had a coat of black paint. I didn't see Dapple in her cage. My eyes were taking too long to get used to the dimness. She was already in Giant George's arms by the time they did.

There were two other cages, both empty. A half wall of rough boards divided this prison in two. I didn't know what I was looking at when I glanced there and saw rubber floor mats rolled up like hay bales, a table holding several metal containers, like freestanding medicine cabinets without mirrors, and in a corner, next to a makeshift counter, a sink on metal legs. It was a normal bathroom sink with two taps.

"I wonder how many litters she already had," said Giant George. "I'm guessing she was scheduled for another one."

His voice sounded strangled and far away. Dapple's head was pressed to his chest, where his heart was. I wanted to open the containers and see what was there, but Giant George blocked me. My job was to go ahead of him, opening and closing doors, all the way to the Jeep.

We'd forgotten to bring a blanket. Giant George took his jacket off. I climbed into the back to be with Dapple. We laid her on the seat and covered her. We covered her. We rode away with her head in my lap. I didn't think she'd ever stop trembling, but after a couple of miles she sighed and let herself fall asleep.

Giant George didn't speed when we reached the main road. I

was so busy holding that dog, I didn't realize we'd gone by the turnoff to the Sanctuary and past the inn. But eventually I looked and saw that we were heading . . . where?

"Where are we going, George?"

"You'll see. It's not like we can take her back to our place."

He said that as if he expected me to have figured it out on my own. But I liked the way he said *our place*. There was an *our* and it seemed I was in it. I really heard that. I didn't care that I'd been so ignorant about things like "people breeding dogs a certain way, based on orders from customers."

"Dapple's asleep," I said, my voice low.

"Good."

"Was insemination stuff in those cabinets?"

"Yeah, insemination stuff. And probably birthing stuff too."

"To sell puppies?"

"Yeah."

"But why. . . ."

"Don't ask. I don't know why. I mean, if you start wondering why people do things to dogs, you could go crazy. But maybe they were into a type of breeding where you want to put different breeds together and see what you get. Dapple's a hound, so maybe they had orders from hunters to fill. That's as far as I can go with guessing. Like maybe there're hunters who would love to have a mix that combines great things from purebreds, or other mixes. Maybe the people in that house were filling orders. Or maybe it wasn't for hunting. It could be a competition thing, where people really like to win prizes. Or maybe it was totally something else."

"Like what?"

"Evie, I don't know."

"Maybe it's a sort of lab," I said. "Maybe they're experimenting with mixes, like they're trying to make a new breed of hound. I *hate* them."

"Hate can be a good thing, sometimes," he said.

A few more miles went by: high snowbanks, evergreens, a cleared pond where people were skating, most of them children. I saw four free dogs paw-skittering on the ice and another one at an edge, prancing about.

I said, "What about the empty cages?"

"I don't know anything about them."

"Would you think I was crazy if I said I smelled something weird in there? Like, a smell that wasn't dog poop or pee?"

"I didn't smell anything weird."

"Well, when I smelled it, I had the feeling that dogs were in those cages not so long ago. I had the feeling they were sick. And maybe they even . . ."

I couldn't say any more. Giant George took a hand off the wheel and reached back. I put my hand in his. His skin was sweaty and warm when he squeezed my fingers.

"I wish we could know what movie they're watching on the huge TV," he said. "You know what I wish it is? *Zoltan: Hound of Dracula*. Or, even better, *Cujo*. Or both of them, back to back. That would be perfect. You ever see those?"

"I never did," I said.

"How about *Pet Sematary*?"

"No. I was thinking more, *The Hound of the Baskervilles*," I said.

"That's not scary. That's just boring Sherlock Holmes. The only thing interesting about Sherlock Holmes is, he got addicted to co . . ."

The second hard *c* stopped as if cut with a knife. I could feel him saying to himself, uh-oh. I had to wonder how many times he'd reminded himself not to bring up that word. It almost didn't matter, not even the surprise of it, not when a dog who came out of a hell was resting her head in my lap. I was sure she knew this was the last time she'd need to be rescued. Her gentle breathing seemed to me the softest, sweetest thing there ever was.

I finished the word for Giant George with my hands on Dapple and my eyes not meeting his in the rearview.

"Cocaine," I said.

He looked embarrassed. "Well, yeah. I really didn't mean to bring it up. We don't have to talk about it."

"Then we won't."

"Okay. But Evie, I just want to say, don't be thinking anyone snooped around in your life. I just heard them, like, discussing you. It was a couple of days ago. It was only about one minute. I don't even know anything."

"I don't want to talk about it," I said.

"Don't be mad."

"I'm not mad."

A gas station was up ahead. He signaled and pulled into it. But he didn't drive to the pumps. He went to the side near an air machine, where a burly, rough-looking man in a puffy black parka was putting air in the tire of a van, the kind of delivery van that doesn't have windows. On his head was a kerchief, tied in place like a pirate's.

"Welcome to the Network," said Giant George.

"The what?"

"Network. Just watch."

What happened next happened so quickly, I felt like an extra in a movie of pure adrenaline and action, and no one had shown me a script. As soon as we came to a stop, the pirate finished what he was doing and waved to us. It was a signal. Giant George leaped out of the Jeep, flung the back door open, and reached inside for Dapple, pulling her away from me. Her eyes opened wide. I saw her terrified look, heard her gasping, then Giant George's calm voice as he whispered, "It's okay, it's okay."

The pirate went into the driver's side of the van. Someone else was in there, opening the side panel from inside. I saw arms of another parka, an orange one, bright orange, neon. I saw Giant George placing Dapple in those arms. I saw his jacket tossed out to him.

The van reversed, turned. The direction it took off in was opposite the direction of the Sanctuary.

I returned to the front seat, a regular passenger again, and that was when I started crying. I couldn't stop myself from thinking about those empty cages. Giant George patted my knee clumsily. He was back to being a big teenage boy.

"I don't have any Kleenex," he said. "I wish I did, but I don't."

I wiped my nose and eyes on my sleeve. He looked at me like he thought that was cool.

Then I waited in the Jeep while he gassed it up and went inside to pay. Dapple wasn't ever going to be in my class again. I wondered if Josie would miss her, or if Hank would, or Shadow, Tasha, Boomer. And what about Alfie? And what about the Scottie Dora, still in the infirmary? I hadn't even met her yet.

When he came back, the first thing Giant George did was tell me not to ask him where they were taking Dapple. He didn't know. The second thing he did was ask me if I wanted to stop on the way back for a burger or something. No, I did not.

"I hate it that Dapple won't be in my class," I said.

"That's okay. You'd probably fuck her up even worse than she is."

I'd been doing so well. I'd been sitting there holding myself together. I felt my face sliding into a wail, as if he'd decided to shatter me, and he'd hit on the best way to do it. And I lowered my head and cried all over again, harder, really hard, trembling like a broken dog, soaking myself.

"I was kidding! Evie! I wanted to make you laugh! Tell me you believe me I was kidding!"

I really wasn't mad at him. But I didn't stop crying until we were nearly up Sanctuary Hill, the sun beginning to set, a red glow in the sky like a slash mark, like a cut. Soon I'd be seeing the notes on Dapple again, this time with one word added: *Networked.*

Twenty-One

MRS. AUBERCHON WAS in the kitchen, looking at a barely touched bottle of vodka left behind months ago by a guest. She'd kept it high up in a cabinet where she stored things she never used. The days of making treats at the inn were over. Mrs. Walzer had fallen while attending a church social. She had broken her hip.

It was too soon for a visit. Mrs. Auberchon knew from making phone calls that Mrs. Walzer was still drugged.

She'd already spent ten minutes imagining herself as a temporary replacement baker, as if a broken hip took as long to fix as a broken fingernail. In no time at all, she had imagined, Mrs. Walzer would sail through the doorway, taking over again. But Mrs. Auberchon couldn't kid herself about her ability to make treats. She'd be overwhelmed. She'd have no talent for it, same as with singing.

Cranberry juice would be nice to put vodka into. She had a can of concentrate in the freezer, also a can of orange. Cranberry and orange together in a pitcher might be just the right thing. She could call it a punch.

It wasn't as if the dogs would be heartbroken about no more

homemade treats. They wouldn't even notice, the same way, she knew, years ago, dogs didn't care that the Sanctuary had to stop feeding them straight from their own gardens, their own pantry, their own freezer, their own frequent trips to the market, the butcher, the shop that sold fish, the farm that became a development of new houses but used to sell eggs and chickens and sometimes ducks from their pond, at prices very close to being charity. Then one day, like a shift in the turning of the earth, so that suddenly you were looking at a different part of the sky, there were no more staffers up there to be spared for the cooking. There were twenty, there were fourteen, there were ten, there were seven, there were four. The dog food became dry nuggets in different sizes, arriving in giant sacks from a feed store somewhere, from orders placed online. That's what would happen with the treats, and it was terrible, and here was an excellent bottle in her hand, vodka made from potatoes, she read on the label.

She'd never tried vodka from potatoes before. It looked very blue-ribbon, very expensive. The liquid was clear as tonic water. The bottle itself was as pretty and shapely as if it held perfume, and Mrs. Walzer was on morphine in a hospital bed, and look what was happening here.

Tonic, she said to herself. *Perfume.*

She was alone. No one was coming to see her. She only kept the wood stove going for the sake of the pipes.

The satisfaction she felt when she heard of the spotted hound's rescue had not lasted long. Soon photos would come, along with news of the new location, but Dapple was gone, because that's what dogs did: staying and leaving and never coming back. Why didn't they ask her if she wanted to be in on that rescue, not just sit still making phone calls? She knew she would have declined. But it would have cheered her up to be invited. They knew about Mrs. Walzer's hip.

She looked out the window. No one was in the pen. No one was out for a walk. No one was dragging a trash can into her sight for a dog to jump over. No one was sitting at her table eating a roasted chicken without a knife and a fork and a plate, or eating the last of her bacon, or slouching around in the lobby with a bowl of Mrs. Walzer's granola.

The light was gray, the snow too old, the wind too biting and nasty. She'd been keeping herself only in the kitchen and her room, like a shut-away, like she was ill, like she needed medicine. And she was getting nowhere with Dora the Scottie, not even after hours and hours of sending her voice into the infirmary, talking herself into hoarseness. That dog was mending just fine postsurgery. She should have been up and about and wagging her tail by now, not lying on a bed in the corner like a terrier in a coma. Whose job was it to get some light in those eyes, some sparks, some sign that yes, even after everything that happened to me, I want to be alive?

It was the job of the Warden. But what if she'd lost her touch? What if she'd run up against a dog she couldn't get through to, in any way at all?

Medicine, Mrs. Auberchon said to herself.

She had read that dog *Black Beauty* from start to finish, leaving out the worst parts. She'd read her Beatrix Potter and bits of every book she had, plus things about terriers she'd found online. But nothing had worked, not even Evie's application and "I want to talk to aliens," which Mrs. Auberchon had saved as a last resort.

There wasn't a library in the village. She could order new books at her keyboard, not that money was in the budget. She'd pay for them herself. She wouldn't mind. But they'd take forever to arrive. Should she fix the cranberry juice first? Should she fix the orange juice first? Should she never mind calling it punch and take it straight, maybe a couple of sips right out of the bottle? How sweet it would be to feel warmed! How glad she would be

for the burn of it, the stirring, the healing on the way, the calm-
ing of her nerves, her tension, her unhappiness!

Mrs. Auberchon undid the cap. She was standing at the counter near the sink. She stepped sideways, tipping the bottle so the
mouth was close to the drain. When half of it was emptied, she
paused, and paused again when there was only enough to fill a
shot glass. Then all of it was gone.

She ran hot water on the label until it loosened enough to peel
off. The bottle was too attractive to throw away. It didn't have to
come to its end. It could have another life, perhaps as a vase, perhaps as a candleholder, bright wax dripping down its sides, hard-
ening, lasting, staying. She filled the sink with sudsy water and
stuck it in there to soak.

She was now good and mad at that dog. The dog was *rescued*.
That dog was *saved*. Terriers could be obstinate, but honestly, this
one was way out of line. This one had gone too far.

She had printed out the notes, had kept Dora's story beside her
all those hours of reading. She thought of her salt-and-pepper
fur, clean and smooth from the grooming she didn't want done.
She pictured Dora's short legs, inert as she lay on her side: the
legs of a dog who didn't care if she ever got up again and used
them. Her muzzle was black and the hairs were a little spiky,
like the gray-black on top of her head, like she'd gone punk in
the days when punk was a fad and she'd never outgrown it. Her
stick-up ears were all black, as were loops around her small eyes,
like a raccoon's, or a miniature version of a panda's. Her tail was
a loose, frizzy braid of black and gray, looking soft and also wiry.
Mrs. Auberchon had never seen it move.

The bottle in the sink water had floated to the top like a lesson
in buoyancy. Mrs. Auberchon clamped her hand on it and held it
down until it filled, as if drowning it. Then she picked up a towel
and wiped her hands dry and went into her room, to look the
notes over again.

Dora. Female. Terrier, Scottish. Black and gray. Age approximately nine or ten. Urban, high-density neighborhood. Was found by landlord of apartment building after repeated complaints from neighbors of barking, which the landlord was slow to respond to, as he was slow to respond to all complaints. Not possible to know precisely how long she was there, following abandoning of apartment by its residents, after rent default. Animal control officer was called in. Several neighbors were questioned. Animal officer reported estimation of alone time as five days to a week. Several bowls had been left, presumably of food and water, reported by officer to be empty. Also reported was her name of Dora. Was taken to shelter without veterinary affiliation or funds for medical care. Dehydration, not severe, was treated by shelter staff, but symptoms appeared of stomach/intestinal disorder. Was sponsored by employees of nearby auto-body shop who often contributed cash for emergencies. Was taken to heavily burdened animal hospital, where she was diagnosed with a routine dietary ailment that would pass on its own. Was not kept in hospital for observation. Remained listless and problematic at shelter. Was then referred to breed rescue group, which sent a representative, who decided to send her here, rather than foster, due to acute psychological withdrawal, which had seemed a greater need than physical state. Was examined upon arrival and immediately scheduled for surgery to remove blockage of ingested nonfood material, specifically, a significant amount of wallpaper, the glue of which presented a threat of toxicity. Following successful surgery, remains in infirmary. Intravenous medication no longer necessary. Other medications minimal. No sign of infection. Does not appear in pain. Has been carried outside of isolation to other areas, but those efforts have been suspended. Becomes highly agitated everywhere but infirmary, several times to point of fear of seizure. No further details at this time. Outlook: Unknown.

Well, thought Mrs. Auberchon, damn her and damn her again for not giving one tiny flick of her tail to Evie and her aliens! And looking the whole time like she was bored!

Not one thing Mrs. Auberchon had read to her was boring! Beatrix Potter! It was true that Peter Rabbit, as a character, wasn't always a hit with the dogs. But no dog ever, in all these years, had scorned Jemima Puddle-duck. Who did that Scottie think she was, scorning Jemima Puddle-duck? And Mrs. Tiggy-winkle! She had scorned Mrs. Tiggy-winkle most of all! Mrs. Tiggy-win-kle! That helpful, kind hedgehog, alone in her cottage, her life all chores and laundry!

Mrs. Auberchon reminded herself that agitation can lead to a seizure. She needed to be calm. She needed a cup of tea. She needed to be strong. She saw what she had to do. She'd have to tell that terrier once and for all, loud and clear, that enough was enough.

She would have to do it in person. There was no other way. She was going up the mountain.

Twenty-Two

ADOPTION. THE ULTIMATE of ultimates for orphaned dogs, even Sanctuary dogs who seem to have zero potential for ever being wanted by anyone in the outside world.

One night in my former program, some of us were watching TV. A commercial came on for a humane society group looking for donations to help shelter dogs get adopted. Five or six dogs were in the ad, looking at the camera from behind metal webbing of a fence or kennel or crate. I had to look away from those eyes. I was still in no shape to consider the possibility that anyone in the world might be worse off than I was. But the girl beside me had a question, to which no one responded.

This girl happened to be famous. She was a star in a network drama, not a soap opera, but a prime-time one, big ratings, long-running. The writers wrote her out for a while so she could *clean up her act*. That was how she put it. She'd been acting since she was in kindergarten. She asked us, "How do you think the director gets those dogs to look so miserable?" At the end of the ad was a number to call and a website address, but no one wrote them down.

Adoption is good. Adoption is *noble*. Adoption means *a home for someone homeless.* To hear the news that a dog is being adopted is a great and wonderful thing.

But I couldn't believe it. Hank? Mr. Obsessive? Mr. Brawny Lab-Pit? Mr. I Hate Wooden Objects? Mr. Jumper? Mr. Attack Dog of Broom Handles? Mr. Don't Walk in Areas of Trees Unless Checking First for Fallen Branches?

Of all of them, he was the first?

I wouldn't have remembered seeing the adoption commercial if I hadn't just found out that Hank would be taken away. He had terrible manners. He was still a beginner in basic obedience. I felt like a teacher being told that a pupil is quitting school forever, after just a few weeks of second grade.

We hadn't even made it to the agility part. I wasn't going to see him jump hurdles.

His adopters feel that the name Hank is all wrong. They're calling him Basil. They live somewhere that's a desert. Their favorite plants to grow in their gardens are their many varieties of basil. They're experts with that herb, and win awards at plant shows.

Basil is dumb for him and also sissy. No one cared how I felt about it.

Call. Another Sanctuary staffer — Forest Green — now has a name. I'm guessing her age to be high sixties. She has fluffy reddish-brown hair like a Pomeranian. I thought at first she dyes it, as there's not much gray, but then I looked closely, and she doesn't. Unlike the other three and pretty much everyone else, she isn't taller than I am. We see each other eye to eye. Her name is Louise. What I thought was a fantastic tan is her regular skin, but then, all that shows of her, in her turtleneck and sweats, is her face and her hands. She's Mexican.

I felt I should call her Luisa, as a way of making up for rigid self-centered Americans making everyone whitewash who they are. It turned out her name is Louise for real. She was gentle with me when she let me know I was stereotyping. I wanted to melt into a puddle a dog would rush over and lap up. But she doesn't have a Spanish-sounding accent.

She came into my class to *be my teacher*. Everything about her told me something was coming that I couldn't discover for myself — not in real life, and certainly not in a textbook or a manual. I remembered the story I'd told Boomer of the student monk and the fallen leaves. I remembered that, in the next part of it, while he was sweeping the patio, the older monk came over and picked up a leaf that only recently was part of a tree. He curled it, held it to his mouth, and blew into it, in some highly trained, skillful, Zen-like way, producing a soft and beautiful whistle. "For this, you need organized instruction," the older monk said, because of course when the student tried it, all he did was cover the leaf with his spit.

Louise is someone who gives the impression of having many years of experience in yoga, even though she never once did it, or even considered it (I asked). She has a stillness that isn't stiff, a voice that hardly goes above a whisper. She ordered me to stand in a corner and observe her. It didn't feel like an order. It felt like a good idea.

She lined up the dogs in sits, Tasha and Shadow and Josie. Not Dapple, gone forever. Not Alfie, flat on his side, stretched out for a nap against a wall. Not Hank, busy with a bath and getting groomed.

That woman's calmness went into the dogs as if she'd put them under a spell. She had no treats. She only had herself. I was awestruck. She backed away from them a little more each time she did a call.

"Shadow, come!" Josie and Tasha didn't move as Shadow trotted to her. When he reached her, she leaned and patted him and told him to go back, and he did.

"Tasha, come!"

You'd think Tasha was in a ballet class, the way she stepped so lightly. You'd think she had a tutu on, like a dancing hippo in *Fantasia*. She didn't jump Louise. She didn't drool for a treat or try to tear off a sweatsuit pocket to see what was inside.

"Josie, come!"

For Josie, that whispery voice was louder. The little white dog heard her name just fine. But for who knows what reason, she decided to ignore it. Maybe she wasn't in a mood to do anything she was told. Or maybe she wanted to find out what would happen to her for being so obviously brazen.

"Josie, come!"

Again the same thing. And again. If I were in the position of the caller, I would have stomped right over to Josie to give her a piece of my mind, probably at the top of my lungs, to make sure she got it. Louise wasn't rattled, or even worried.

"Bad dog," she called out, in a matter-of-fact way. "*Bad.*"

Josie looked like she was thinking over what that meant. She looked like she was having an inner struggle, wondering if she wanted to be someone connected to that adjective. I loved what it was like to watch her decide, well, no. She went to Louise in a rapid strut that was just like the walk of a fashion model on a runway. She was totally posing. She had made up her mind that she was fabulous.

I thought Louise would want to punish her in some way for the brazenness. But she was only thrilled to have Josie with her at last. She looked down at her with eyes full of praise, and even though she didn't say to me, "Evie, never, ever give a dog who comes to you anything but love," I heard that rule loud and clear, because, duh, if you call a dog to you and then you're in punishment mode, what's going to happen the next time you call the dog, and so what if you had to call the dog many times? Probably, also duh, the next time you call the dog, the dog will come faster, because of the *yay* you're giving.

Positive reinforcement isn't only about food treats! So I understood all that, and then I made a bet with myself that Josie wouldn't allow Louise to pat her.

She allowed Louise to pat her, lavishly. Josie, I was messaging her, not that she knew. I *hate* you.

Over and over it went. Call, come, one by one, with Louise backing away from them a little more each time. Everyone responded on cue. On the last round, when Louise was as far from them as she could get, she altered her tone into something more lively, like she was really excited. She called to the three of them at once. They took off like horizontal rockets, running to her with their tongues out, their paws barely touching the floor.

I put my hands together, clapping for them. Then it was my turn. Louise signaled to me to get them to run back to me, and I went, "TASHA-SHADOW-JOSIE, HEY! COME ON OVER TO ME!"

The three of them crowded around Louise and plunked down on their haunches and looked across the room at me. I really thought I was getting a unanimous "no," and not in a brazen way. I was starting to feel hurt, as if they'd secretly conferred like a jury, in dog talk, and decided I was guilty of being a human they'd never want to go to.

But they were only taking a rest. I wasn't like a student monk with a leaf. Or I was like a student monk with a leaf who got the whistle in one minute. The dogs acted as if running to Louise was practice for running to *me*.

I thought, maybe a command to a dog can be made like an *invitation*.

Note to self: try to remember that.

Goodbye. When the man and woman came up the front steps of the lodge, I happened to be near a window. I thought they were Dapple's owners, coming back to claim her again. They weren't. I should have noticed the different car, an SUV, impressive, a Lexus. A picture of a cactus was on the license plate. The leash they brought was a leather one, thin, strong, top of the line. The collar they brought was lined with sheepskin. Boomer met them at the door. It was time to say goodbye to Hank. I didn't do a good job of it. I just patted him and told him I was glad for him but not for myself, which I hope he understood meant, "I already miss you and it hurts."

Haiku. I tried to write a haiku about him. It didn't work out. I kept imagining him taking part in a totally international, major event, full of pomp and circumstance and drama: an Olympics for dogs. I pictured him gold-medaling in every event they had for jumps. Then I pictured him at the bottom of Sanctuary Mountain, getting ready to hurdle it. When he was up in his arc near the top, he'd keep going, like he was aiming to join the stars. It was night when I was having these thoughts. I looked up at the sky. I realized that the white powder above me was the Milky Way.

Then I tried to write a haiku about how I'd thought the mountain was so big and high, and it really wasn't, and that's why people stopped skiing here. That one didn't work out either.

Housebreaking. I read an article about putting diapers on dogs. I went around for a while imagining Alfie in a diaper. But I don't think that's the answer. Tasha would think he had it on as a special present just for her. She would think ripping it off him after he filled it was the best thing that ever happened to her.

Alfie pooped in my class today when the only human was me, and I cleaned it up and didn't tell anyone. Tasha and Josie just wanted to smell it, as if maybe there'd be a different odor when it was on a floor indoors, but I noticed Shadow looking at Alfie with disapproval, frowning in a way that maybe Alfie noticed, male to male. So there might be some peer pressure going on. (To be continued.) (Or not.)

Insemination, artificial. Now I know about breeding without dog-to-dog mating. Probably the husband and wife in the ranch house with daisies on the kettle couldn't take the risk of having boy dogs turn up at regular intervals for short-term visits. So where did they get the sperm?

"From sperm sellers, Evie," said Giant George.

I can see where the husband and wife would find it easy to load a carton of puppies into their Buick, then drive them to a buyer. Maybe the buyer met them at the same gas station where the pirate and Yellow Jacket were waiting for Dapple.

Network, the. I don't know anything about it yet. I'm in a country where I don't know the language. I'm at the fringe of a galaxy that won't offer me a spiral arm. No one tells me anything.

"You're so impatient," said Giant George, like he's twice my age. "Aren't you supposed to be able to *speed down?*"

I didn't react. He takes it out on me that he keeps walking Alfie and can't get him trained. Shouldn't he be in school? Shouldn't he be doing something such as reading *Hamlet* and getting obsessed about it, like a normal teenager?

"I only read nonfiction about dogs," he told me.

No. (Note to self.) When you say no to a dog who's doing something absolutely unacceptable, would you please learn to stop being such a wuss about it? Everyone can't be a Louise. Stop acting like Louise imprinted you, like you're a baby duck.

Obedience, types of. There needs to be another word for the kind of obedience that's the kind I want dogs I train to give me. But I go blank when I try to think of one. So I guess I'll stick with "invitation." Or more specifically, "an invitation, dear dog, to which you really need not to RSVP in the negative."

Play. Tasha puts her jaws on Shadow's neck as if she plans to remove his throat. Shadow tips his head and lets her chew him. That, I've figured out, is playing.

Tasha puts her jaws on Shadow's neck like she's interested in finding out what his fur is like, through the sense of taste. Shadow narrows his eyes and shows his teeth. That means not playing.

Assignment to self: either never let Tasha near Shadow, or figure out how Shadow knows her intentions toward him, before her jaws get hold of his neck.

That might be too advanced for me. I might be experiencing impatience.

Racing, greyhound. Quietly, Louise mentioned that it might be useful for me to search on my own, in my room, for videos of greyhound racing, not that she'd ask me later if I'd done so. It was entirely up to me. She also suggested that I look at their faces.

I didn't want to do it, which I know was totally counterproductive of me and also *childish,* like, do not even tell me what to do with my own Internet time. But that was from being used to looking things up on my own, just because I'd thought of them myself. I only resisted a little while.

I ended up hitting video frames into stills so I could look at the faces of dogs who'd just crossed the finish line. The question I wanted to answer was, does anyone look like they had a good time on that track, aside from what you'd expect in terms of being exhausted from giving it your all? I could not answer yes to that question.

One of the videos led me to a blog of a genial, folksy former newspaper publisher who took up greyhounds in his retirement. He races his dogs all over America. His initials are the same as Mark Twain's, and that's who he compares himself to, calling himself the Mark Twain of dog sport. The theme of his blog is how happy he is, how he learned to mellow out and find meaning and satisfaction by being part of the animal world. Even at races where his dogs perform badly, he's still happy. All the dogs he owns are under the age of four, although he started buying greyhounds nine years ago. I posted a comment. I said I was new to his blog and I'd love to know what happened to the dogs he'd owned before, the ones too old to race. He didn't answer. The next time I checked, my comment had been removed.

I must not feel sorry for Alfie. I must keep just saying no to pity.

Scum, human. I understand the reason why people would run a breeding business in secret, where dogs they cause to be pregnant are kept in cages. It's the same with people who would push a dog out of a car in a strange place, by way of abandoning the dog, and the same as humans who would keep their dog on a chain, et cetera: they are scum. It's not enough to say you hate such people. You have to also say they are scum.

"Evie," said Giant George when I told him this, "wait till the pitties arrive."

I'd forgotten the pitties were coming.

Second chances. "We're big believers in second chances," said the man of the couple from the desert, putting Hank's new collar on him. Meanwhile, his wife was holding the new leash and nodding in agreement, while also stroking Boomer, who'd placed himself close to her. He'd never miss a chance to be patted.

Hank knew what was going on. The instant he felt the soft fleecy lining of that collar, he sighed and went relaxed. I hadn't known how much tension was inside him until I realized it was gone, poof, like turning off the current in bad, buzzing wires. By the time the new leash was snapped on, he was Basil. He'd erased us. I remembered that Second Chance was the name of the organization behind the adoption commercial I saw.

Sex. This is the first time I ever lived somewhere where no one is having sex. I just wanted to mention this.

Tomorrow. I still haven't met Dora. I don't remember what I read in the breed book about terriers, Scottish. I haven't had time to look it up. I've read the notes on her. I'm trying to gear up for whatever's coming with the pitties. I can't do everything at once.

I keep telling myself, "I'll go see Dora tomorrow." I don't think I'm being a coward about what I have to know, when it comes to things I'd rather never hear about. More scum things: a dog left alone in an apartment people moved out of. Forever.

Maybe there's a limit to how much one person can take in.

Or maybe there is only infinity about that, like pi.

Volunteers. I think there are twenty of them altogether, coming and going in no set pattern, some more than others: men, women, all ages, but all grown-ups. They come from the village and the towns off the main road. They seem to have a sort of club. Mostly what they do is take the dogs out for exercise. They all appear fit, and tend to leave their cars at the bottom of the road, so probably it's exercise for themselves as well.

I heard the two staffers whose names I don't know yet, Navy Blue and Dark Gray, talking about an upcoming meeting of upper-level volunteers. The subject of the meeting will be the pitties.

They didn't invite me to the meeting. It was in the dining room. A volunteer from the one pizza shop in the village arrived in his delivery car with a stack of cardboard pizza boxes. I was with Boomer, near his crate, when he came in. I had Josie with me too. She was in my lap. Every time I tried to pat her, she snapped at me.

We all paid attention when the pizzas appeared. I went down there later to see if anything was left. I found two slices of pepperoni and tore them up for Boomer and Josie. They fell in love with me for about ten minutes. Boomer drooped and went to sleep when the last bit of crust was gone. Josie licked my fingers, one by one, slowly. Then she nipped me. She was angry that I'd run out of everything but skin.

I told her *no* in a much stronger tone than the tone of a wuss. I couldn't help laughing at her. That's how cute she is. (Working on that.)

I'm never eating pizza again. Pizza is what the scum ate while we were rescuing Dapple.

When I was looking in the boxes to see what was left, a few volunteers were still there, sitting around a former ski resort table: one woman, three men. They were murmuring earnestly, somberly. I think they'd lowered their voices on account of my appearance. Except for one man, they were well up in middle age. They reminded me of deans I used to know, also professors. The one young man looked like the Romeo in a *Romeo and Juliet* I saw in a summer-theater production when I was about twelve.

I remembered him because it was the first time I fell in love. All I could do about it was go home and memorize the lines of everyone who spoke to him in that play, so I could walk around speaking to him.

I took a lot longer than I needed to, gathering the two pizza slices. I caught his eye. He smiled at me. I had a tiny moment of, oh! But his left hand was cupping his chin and I saw that he wore a wedding ring.

Note to self: interact more with the volunteers, but not that one.

Here came Shadow. Here came Tasha, overtaking him. They knew about the slices, the pepperoni, and now Alfie did too. He just showed up, tiptoe walking, looking for a spot where he could lie down and make believe he was a statue.

They were fully united. They were appalled. They accused me of playing favorites. Tasha looked at Josie as if she had the right to eat her, and Josie, in response, felt that I couldn't be trusted to protect her, so she scooted to Boomer and pressed herself against him, looking as small beside him as a chew toy.

Boomer sleepily opened his eyes. Alfie reminded everyone that greyhounds have very sharp teeth. Shadow tipped up like he was starting a howl, but he stopped himself. He remembered he'd been told a hundred times, by me and everyone else, that howling indoors is only a good idea if he's trying to save someone.

Five dogs were looking at me. It occurred to me they were upset about Hank being gone, Dapple gone too, even though they didn't get to know her. So I told them a story. I told them it was a true one. I told them how Giant George carried Dapple out of that house. I told them about the gas station and the pirate and the yellow arms that reached for her.

Then I promised I'd give them treats of human food in the very near future. Dogs don't know that word. But I do.

Twenty-Three

THE MOUNTAINTOP WAS full of wind, icy and blustery. No one in her right mind would have ventured out in this, but Shadow needed a walk. He was with me on a leash. I'd felt he needed after-lunch exercise to work off his acute depression, which he was feeling for a very good reason. Also he needed some confidence. He had flunked the pop quiz Giant George gave him to see if it was time to send out his SAR applications.

If the five basic commands are fingers of a hand, Shadow was okay with three: sit, come, stay. He really had those, all aces. He'd stay put in perfect position, even if you walked away from him to another room. He'd come in a flash; it made no difference if he felt he was doing something more interesting than rushing to your side. For a sit, you didn't have to speak. A tiny pointing downward would do it. Sometimes he'd have his bum on the floor with just a lean of your chin toward your chest, unlike Tasha and Josie, who'd be standing there, unless the instructor was Louise, saying things like I'm not in the mood, or I can't hear you, or I don't want to lie down because that's what Alfie does and I don't want to turn into Alfie.

Lying down for Shadow was a finger that was on the hand, but he didn't have a clue what to do with it. Maybe he'd learned from the girls that it was uncool to act like Alfie. Maybe he had reasons of his own from all that old infinity of his, tied to his chain on the same ground he peed and pooped on. Sometimes when he lay on that ground, it was hot against his belly and penis. Sometimes it was muddy, cold, crawling with bugs — didn't anyone care what he used to lie down on? Giant George gave him three tries only. All Shadow would do with that command was say no. He was polite about it. He was completely: I would prefer not to. So that was an F on the quiz, for which I blamed myself. I thought I'd done a good job of getting him to wipe out all those memories.

The command for dropping was worse. It was F-. It was a finger of the hand that hadn't grown in. The fault was mine. All along, I was supposed to throw him tennis balls he'd find and bring back, dropping them at my feet right away, not after half an hour of keeping a ball to himself, poor boy, cherishing it, his possession, his prize, when he never had anything before but the chain he was on and the collar that held it, the choke one, digging in, a necklace beneath it of worn-away fur and infection.

Giant George should have given me a heads-up about the pop quiz. I could have made Shadow do some cramming.

The only reason he ended up having the ball in his mouth no longer was that Tasha sneaked over to him and stole it away with her teeth. She chomped it until it was crushed, and so were the spirits of Shadow. Giant George refused to throw another ball and start over. He wouldn't average Shadow's marks to low B, the minimal requirement to get through the first door of Search-and-Rescue. He was all, stop looking bummed out, Shadow, and get busy with some learning. But that's probably something to be expected in a boy his age who hasn't read *Hamlet*.

We were walking on trodden snow paths with our heads low. Shadow was on a leash out in front of me, the two of us proud of ourselves for being stronger than the winds, which were trying to blow us over. I left it to him to decide when it was time to go back. When he finally did, he picked up the pace, pulling, as if he realized we were about to die if we didn't get out of this soon. He was covered in snow. His eyelids were crusted. I was so wind-lashed and freezing, I'd gone past the point of thinking I might ever be warm again.

We had to cross the road to reach the lodge. Of course there wasn't traffic. It was only a habit that made me pause and check. I'd also read an article about the danger of snowmobiles zoom-ing like race cars in the middle of nowhere and killing cross-country skiers, people on snowshoes, normal pedestrians and dog walkers like me. I looked down the hill, peering into a land-scape of crazily moving, whipped-up snow, in clouds and sheets and mini-tornadoes, and there, far below, in a momentary break in the action, which lasted about two seconds, I saw a mirage of Mrs. Auberchon, trudging upward, bent low, her head hooded, her purse on her arm.

Or maybe I should say I was hallucinating, which I felt no one should do except old-time hippies flashing back on what hap-pened to them with mushrooms, LSD, hallucinogenic mix-and-matches. I'd heard stories in my former program that *terrified* me.

Hallucinating Mrs. Auberchon! It really shook me, same as when I thought I heard her talking in the infirmary on the day of Dapple's rescue. Yanking at me, Shadow was saying, *come!* I hurried forward, shaking my head vigorously, like a dog, as if that would take care of it. I had the feeling Mrs. Auberchon was haunting me. I felt she was trying to take up space in my brain as if I were her inn.

But after I dried off Shadow and settled him down and took a hot shower and looked up articles about people seeing mirages in lands of extreme snow, I was all right. It's not just deserts that are places for people seeing things that aren't there. Mirages are as normal in snow as in sand.

I wondered if Hank would see mirages in his desert. It felt good to pretend I could message him even this far away, wishing him wonderful visions: a steak bone, an agility course of all hurdles, me.

I was in my room with a little free time. My door wasn't locked. I heard a knocking. I thought it might be Giant George to say he was sorry he forced Shadow into that test without telling me.

But walking in was the woman on the staff I knew as Navy Blue. Agnes was her name. If she were a flower, she'd be a primrose, a pastel one, maybe pale blue, emphasis on the *prim*.

She was the tallest of the four of them, and lean like a greyhound, with sharply chiseled features and a hairdo like a cap of gray that always looked as if she'd just had a clipping. "Agnes," I was mentally writing, now that she'd introduced herself, "approximately seventy-four, crinkled around the eyes, also the mouth, where the wrinkles are clearly from age, not from laughing. Do not antagonize. Do not attempt to pat." She had changed her outfit to ladylike jeans that were ironed—*ironed!*—with creases down the legs in perfect lines of denim corrugation. Her blouse was dense with flannel and plaidness, and tucked into the jeans precisely. She didn't need a belt; her waistline was elastic. The laces of her sensible rubber-soled shoes were exactly as long as they needed to be, and tied in perfect bows. I think she knew she didn't have to tell me to never call her Aggie, or just Ag. It was the first time I'd ever looked at a heavy flannel shirt on someone and thought of it as a blouse.

My room was in a state of almost extreme disorder, not only from clothes around everywhere in different stages of being clean, which I'd come to define by how much they smelled of dog and my sweat. By now I had kitchen privileges. Things I'd brought up from downstairs were taking up space on the carton I'd shipped my clothes in, with its holes and scars from being attacked by Tasha. This was my tabletop for boxes of crackers, a jar of peanut

butter, another of jam, a tin of cookies I kept refilling by pilfer-
ing more into my pockets, a few utensils, a jar of peanut butter I'd
used up but hadn't thrown away. I was always hungry, even though
at meals I ate more than all the staffers put together, like I was in
training to outdo Giant George. I didn't have access to a scale, but
I was definitely putting on some weight, and not in a bad way. It
was more like I was filling in a missing dimension of myself.

I didn't mind that meals were non-talking events. No one laid
that out for me as a rule. It was more a communal habit. The ears
of the staffers were tuned to the sounds of the dogs, Boomer in
the front, the others in the kennels below us, Dora the Scottie in
the infirmary, and the volunteers too, if any were around. Except
for meetings, volunteers were never invited to the dining room.
It was a zone of quiet where all noise was gentle: the tinkling
of silver and glass, the sound of water poured from a pitcher, a
chair creaking lightly, the crackle of a log in the fireplace, the
wind far away outside, not harsh and huge but soft, as soft as a
lullaby. Anyway, at mealtimes I was too hungry to do anything
but eat and rush to whatever I had to do next with the dogs. If
I'd stopped to consider that there were moments in every day
when I was very, very peaceful, I would have made fun of myself
for being such a mushy self-liar. I would have remembered that I
was someone who flunked yoga after only one class, like that was
something in myself I'd never actually be able to change.

To my relief, in my doorway, Agnes said nothing about the
mess of my room. She didn't come all the way in. She told me she
had two questions for me. She spoke to me without emotion or
disapproval, from high in the air of her height.

The first question was, had Mrs. Auberchon given me the message she was meant to give me, the one that was sent to her as
an email, when I was staying at the inn? She was asking about
it because among the staffers there was worry and even distress,

for calls were coming to the Sanctuary that were very confusing. Mostly, these incoming calls were voicemails, as the staffers had enough on their hands without rushing to the telephone every minute. There'd been emails too. Agnes recalled that the message Mrs. Auberchon was asked to relay to me had been left with her on the last day I was down there.

Flustered, I didn't wonder what she was talking about. I was too busy noticing something familiar in the way she put words together. I didn't figure out what it was until she asked the second question. Had I looked at the notes on Alfie?

She was the notes writer! And it wasn't just the pattern of her voice! She looked like her handwriting!

The notes on Alfie were on a piece of paper slipped under my door. I didn't remember when, I mean not in terms of time. Time for me at the top of the hill was something that moved about in colors of light and shadows and darkness, in the shifting, floating differences between sunlight and starlight, day clouds and night clouds. If I measured it at all, I measured it by the movement and smells of a meal being brought to the dining room, the sounds of dogs waiting for me when they arrived for class before I did, the intervals between walks and bathroom trips, barks and quiet, the feel of my body craving rest, the feel of plunging without thought in my bed down a hill of nothingness into sleep, then waking what felt like an instant later to barking, barking, barking and being hungry and *oh my God I can't be late for breakfast.*

The Alfie paper had appeared before a breakfast. I knew it was about him. I'd glanced at it long enough to see his name at the top, the first word.

It had to be around somewhere. Again I answered yes. I had read the notes on Alfie. Of course I had!

Agnes didn't leave my room as much as she stiffened up her back even straighter and withdrew in her no-noise shoes, quietly closing my door. I found the piece of paper after nearly giving up. I'd forgotten I had placed it on the tabletop of my carton. It had slipped between a cardboard side and the wall.

"Alfie," I read.

Male, neutered. Greyhound. Age most likely three. Weight: fifty-eight pounds. Was taken with several other racing dogs from highly unethical persons, under Sanctuary guidance. Due to secrecy of the operation, and to protect the rescuers, location must never be revealed. After veterinary attention, a breed rescue group assumed responsibility for fostering and basic training. They were able to place the other dogs in homes. Ultimately they arranged to have Alfie transported here, due to findings of extreme alienation, complicated by his failure or refusal to learn habits of domestication, which make adoption an outlook not to be considered.

And then I read this: "Evie, please come to the dining room. I have a question of great importance concerning phone calls and messages. I am eager to have my question answered."

Following the notes and message was a signature: "Agnes."

I knew there was a jail in another part of the lodge, along with the infirmary and a holding area for new ones and sequesters. I hadn't seen it. I hadn't ventured out of my own little orbit, not even to visit the kennels or snoop around the office or find the living quarters of the staffers and Giant George. I liked my own neighborhood: a hall of only one occupied room, mine. I liked my routines of class and dogs and the dining room. Was there a jail I didn't know about, for trainees?

I pictured myself opening my window and being transformed to a bird, a paper airplane, snowflakes, anything that could join the wind and disappear. Where was my *phone?*

I found it in a bureau drawer. My plan was to text Giant

George for help and advice, throwing myself at his mercy, his inner hobbit. He'd hold it over me, but it might be worth it, I was thinking.

Something stopped me. I remembered that I was older than he was. I was *educated*. I was a Rottweiler like Tasha!

I returned the phone to the drawer. Mentally I went back in time to the moment before Agnes showed up. I'd been about to go online to find out about Scottish terriers — I still hadn't remembered anything about them from the breed book. I was nagging myself about getting around to Dora.

So that's what I did, making notes to myself very firmly, in a memorization way I knew would be permanent. I was totally focused.

Outer coat that's resistant to water, I memorized, plus a soft, short undercoat. Alert, good watchdog. Independent. Small, strong. Natural charm, which alternates with *don't fuck with me* (my words, not from a breed chart). Stubborn. Bold. Hunter of hole dwellers: foxes, weasels, badgers, Scottish Highland pests of all kinds. Sturdy. Adorable. Expert at competition, winner of best in shows all over the place, very often, lots and lots of prizes. An American president who had one was Franklin D. Roosevelt. His Scottie received more mail than he did. Can be prone to vanity, airs of superiority, feelings of grandeur. Takes stubbornness to extremes when sensing a situation requires it. After swearing a vow of loyalty, will never break it. Has a heart twice the size of its body. Many owners enjoy naming them Scottish names: Dundee, Thane, Duncan, Laird, Abby for Aberdeen. Stoic like an old-time, well, Stoic. Does not have a brain function to recognize size, especially concerning self. Fearless.

Then I wondered if the wallpaper Dora ate in that city apartment had been loose on the wall to begin with, or if she'd had to claw it first. I wondered if the vet who operated on her would tell me what he saw while doing her surgery, if I were to ask him. I wondered why a dog who was genetically incapable of knowing she was little was lying around acting tiny and weak like a quitter.

Then I smelled mealtime, and I jumped up to rush for the dining room to waylay Agnes and tell her I was sorry. I knew I had to do it without offering any sort of excuse. I had to do it as if presenting a fact. And I had to say, not so much in words, but with everything I was, "Okay, so I'm willing *to let you teach me.*" Or maybe, "change me." Or maybe they are the same thing.

I wasn't being suddenly practical, like if I didn't respond to her the right way, I wouldn't get food. Agnes had written something else, in a PS after her signature. I had tried very hard to ignore it. "PS, Evie," she'd written. "In case you haven't discovered this yet, dogs don't tell lies."

Twenty-Four

AMENDS, MAKING. A dog who has a conscience can work at erasing a trainer's memory of poor behavior. This includes acts of aggression, destruction, disobedience, et cetera. The dog can offer the human a signal of let's let bygones be bygones.

A nice sit, followed by a raised paw held out like a bid for a handshake, can take care of it. So can a quick, polite, gracious lick on whatever skin of a human a dog is able to easily reach. There is also the traditional method of hanging one's head, tail down, muscles slack to the point of almost melting. Or a dog can choose to go for a big, dramatic gesture and drop to the floor and roll over, belly exposed like something someone could take advantage of, and bite into.

Conscience. A type of dog who might lose or be robbed of a conscience, which all dogs are born with (I think), is a racing greyhound. Or maybe not lose or be robbed of. Maybe it has to grow, or be grown, or established, like *trust*. And maybe that never happens for greyhounds.

It's good for me to take a moment here to compare myself with Alfie, who's never once looked sorry for his puddles and piles of shit indoors, not even when everyone is telling him in all sorts of ways that what he's doing is *bad bad bad bad bad.*

"Let's get to work on rehabilitating your conscience, Alfie."

I must have said this to him already five hundred times. But I'm not giving up on him, even though not doing so feels like trying to raise the dead. I don't think he's, say, a sociopath or something.

Forgiveness. Tall Agnes is not a primrose. She's not even a flower. She is a terrier, maybe with an undercoat of softness, maybe not.

This is her idea of forgiveness? Smile at me, and tell me she has an assignment for me? I'm in front of her like a belly-exposed dog saying I'm sorry for lying, and I'm going to be, from now on, the most perfect student anyone ever had, and she's not talking about lying or teaching, or even about whatever she was talking about in my room when she was talking to me about messages?

She wants me to write a set of notes for the staffers? On *myself?*

I did a little pushback, very reasonably. I didn't give it away how Giant George brought up Sherlock Holmes and his drug of choice on the day we rescued Dapple. I only said I sort of suspected they had notes on me already. I didn't get into my awareness that they'd put together notes on me from information I hadn't disclosed, and never mind that I had no idea how they acquired it. I could not have been more polite or respectful when I asked, if they had background stuff on me, please could I see what they'd come up with?

You'd think I was one of the dogs, asking that question. I received a big no on it, not that she actually said "no." She just looked at me like, do what I'm inviting you to do, Evie, and it's definitely not open to discussion.

Obedience (which I'm getting sick of thinking about). Another word for it could be *surrender,* in a good way, somehow.

Rehabilitation. How does a trainer of abused rescued dogs

know for sure when the rehab is over? It's not like quitting something because you went too far with it, like a pendulum getting stuck at the extreme of a swing, and it looks for a while like maybe it will never come back. Or maybe they're the same thing, sort of. Maybe the rehab never stops. Maybe it's another infinite, another pi.

Alfie is anti-rehab. Everyone has to step over him to enter the dining room. He's been hanging around in the hall. Today he was so still, I bent down to his level to make sure he was breathing. He didn't want me in his face, but he didn't show me his teeth. I'm calling that a gain. I told him that if I were a member of his family, I'd automatically think his problems were mine too.

He looked at me like, what problems? He was telling me, Evie, the only problem here is *you*.

Rejection. I just found out that Giant George went on Skype with Josie to show her to a potential adopter, a woman who doesn't have kids and is too old to have a baby. It went well until Giant George made the mistake of putting his hands on her ears so he could tip up her head, as she was clueless about looking into a camera. She was sitting on his lap. She must have panicked about getting blocked from the little hearing she has. She nicked Giant George on the chin, like a shaving cut. Unfortunately it bled.

Relapses. They happen. As dumb as this sounds, anytime you take two steps forward, it will probably mean taking one step back. It's not just Josie. Tasha forgot for a moment about not using her size as a way to be a thug. I saw her head over to Shadow, and I knew right away she was about to do a territory thing with him. She wanted to lie down in the exact spot he was in, fast asleep, in a patch of sunlight. I couldn't get to her in time to grab her. She was about to plop herself on top of him. With the mood Shadow's been in, he might have taken that as an act of war. I didn't panic. I did a quick, sincere call to the almost-thug, stopping her with the magic word of "Treat!"

So a relapse can be only an urge, which is then avoided in reality.

Truth. The truth is, every day now, there are moments when I am very, very peaceful. Sometimes it's due to the face of a quiet, solemn dog, or the sky outside my window, or a mealtime in the dining room, or a staffer walking by me and saying hi in a way that makes me realize how all my life, until now, I'd never learned a good way of offering someone a hello. Sometimes it's from a discovery I made on my own in my room, or in a moment of watching staffers pat the dogs, or speak to them, and it occurs to me that *teach* isn't something they feel they should try to do. I don't think they even consider it a verb like any normal verb. It's more that, wherever they are, there it is. It's something they just *are.*

Sometimes, the peacefulness happens to me all by itself, out of nowhere, for absolutely no reason.

Twenty-Five

MRS. AUBERCHON WAS stunned by the condition of the lodge.

All these years, she'd never thought about an outerness to the interiors she visited so freely in the bubble of her computer connections, for that was how she thought of it now: a bubble. In one awful moment, as the hilltop wind was swirling and blasting her, and her body was telling her she'd been crazy to make the walk from the inn, she came face-to-face with a reality that nearly made her cry.

But it was too cold for tears. Instead, she was mad at herself for being as simple-minded as a child. All those hours of all those words, all those streams of her voice, all those sentences of all those books, were gathered together in the place in herself where she was the Warden. The magic of it disappeared. The special purity she loved and depended on became a weak and faltering thing, like what happens to clean air in a room where a window's been opened, and grit and bad vapors rush in.

She wished she could blink and look again and see that it was all as she'd pictured it, based on photos on the Sanctuary's website and in their mailings, although lately their newsletters and brochures were so infrequent, there were almost none at all. They hadn't updated their site in something like six years, she realized. Maybe longer.

They were aging. They were old. They couldn't keep up. Time, Mrs. Auberchon saw, as she approached the front steps, wasn't leaving them alone, like it did in the land of make-believe. The walls of the lodge had a sag to them below darkened timber eaves that looked brittle and tired and fragile. The stonework needed a mason, the wooden exterior a carpenter and a painter, the roof a whole company of roofers. Parts of the steps were crumbly or worn away. Above Mrs. Auberchon's head, the wildly flapping Sanctuary banner took a pause between wind gusts, and she saw that it was faded and frayed at the edges, bearing its dog of white stars regretfully, like a burden too heavy to hold.

Shabby was what everything was—not derelict, not an eyesore, not a few ticks of a clock away from being hopeless. Those things would have made it easier to take, somehow. Shabby was only sad. She was an *innkeeper*. That's what they made her before they also made her Warden. That's what they offered her when they took her in. Oh, they'd told her, don't worry, you've been a housewife; you'll see that the job will be more of the same, cleaning and laundry and cooking and managing, sort of multiplied, with more people.

It made her crazy that her inn needed work, but it was only a little, in the back, the back porch and its roof, minor really: not shabby, not sad.

No one had told her. She could not believe they'd spent all that money on luxury dog treats when it could have been spent on *structural rehab*. Why didn't she let herself have that vodka? Why did she have to go and pour it down that drain? Her bones would be warm, her blood would be pumping smoothly, no muscles would be cramped and aching. Her eyes would be filmed with boozy fuzziness, and so what if the first thing anyone did at the Sanctuary was come over to her to catch scent of her breath, of course pretending only to greet her: Mrs. Auberchon at the top of the mountain!

But probably if she hadn't stood up to the bottle, she'd be down the road somewhere in a heap, having stumbled and fallen into a snowbank. She'd be sinking, getting buried by windblown snow. She'd be getting frozen and she wouldn't even know, and then she'd be getting dead.

Mrs. Auberchon saw that she had something to work with. She was glad she wasn't about to be dead.

Suddenly she remembered how mad she was at Dora the Scottie for her lack of interest in that admirable, hardworking hedgehog. Mrs. Tiggy-winkle! Not only lack of interest but scorn!

Mrs. Auberchon gave herself a shaking to throw off the cape of snow she was wearing. With a burst of heated emotion, she propelled herself to the front door and, without knocking, pushed it open and huffed inside, fearing the worst. She'd never seen the part of the lodge she was walking into, so she stiffened to prepare for more shabbiness, more sadness, perhaps with an overlay of invisible dread and doom, like that hotel in the movie where Jack Nicholson becomes demented with an ax, which, she felt, no innkeeper or Warden should ever see. She'd watched it at the inn with Giant George, on one of those nights when he was new to the Sanctuary and often turned up, because he thought the way she ran it was homey and warm, not that he'd ever said so. After the movie she'd made him stay overnight in a guest room so she didn't have to be alone. He had screamed with laughter at the whole thing, while she was sitting there almost having a heart attack.

She remembered how that boy would plop himself down to be near her, like they were related, like maybe she was his grandmother. But then he took on his Great Dane symbol and didn't come anymore, needy and soft as a puppy.

She had worried for nothing. She found herself in the open area of a training room, crates clean, a comfortable brightness, colors, everything shipshape. No one was in sight, not that she expected a receiving committee, or Evie alone, busy with something or passing by on her way to an assignment, then stopping in her tracks startled, amazed, and actually, for once, speechless. There was no one at all. They must be at mealtime.

Mealtime. How quaint it was, putting it like that. But that was how they put things up here. "Oh, it's mealtime, Mrs. Auberchon," one of them would say, hurriedly ending a phone call. It didn't matter which one was at the other end of the call. They even said mealtime for breakfast, as they said teatime, rest time, nail clipping time, outdoor play time, quiet reading time, brushing time, personal reflection time, meet-with-volunteers time, supervised play time indoors, go-to-bed time, and she'd giggle to herself for the efforts they made to turn their days into slots of moments to squeeze themselves into, when down at the inn, time was slippery and ever-changing. She was the Warden when a Warden was needed, for as long as it took. She was an innkeeper when she had guests (or just one). She'd been a baking helper on baking days, and all along in all the rest of her hours she was a woman on her own, unslotted, *free.*

Well, here she was. She didn't know a dog was standing nearby, looking up at her, until she closed the door behind her and caught her breath. The dog, she realized, had been watching her approaching. He'd just turned away from a window.

She only ever looked at the dogs in confinement and sickness and early stages of arrival, but she knew who this was. The last time she saw him, years ago, six or seven years at least, he was still in his bloom of dog-manhood, still young enough to break the rule of never leaving the mountaintop without a human. He'd been an expert at sneaking away. She remembered what it was like to look out her kitchen and see him coming toward the inn in the loping sideways trot of a golden, his mane waving, his head high, his eyes shining because of course he knew she'd open her refrigerator to him. There were always guests in those days to pour compliments all over him, put their hands all over his fur, even people who only had cats, or nothing. He always knew she'd take her time making the call to the Sanctuary to say she had him.

It had ended so suddenly: arthritis, medical scares. The last time she had contact with him, it was pre-computer. They were using the walkie-talkies. She'd spoken to him as he lay in the infirmary, urging him to get well from whatever it was he was down with. He got well. Afterward he entered the group, like a breed group, of Sanctuary dogs who didn't need her.

"My goodness, you're Boomer," she said, lowering herself to embrace him. She had to hurry and close her lips so he wouldn't French-kiss her. He slobbered all over her face. He didn't know she'd forgotten him.

She noticed the crate with his name on it. How many times in his youth had he left the mountain for a home he was adopted into, only to come back? She didn't remember how many times. It was always something. He had the bad luck of drawing adopters who in spite of their applications and interviews turned out to be people who should only have a dog that was stuffed and bought in a toy store. He was too big, adopters said, or he was a bolter, he was mouthy, he was addicted to dirty underwear. He stank of rotting things he had rolled in, he collected dead leaves in his tail, he did way too much shedding. If you threw him a stick, he refused to return it, and instead lay down and ate it, an entire stick at once, as children eat licorice, and he'd moan with a bellyache, and the vet bills were out of control. He refused to stop jumping on people, and he was terrible as a guard dog, for he only barked if he felt like expressing his feelings, and the list went on and on. Mrs. Auberchon had seen it in his files when Giant George put everything online, for Sanctuary people's eyes only.

But Boomer never came back from a failed adoption with his

tail between his legs. It was impossible for him to believe anyone wouldn't want him, just as it was impossible for him to think
Mrs. Auberchon had done anything, since their last connection,
but wonder how he was. That's what he was saying to her with his
tongue, with the nuzzle of his big head against her, with a paw on
her knee as she knelt beside him. He was telling her too that old
as he was, he was healthy, and also, he remembered every item of
human food she used to give him, although he felt it was tragic
that she had nothing in her pockets or purse to give him now.

She saw she'd interrupted him on the verge of napping. She
wished him sweet dreams and watched him bend his stiff legs to
the floor. A moment later he was asleep.

How she knew the way to the infirmary, she had no idea. She
saw a hall and went down it. She turned a corner, went down a
flight of stairs and down another hall, looking straight ahead all
the while, not rushing but hurrying purposefully, professionally,
all Warden.

There was the familiar dog-hospital whiteness, the tiled floor,
examining tables, wall cabinets, cages, bright cotton window curtains donated from a chain of pet stores, with pictures a sick dog
might find cheering or arousing: socks, meat bones, balls, cats,
food bowls, biscuits, squirrels, little mail trucks of the United
States Postal Service. She didn't seek out the shelf that held the
equipment where her voice came out. She knew it would only
rattle her to see hard evidence that she was now on the other
side. She couldn't let herself become distracted.

Two volunteers, young women, in smocks embossed with the
Sanctuary's logo, were sitting on the floor on either side of the
dog bed the little dog lay on. She lay on her side, her eyes half lidded. Her belly was pinkly pale from the shaving. The stitching
was gone. The scar was a statement of excellent healing. Yet the
manner of the two volunteers was that of watchers by a patient in

danger, as if Dora had had her surgery just minutes ago and the chance was strong she might not survive it.

The volunteers were not from the village. They were strangers to Mrs. Auberchon, and they were murmuring to Dora and patting her with expressions of such sweetness, such anxious concern, such *loving,* it crossed Mrs. Auberchon's mind that the Scottie was having the time of her life in here. She must be imagining herself a queen in a fairy tale. Mrs. Auberchon never read stories of royalty to dogs, because she believed in democracy. But really. No wonder that dog put on airs!

Mrs. Auberchon stamped her foot to get everyone's attention. Dora opened her eyes, but she didn't lift her head until Mrs. Auberchon spoke. She knew the voice, although she'd never heard it sound like this.

"Dora! You cut that out! You cut that out right now and get up on your feet, or I will throw that bed in the snow with you wrapped up inside it!"

That was the opening salvo. The volunteers gasped, horrified. They also looked a little afraid, as if they thought the Sanctuary had a secret wing that was used as an asylum, and this madwoman had escaped from it.

"Excuse me, but who are you?" asked the bolder of two.

"Oh, I'm just another volunteer," Mrs. Auberchon said, for it would take too long to explain herself, and anyway it was none of their business who she was. She took a step closer and talked to Dora again, this time more quietly.

"Dora, up," she said. "I'm telling you to come. Now. I *mean* it. You *come.*"

And suddenly the black and gray dog took possession again of her staunch little wire-fur body. She let out a sigh. A quick little twitching began in the upward points of her terrier ears, like a sign of complaint for being addressed so commonly, so roughly, and then she got up. One of the volunteers had to move to give her space. She stood wobbly. The volunteer held out her arms, ready to catch her, but Dora didn't fall.

She didn't come, but you can't have everything your own way, felt Mrs. Auberchon. She walked around the cushion to let the other volunteer, clearly the one she favored, pat her and praise her. On a wall hook nearby was a new collar that looked her size, and a short leash. Mrs. Auberchon pointed to them and told the unfavored volunteer to put them on her. The command was obeyed at once.

"All right then. Take her upstairs," said Mrs. Auberchon. "You can carry her on the steps, but otherwise, keep her walking."

The favored volunteer looked alarmed, in spite of the fact that Dora was perking up. Her tail wasn't wagging, but it was out. It wasn't limp. Her legs weren't buckling under her. Her eyes were the eyes of a dog who's ready to be on the move. Mrs. Auberchon didn't take it personally when she realized that Dora's motivation to leave the infirmary was to get away from her. Instead, she felt moved with a secret admiration. She wished she could message her, human mind to dog mind. If she could, she would say, "I hope I never see you again," and the meaning would be instantly known as I hope you're never sick; I hope you're never in Solitary; I hope someone adopts you soon, and gives you a crown and a throne.

Dora wouldn't look at her.

"But the vet! The vet said she has to take things really—"

The favored volunteer was doing her best to put up resistance. Mrs. Auberchon decided to interrupt her with a queenly little frown of her own.

"The vet," she said calmly, "isn't here, and I am."

She kept the frown until Dora started off on her exit, serenely and slowly, neither pulling on the leash nor being pulled. Right away the terrier took the lead, and when the favored volunteer stepped in line to follow, a procession was formed. It was going, Mrs. Auberchon knew, to a reunion and reception in the Sanctuary's upper chambers.

Her job here was finished. They didn't need her upstairs. She thought for a moment about looking around for Evie — but what was there to say, after hello, how are you, how are the dogs, how are things with your training?

On her walk up the road, Mrs. Auberchon had remembered the email from the Sanctuary asking her to take care of the problem of Evie not being in touch with people she was supposed to be in touch with. That was a potential subject. But not really. Too much time had gone by.

She couldn't talk to Evie about Mrs. Walzer's broken hip. Evie had never met Mrs. Walzer. She couldn't talk about Dapple's rescue, not even the part she had played in it, for it might raise the issue of why wasn't Mrs. Auberchon invited to go along, which she would have said no to, but it would have been nice to be asked.

What about Hank?

Absolutely not. She couldn't talk about Hank's adoption. She'd be too afraid of blurting out how she saw Evie that day with the jumping and the trashcan, which might lead to making an impression of herself as a lonely middle-aged busybody snoop, as if she had nothing better to do than spy out a window at a guest.

She didn't need to check up on Evie and see for herself how she was. She wasn't her mother! She didn't even *like* her!

In a corner of the infirmary was a small refrigerator. Mrs. Auberchon knew it contained refreshments for volunteers. She would need some fortification. She picked out a small bottle of apple juice and a couple of bars from a package of those fruity, nutty health-food things that didn't need refrigeration, but there was nowhere else to put them. She placed the refreshments in her purse, then stopped at the toilet for volunteers in the hall so she wouldn't have to pee in the snow like a dog. Going down, there'd be nowhere to give her shelter for a rest, but at the bottom was a copse of young hemlocks she liked to look at on her bus and cab rides to and from the village. She'd have to stand up in the snow, but that was all right. She trusted her boots. It would be just the right place for a little winter picnic for one.

She left the back way, stepping into the cold and the wind with the feeling she was a hiker who'd made it to a summit, and going down would be better than going up, even though she'd never in her life hiked anywhere before. When she rounded the lodge and entered the road, she wondered if Boomer, awake from his nap, was watching her out the window. Or if anyone else was. But she didn't turn around to find out. She wanted to spare herself another sight of all the *shabby.*

This mountain did not deserve shabby! The dogs did not deserve it! The dogs were supposed to come here to learn to lift up their heads, be proud, become *renovated!*

Oh, but those staffers were getting so old. Every one of them was old enough to be Mrs. Auberchon's mother. But why couldn't they be at least a little connected to reality that wasn't about dogs, such as reality about walls, stone, wood?

They were maddening. They'd let things go as if they felt aging and wear and tear and all the natural forces of reality had nothing to do with them! They were idealists! They were so wrapped up with their ideals that they didn't know a sagging roof from a tree or a cloud or a paw of a dog. They didn't even concern themselves with generating income from tuitions. Their so-called training program had fallen like crumbling walls! They only had one trainee, and it was *Evie.*

Mrs. Auberchon didn't know if it was good for her or not to be upset, but getting all worked up about the shabbiness gave her the steam she needed to make it to the bottom of the road without reminding herself of her own age. She hiked down at a snappy clip, her breath making streamers of clouds, like something coming out of an engine. There needed to be magic, she was thinking as she paused for her picnic.

The lodge, she realized, was like a lonely old dog no one paid attention to. There needed to be an Anonymous to rescue the poor lodge. What about all those volunteers? Some of them were *loaded*. But of course you couldn't count on volunteers to tune in to non-dog reality. They were all idealists too.

Leave it to Dora, Mrs. Auberchon felt. You'd think she had planned this whole thing, lying there on her cushion like a queen. She'd known perfectly well the Warden would show up in person! And see with her own eyes what was what!

Well, the rescue couldn't be something to rush into. Spring, Mrs. Auberchon decided. Late spring.

This wasn't the way things were supposed to go. Only the other day she felt herself drifting closer to the moment when she'd know it was time to start thinking about her own future. So far, all she had in mind was "somewhere that isn't here." That, and maybe an inn, a brand-new one, nested in the middle of the somewhere. She'd already spent a lot of time imagining herself a guest, waited on, fussed over. Nothing was specific about it. Just "a guest for the rest of my life."

And there it went, popped like an actual bubble. She had the right to a moment of bristling, growling, showing her teeth, even though no was around to see her.

Damn those old women, she thought, crunching into her energy bar. And damn that little dog.

Twenty-Six

AGILITY, EQUIPMENT. A day was scheduled for UPS to deliver components of a basic agility course. The equipment could be used outdoors and also inside.

The agility things were paid for by an anonymous donor. Activities involved in the course were jumping; running in patterns of the letter S through a row of objects (like highway cones) that needed not to be knocked over; getting oneself through a tunnel; getting oneself up and down a stand-up pair of joined surfaces in the shape of an A without a crossbar, which were ordered in two sizes, for small dogs and big dogs, not that I expected Tasha to give it a try of her own free will.

I was confident the UPS guy would be able to make it up the hill. Meanwhile, as he was out there steaming toward the turn of our road, the staffer Margaret decided this would be a good day to undo her experience of falling and witnessing Dapple put into the Buick of the scum.

Margaret took Shadow with her for a walk, retracing her steps. As I heard it, from Giant George, the UPS truck met up with her and Shadow around the halfway point. The driver had to stop. They were in the middle of the road. They had a conversation about the nature of the delivery while the truck was at a perilous angle, and what did Margaret tell that driver to do? *Back down and go away because, on behalf of the Sanctuary, she was refusing acceptance.*

Why would a staffer not want equipment for an agility course for abused rescued dogs? Because it still was winter and the snow was too deep for putting it outside. Because they couldn't have it indoors because there wouldn't be room because *the pitties were coming on a Network transport, and they'd picked up a few more on the way, and they were about to take everything over.*

Mrs. Auberchon was called. She refused to take the equipment at the inn. The classroom/indoor porch behind the sliding door in the lobby was too small for it. Anyway, that room wasn't meant to be a playground. That was her reaction.

The agility course is like Dapple. I don't know where it is.

Alfie, more notes on. I've put together my own notes on Alfie, and not because I'm ignoring my assignment about "notes on Evie," which I am, in fact, very actively ignoring.

I've done some searching. My first impression of him as a dog who used to live in a stable was wrong. Without realizing it, I confused him with horses. I was thinking only in terms of racetracks, racing. Greyhounds are penned or crated. He had it in common with Dapple, I think, that home was some kind of a cage. I don't think he had it better than Dapple in terms of having the chance to be out and running on his own, just to do it.

I've decided he came from Florida. That's the state with the most greyhound-racing tracks. Other questions, I can't answer, not even by making something up, based on solid information. For example, in his training to be a racer, how many rabbits did he have to chase, catch, and kill, while being kept in a fenced enclosure? Probably there were rabbits and he chased them — that seems to be pretty standard.

It's impossible to know how long he was given nothing to eat, before being placed in the pen rabbits were introduced into. It's also impossible to know what was done to him on days he was scheduled for a race he didn't feel like taking part in, like he was asking for a holiday or day off for personal reasons. But when trainers use *electronic devices as a way to stimulate dogs into proper performance,* no scars are left behind on their physical selves, not that I'm saying his trainer had zapped him. It's just a theory.

Alpha, new thing about. Head high, looking sure of herself, Dora the Scottie walked into my class.

So I'm adding to what I thought before about alphas, which wasn't, it turns out, everything there is to know. Sometimes alpha-ness is not completely bad.

This is not like saying that maybe there are positive aspects in the whole idea of domination for one and submission for everybody else. It's not, dictators can be pretty benevolent, especially when they're compared with pure thugs. It's not, bullies can be useful to have around. It's not even about wolfness and let's have a pack because packs are cool and being an individual isn't.

How did the other dogs know what was coming at them in that almost elderly black and gray terrier body?

Suddenly here she was, strolling in, not hesitantly, not looking around to check out what was what and who was who. Right away, she was the one who had to be looked at, and while the see-the-new-student business was going on, she was privately asking herself if it was worth her time to stick around, as if she had many other items on her agenda, all of them more worthy of her than anything happening here.

I think it took Dora less time to become Chief Dog than it takes a greyhound to run a race on a track of something like six hundred yards. Dog races are measured in yards. Dog races happen *fast.*

Staffer Margaret was present to "give me instruction," as she put it, on how to get Shadow and Josie and Tasha to play with dog toys, and also one another, without crossing the line into one of them saying to the others, my mood just changed from having fun to becoming your enemy. I wasn't exactly open to instruction from Margaret. I felt I was fine on my own. What could be complicated about getting dogs to play with toys and one another? I already knew the difference between play looks and fight looks. I was feeling very advanced.

In fact, Margaret seemed to barely pay attention to me and the dogs. She stayed to the side, being elderly and frail. I could tell she was nervous. Maybe her thoughts were filled with the coming pitties, but I had the sense that fall of hers had really scared her, like she'd have to spend the rest of her life being worried about falling again, which I tried to be understanding of, as I'd tried in college to be understanding of King Lear, that extremist alpha of a father.

I wrote a paper in an all-Shakespeare class about how maybe you have to be old yourself to feel some sympathy for him. It wasn't that Margaret was Learish exactly. But when I factored out the pitties and her nervousness, I was left with non-sympathy. I could not believe she had forbidden the UPS guy from coming up the hill.

I thought that was personal *tyranny*. But of course she didn't care how I felt. Meanwhile, I was putting myself between Josie and Shadow because Josie had decided that playing with him meant biting his legs like he was her chew toy, which meant that Shadow was conflicted about being gentlemanly and tolerant, especially toward a smaller dog, and he was showing some teeth and doing snarls of *fuck off me you yappy little jerk, before I get mad!* And Tasha had just torn open a stuffed duck. She was disemboweling it. The thing had one of those plastic squeaky things inside, which I had to make sure did not go into her mouth, and also that she didn't swallow an amount of stuffing that would wad in her guts and require surgery. What to do? Go to Tasha? Separate Shadow and Josie, who chose to stop leg biting for a moment so she could stare at his penis? She looked like she was contemplating biting him there just to see what he'd do. Poor Shadow was so in the habit of never wanting to lie down, he couldn't think fast of protecting himself. And all along, Alfie was such a total dog zombie, I had to wonder if maybe there are really such things as zombies. Also I had to keep checking him to make sure he was actually breathing.

Okay, I needed some instruction. I wasn't aware of looking to Margaret to signal her to please step in and be my teacher. I don't think I had time. She was on it. I couldn't believe I'd thought she wasn't being attentive. Suddenly, at exactly the right instant, she called out, as if talking to nothing but air, "Dora! Dora, come!"

Her old woman's voice was big with strength and vigor. I'd had no idea of the dog waiting literally offstage, poised to receive her cue.

"Evie," called out Margaret. "Please do as I tell you. *Relax.* Just stand still and relax and be *calm.*"

I watched a smile come onto her face, softening her, like she'd formed it on purpose so I'd catch it, and soften too.

And here was Dora. She went straight to Margaret and paused to look up at her so Margaret could admire her and tell her how amazingly perfect she was, in every way, which Margaret did, with just that same smile, plus a nod of her head. A second movement of her head — a tipping, a slight one — indicated that Margaret wanted Dora to start with Tasha. So Dora strolled over to Tasha and took the duck from her mouth, entrails dangling. The squeaker dropped to the floor, and I grabbed it.

Tasha appeared to feel that being robbed by Dora was wonderful, and now I know what it means to drop one's jaw in stupefaction.

Drop the duck and work the room, Dora, Margaret wasn't saying. I mean, she wasn't saying it in words. She was just moving her head a different way, in a more circular tipping, as anyone would do who had a neck crick or shoulder tension. It was actually so discreet, I wouldn't have noticed, if I hadn't been watching her closely.

Dora brought the duck to a corner and left it there. An invisible spotlight was shining on her. We all knew it. Of course she knew it too. She walked around, slowly, her eyes busy, checking everything out, letting herself be stared at.

Shadow went starstruck. You'd think a diva had stepped off the stage of an opera and come into the audience to say hello to him.

Josie was saying to her, I swear to you, I'll yap at, and also bite, everyone here except you.

Alfie lifted a front paw as Dora passed him. If she were closer, he would have touched her, so it was more like a wave, or a salute. No one crowded her. No one sniffed her bum. A decorum entered the atmosphere.

Then she came to me. I didn't get down to be close to her. I looked at her with my face as close as I could get it to a replication of Margaret's smile. Dora knew I was sincere in welcoming her. I think she was grateful to me for pretending in front of the others I didn't see that, inside the terrier body, behind the terrier eyes, was a dog who was alone in an apartment she used to live in with people, who had left her. I wondered how long she waited until she realized they would come back never. I wondered how long she had gone without food before swallowing her first mouthful of wallpaper.

Dora. I told her with my expression that I would do what I could to wipe out her memories like a virus. I saw that behind the shine of her eyes there was a blankness. I didn't blame her for disbelieving me about what I wanted to erase.

Then it was feeding time, and oh my God Margaret patted me on the arm. But it wasn't to pat me. She wanted me to walk with her to the dining room. She wanted to lean on me, not that she said so. She just looked at me and dared me to be strong and walk in baby steps and make her feel safe. If she asked me to carry her, I would have done it, even if I had to be sore from it for the rest of my life.

This was just a little while before the pitties arrived. I was hoping the new decorum of the dogs would last.

Connection. Josie went on Skype with Giant George again to meet and greet a potential adopter.

Again it was a woman past her childbearing years. Josie behaved perfectly. The woman was an urban professional, Giant George said, very prosperous, very up in whatever corporation she was with. "I feel such a connection with you," the woman said to Josie. "I'm white, I'm on the small side, I have a Unitarian mother and a Catholic father, so I'm not a pure breed." She explained to Giant George that everyone she knew had purebreds, many of them designer-level in quality. She was willing to stand out from her crowd. She was going to love how it felt to take in a rescue, she said. And Josie was a terrific size for her lifestyle and environment.

But then came the *but*. The woman started talking about what she meant when she talked about connection. It was more complicated, she said, than a feeling, or having personal details in common. A dog she adopted had to connect to who she was. When you walk a dog on a sidewalk, or go to the park, she said, you are saying something about your basic identity.

The woman could tell that Josie couldn't express the right thing about her identity. So there really wasn't a connection. She was sorry, but she was sure that people were getting in line to try to be lucky enough to have her. She was such a cute dog, very sweet.

Giant George said we should be glad Josie didn't go to her, only to be returned, or put into a shelter, which we'd never know, as our connection to her would be severed.

No word on Dapple. No photos from the adopters of Hank, or even a message.

Giant George told me he felt a connection with the sled pups. The guy in Alaska who had them now had promised to keep in touch, but all he'd sent was a two-minute video of youthful huskies romping in snow and knocking each other over. They were too far away to be recognized.

And Giant George asked me, "Which one of the dogs do you have the most connection to, Evie?"

"I don't play favorites," I answered.

"Okay, but who is it? It's Tasha, right? Was I right about you being a Rottweiler?"

"That's actually none of your business," I said.

Dogs, fighting. No one advised me to do homework on pit bulls who've been rescued from lives of fighting. So I was putting it off. I was out of the loop, out of a club I wasn't invited to be a member of. That club was the Network.

Then I came upon Giant George watching something on his laptop. He was sitting with it on the floor in a hall. I could tell he wanted to be private, but I looked anyway. On his screen, a man of about forty was talking, perhaps in an interview, perhaps with a member of his family, or a close friend. Something was very intimate about it. The man was white and rugged, in a Clint Eastwood sort of way. His eyes were liquid, brimming. His face was a face of raw, awful sorrow.

"I loved that dog," I heard him say. "I thought he'd have another couple years. Honest to God, all the rest put together, they're not half what he was."

Giant George closed the laptop when he realized I was there. His expression was so hard, I began to worry that he was revealing himself as stunted in the area of feeling sorry for a grief-stricken human. I wondered if I should be alarmed about him, sitting around (I thought) heartlessly watching videos of people whose pets had died.

He didn't want to tell me what it was. But he had to say something. I wasn't going away until he did. He confessed he'd made his way into a website he was not a member of. He admitted he knew a few things about hacking.

"That guy," he told me, "is talking about a dog of his he trained to be a fighter." Maybe he would have said more if I looked like I was ready for more listening. But I wasn't.

Dogs, grooming. On a visit to Boomer, I noticed a brush on top of his crate. He noticed right away that I had noticed it. He came out into the open, looking up at me, so I picked it up. He didn't know I'd never brushed a dog before.

At first I was wussy about it, making short, light strokes, hardly leaning into it at all. But then it came back to me that before I had short hair, back in my college days, I had very long hair. I started brushing him from personal experience. I loved the way he tipped up his head so I could do his mane.

In came Josie. She watched for a while, looking jealous. It occurred to me that she might not think of brushing as patting, so I asked her if she wanted me to groom her, even though her fur was so unhairy. She did!

Soon the sounds coming out of her were almost like purring. Boomer was a good sport about it. She let him lick her muzzle. I faked her out a couple of times by running a hand along her back instead of the brush. She didn't reel about and snap at me. But I was careful not to push that too far.

Dogs, photographing. A volunteer who has a job as assistant to a photographer of weddings and other special events came to take new pictures of everyone for putting on adoption websites. We decided to include Shadow as a maybe-adoptee, in case we'd have to give up on SAR for him. Only Josie cooperated. There was some tension in the air. They knew something was going to happen, even though they didn't know what.

We had to put three of them on leashes for the picture taking, even Dora, who has a jumpy streak, on top of I'm someone who doesn't like being told what to do. Alfie came out in every shot with his eyes closed. Josie sat so pretty. She hasn't given up.

The pit bulls, Giant George told me, wouldn't have their pictures taken until after they've lived at the Sanctuary for a while, probably at least four or five months.

They're going to be sequestered, he told me.

Losers, dogs who think they are. I wonder how many races Alfie won, and how many he lost, and how many he lost very badly, crossing the finish line as the last one, the bottom dog, the failure. Maybe he didn't care one way or another. But maybe he did.

He'd been "taken." When his rescuers showed up, was he even a little bit glad? If he wasn't, had he already confirmed with himself, in dog talk, that he was fully a loser, in every way?

It's not just him. I've seen "loser" in all their eyes, in the way I've noticed them gazing off blankly in idle moments, feeling that maybe being thrown from a car by your owner, or being left in an apartment alone, or being kept outdoors on a chain, et cetera, was actually something they *deserved.*

When I told all the dogs that there were dogs on the way who had it worse than they did, and they should be glad they'd never been put in a fight, they didn't look at me like they felt better about themselves. It could get a little low in my classroom. I wished I was the kind of girl in high school who tried out for cheerleading and made the squad. I wished I knew some cheers, especially the ones near the end of a game when your team is getting creamed and there you still are, buoyant, bubbly, jumping around, waving pompoms.

I hated it when the dogs looked at me like they thought they were losers. I keep saying, "Would you wipe that look off your faces? Would you please erase all that stuff like a virus on a computer?"

Surrender. Maybe in its good sense, it doesn't have to mean "go submissive." I've been worrying about that. When I invite Shadow to give me a ball I threw him, or I invite Tasha to consider being forever a non-bully, am I standing there like a dictator, ordering them to obey me *or else,* even though I'm not aware of the "or else"? I'm wondering this because Margaret mentioned to me that she thought I was getting *rigid.* No one had ever used that word about me before. Margaret said it's normal for this point in my training program. I don't know what she meant by "this point." There aren't any points in my program. There isn't even a program, just me and dogs and the sun in different places in the sky on top of this hill.

Maybe she didn't criticize me because she was annoyed that I disagreed with her about postponing my agility course. Maybe she was teaching me.

I thought of a counselor I had in my old program, a former hippie who was also a veteran of Vietnam. He became a hippie when he got out of the army, even though the days of hippies were in decline by then. I had a massive crush on him, unrequited. It was against the rules for a staffer to do anything with a resident but be a staffer. But personally, to take the edge off some tension I put out to him, as I was having an identity as someone who didn't believe in obeying rules, he told me he never involved himself with white girls, as a rule. He was frank about it. To deal with that, I had to write names of Morgan Freeman movies on the request list for DVDs, so I could sit around looking at Morgan Freeman, pretending he was my boyfriend, in spite of our age difference.

He actually sort of looked like Morgan Freeman. He called

himself my teacher. Counselor, he felt, was too nice of a word, too polite.

"I'm going to take you apart, and I'm not going to put you back together, Evie," he told me, after the crush had worn off. I was sitting there starting to hate him. This was being a teacher? This was rehab?

"Surrender, Evie," he told me, like he was riding a broomstick up high, skywriting, like I was Dorothy.

He didn't think teaching me meant teaching me how to put the pieces back together. He was, figure it out your damn self.

He left that program before I did. We couldn't keep in touch, another rule. But he didn't break me when he took me apart. If he did, I wouldn't be here.

So I'm saying to Margaret, sort of, about the rigidity, thanks for the tip. And I'm saying to the dogs, I won't break you. I mean, I won't make you worse than how much you're already broken.

Treats, random. Besides giving treats to say "good job," or to avoid bad behavior, there's another element of *positive reinforcement.* You give a dog a treat for no reason, as a surprise, like a gift when it's not your birthday. I love how they always get startled, especially when you single out one of them, away from the eyes and noses of the others. They're looking at you like, what? What? What did I do wrong now? And you hold out a treat and smile and say, "Oh, I wanted to remind you I think you're cool." This amazes them every time. They never get used to the randomness.

It's not spoiling them. Abused rescued dogs can't have birthdays. I bet that every day in America, non-rescued dogs wake up to their people saying to them, "Happy birthday!" Probably many of them receive presents, perhaps a party too. People with rescued dogs can make up a birth date, sure. But it's not the same thing.

We're not getting treats anymore from Mrs. Treats in Mrs. Auberchon's kitchen. I don't know why. We're getting them in bulk from the feed store, like the food. But the first time the new treats appeared, they came in a delivery of just treats.

This was a truck that was not turned away. The driver was a guy with a wedding ring. In the cab with him were his own dogs, a pair of friendly, happy young collies, brother and sister. It was obvious that their natural desire to be out herding a flock of something had been modified to fit their lifestyle. They and the guy were crazy about each other. They rode everywhere with him, herding traffic out the window glass, the guy told us, with their eyes.

While the guy unloaded the bags, one of the staffers gave permission for the collies to visit my class. It was a good opportunity to see how our students would act in the presence of strangers from the outside world. I coped with the surprise very well, expecting the worst, ready to stop Tasha from being a bully, Shadow from howling at them, Josie from biting them, Dora from bossing them around and demanding that they bow to her, Alfie from ignoring them, when it wouldn't kill him to pick up his head and say hi. But nothing happened.

It was the same as if those collies and the Sanctuary dogs belonged to two different species of aliens, from two different planets, with nothing to say to one another and no means to say it, even if they did. The visiting dogs remained at a distance, staring silently, getting stared at back. Not even Tasha went over to them, which would have been her job, as the biggest.

They weren't being indifferent or antisocial. I don't know how I knew what was happening, but I knew. Truly, in their own minds, they recognized the huge abyss between them; they had nothing in common. The collies had a person. The collies had a home. No human had ever hurt them. They had zero awareness of such a thing as "homeless dogs hurt by humans."

I was sure my dogs felt they were looked upon by the visitors as losers. When the visit was over, the sense of relief in my class-room was like the removal of a collective collar worn too tightly, finally taken off.

Everyone received treats from a new bag. They didn't care that the treats were not homemade. "Those collies were snobs," I told them. "They were boring, ignorant snobs."

Two-ball. Louise returned to my class to give Shadow a lesson on Drop It.

She had me keep the other dogs to the side, Tasha on a leash and Dora too, because Dora didn't like anyone doing something she wasn't involved in. I sat on the floor with Josie in my lap. Alfie was beside us, inert, his tail tucked in, his sleekness and smooth-ness curving like half of a hoop. He was letting me pat him with the hand that wasn't holding the two leashes.

Tasha and Dora settled down. I think the dogs knew we were playing the part of an audience.

With all her quietness and calm, Louise called Shadow to come to her. Of course he went rushing. He adored her. She spoke him into a sit. In her hand was a tennis ball. She made him wait for the throw until he started drooling for it.

She didn't fling it far. He shot after it and, as usual, hung onto it, looking like he'd rather stop breathing than give it up. She didn't call him back. She didn't tell him he needed to go and drop the ball at her feet.

"Shadow, look," she called softly, reaching into her pocket.

And it was, oh my God she has another ball.

She held up the second ball, her arm pre-throw. In the audi-ence, we were riveted. Shadow turned toward us as if asking for advice, but he knew he was on his own with this. He went rigid with perplexity, Hamlet-like with indecision. He wanted that other ball. He also wanted the one in his mouth. I don't know how he knew he had to return the first one to have the second. But he knew.

"Come and drop, Shadow," called Louise.

He was so conflicted, some pee dripped out of him. It was only a little. No penalty. He watched Louise bounce the second ball, catch it smartly, bounce it again, again, again. He couldn't bear it. He moaned and let out a half bark and streaked to her, skidding to a rest just beyond her. Then he reversed himself to stand in front of her. Up went her arm.

"Drop it," Louise commanded. "*Drop* it."

Shadow opened his mouth like the day he first barked again, in the snow at the inn. The ball landed on the floor one instant before Louise tossed the second one.

Off he went to get it. Down she bent for a pickup. Again she raised her arm, poised for another throw. When he brought the second ball to her, she didn't have to tell him what to do. He dropped it at her feet and went into a sit to wait for the next one. I looked at the way his body trembled with excitement. His tongue was out and so was his tail.

It took eighteen times (I counted) of two-ball back-and-forth before he graduated into being okay with having a ball in Louise's pocket that was hers, unthrown, and a ball that was tossed, which needed to be brought back and dropped.

The dogs were soon bored with the show. They went into states of drowsing. Tasha snored lightly, as if she'd decided on her own to make some background music.

I had never felt so awake.

Twenty-Seven

SPRING WAS ALMOST coming. The level of snow was lower than the top of my boots. I was out in the yard with Tasha for leash work, while doing some planning for the agility course. On a short leash, Tasha had to walk with me to blaze a trail for fence lines around an imagined playing field. I had realized that we needed a fence before the equipment could go in. That's how I was okay with being respectful, for now, about the decision to block that UPS delivery. My eyes were on the future.

Alfie was with us, in his own way. He was wearing one of those woolen, blanket-like dog coats from the closet of stuff the Sanctuary receives as donations. Lying nearby in a hollow I'd dug for him with Tasha's help, he looked bundled up and content. I'd come up with a theory that he didn't want to pee or poop outdoors because, like any new transplant from a warm climate, he hadn't yet developed a good relationship with winter. I was trying to put his problem in a reasonable light. I wished I could have let him know how much I'd been thinking about him.

I was feeling proud of Tasha. She was turning into a pro at being leashed. Whenever she pulled too hard, forgetting to be mindful of a human arm connected to her, she turned to express her feeling of, that was a little mistake, not a relapse. When she jerked too roughly, she was willing to apologize. I'll try harder not to do that again, her eyes would say. This was something that came from Louise. She was the one who'd handled Tasha from the start. You don't have to be big yourself to hang around with an enormous dog, she had told me. I'd seen what she did when Tasha yanked her so strongly, her eyes watered from the arm and shoulder pain, never mind the fear of being toppled and possibly dragged on the ground, like a plow attached to an ox. She knew Tasha hadn't meant to hurt her, but she'd let out a cry of *ow, you hurt me!* She appealed to the Rottweiler's conscience. With Louise, who never otherwise raised her voice, it only took a few times for Tasha to get it. With me, things needed to be a little more dramatic, as in, *Tasha, I'm in agony! Stop trying to kill me right now!*

Right now I was humming to her. It was opera this time, from *The Marriage of Figaro*. My pacing had made me think of what happens right after that major arousal of an overture: Figaro counting off steps around the space of his future marriage bed.

In between hums I was telling Tasha about the time a company of puppet people came to my college to put on *Figaro* with lip-synching marionettes. The music and voices came piped through speakers. This was when Formerly Known As Made Me Happy and I were still new with each other. We went to see the show because we felt we should do something together that wasn't about sex. But we didn't last long. While Figaro the marionette took his steps, his soon-to-be-wife, the marionette Susanna, looked at him with eyes that were asking, even though she was wooden, "Why should we wait for a bed?" Formerly Known As Made Me Happy and I went into a mind meld because of the power of suggestion. We jumped up and rushed out. It was late autumn. We made love in fallen leaves under trees behind the theater. I loved what it was like to go back to my room and look in the mirror and pick leaves from my hair and point out to myself, oh my God I just figured it out that I'm sexy.

"But I don't want you to think all I think about these days is how I never have sex, Tasha," I was explaining.

That was when the Buick of the people we rescued Dapple from appeared, its tires crunching on the snowy road. I recognized that car right away. It came to a stop as soon it reached the flattening where the Jeep was. Its fender was almost touching the Jeep.

A woman was at the wheel. She wasn't wearing a coat. She wore a collared big sweater and a knitted cap, both of which looked homemade. The man in the passenger's seat wore a similar cap and sweater. Hers were blends of yellow and turquoise. His were blue and brown.

They were not ugly-looking people. They were not people whose faces looked like faces of criminals. They looked neighborly and agreeable, with ordinary, middle-aged human skin, ordinary eyes, ordinary everything. The first thing I thought of was how unbelievable it was that a woman who was a knitter would sit in her kitchen or living room or bedroom, knitting, while down in her cellar, Dapple was in that cage. I'd known knitters in my former program. If you wanted to hang around someone who'd be nice to you, you sought out a knitter.

Then I remembered the grieving owner of a fighter on Giant George's laptop, talking about loving his dog. He didn't look like a criminal either. My hand holding Tasha's leash tensed up. Maybe it was the change in my grip that alerted her. Maybe it was something else. Maybe it was dog ESP and she *knew who these people were.*

The man opened his door and stepped out of the Buick. He clung to the open door to keep his balance. It was icy over there. Of course he wouldn't know I was a trainee, not a Sanctuary staffer. He shouted to me in a tone that wasn't belligerent, wasn't hostile in any way. He was almost polite about it, as if he needed to yell to merely be heard.

"We're here to get our dog! People can't be taking other people's dogs!"

He was looking at the front windows. He seemed to think Dapple would be there with her spots and sadness, pining to go home with them. But the dog in the window was Boomer. His barks came out to us muffled and old-dog weak, which didn't matter. He was definitely sounding an alarm.

I didn't let go of Tasha's leash on purpose. Gone for the moment were all her lessons. We had entered a state of emergency, she felt. She had to serve. She had to protect. She had no other choice but to activate her Rottweiler genes and *go for it.*

She was yanking me in a way that made me concerned about my shoulder in its socket. Even though I had gloves on, the loop of the handle pressed into me. I told myself that if I didn't let go of the leash, I'd never have the use of that hand again.

I saw her bare her teeth. I saw the opening of her Rottweiler jaws. I heard the snarl coming out of her, low and raspy and rumbly, and I knew, for the rest of my life, I'd have a sound built into my memory to go along with the word *menacing,* with a *very* in front of it, perhaps two or even three.

She took off toward the car at a gallop, dragging the leash in the snow like an extra tail. I didn't see Alfie getting up to his feet to join her. You'd think an alarm to run a race had gone off in him, even though there wasn't any track, and it seemed to me that everything he knew about running had been coiled in his body, tense and ready, waiting for a reason to explode. He shot by me in a flash, in a silent, glorious streak, his paws barely touching the ground.

I must have failed to tightly secure the straps of his dog coat when I'd put it on him. It flew off his back in the middle of his dash. Then it lay in the snow like the shell of a bug a butterfly just emerged from.

Hey, Alfie, I messaged him, even in that chaos. I want to see you run someday for no reason, just to do it, and I want to see you as happy about it as a goddamn brand-new butterfly. I'd caught a glimpse of his face, his eyes. He was grim and fierce. He looked as if some drug had entered his system, some upper.

Tasha was mad that he beat her to the Buick. She was even madder to find that the man made it back inside, door closed, before either dog reached him. I couldn't do anything but watch them rush around the car, jumping the driver's side, the passenger's side. Screaming barks, they took turns: Tasha at the man, Alfie at the woman, Tasha at the woman, Alfie at the man, again and again and again, their nails cutting into the finish in scratches I hoped would never come out.

And Boomer was still barking in the window, and inside the lodge somewhere, Shadow had started a siren of baying. I was about to feel bad for Josie, who was maybe barking too and getting drowned out, but then I saw Louise. She positioned herself near Boomer, with Josie in her arms like a baby. Josie wasn't making noise. She was too thrilled.

Suddenly, at the next window, there was Giant George, holding Dora. She had the same expression as Josie. Their little faces were *ecstatic*. And there was Shadow! He'd jumped up, paws on the sill, copying Boomer. He squeezed beside Giant George and kept howling. No one was telling him to stop.

I could see that the woman and man in the car were having trouble deciding what to do. On the one hand, they wanted to get out of here, even if it meant, perhaps, running over and murdering two animals. On the other hand, they wanted to follow through on their mission.

I remembered everything about those cages, that darkness, that smell. I felt I was on a high. My adrenaline was so pumped, I was almost shaking. I felt I'd never seen anything in real life as thrilling as those two dogs *in attack mode*. I felt that Alfie had plugged into his memory of being trained to be a racer — he was thinking of the man and the woman as rabbits inside that car. And Tasha was finally getting to use her size and her facial expressions to scare the shit out of people who very much needed to have the shit scared right out of them!

Things entered their final stage when the front door of the lodge opened.

Coming out, a coat thrown over her shoulders, was Agnes, descending the steps with all her tallness, all her terrier inner self. She picked her way carefully in the snow, as if she'd caught a fear of falling from Margaret. When she reached my side, she leaned down so I could hear her in all the racket.

She spoke to me calmly, fully composed.

"You lost control of dogs you were in charge of," she said.

I couldn't believe it. We were in this situation, and she was talking to me about me, like the problem out here was *me?*

"Alfie's moving," I pointed out, as if that were the only thing that mattered. I knew I sounded like a child, sticking up for myself and doing it badly. I didn't care.

"Evie," she said, "please don't make the mistake of imagining he loved to run, just because you're seeing him love it today."

Around and around the car he went, faster than Tasha. He didn't slip on the ice like she did. She was starting to get weary. He looked like he was just warming up.

"But he's having a good time," I said.

She didn't look at me with disappointment, or as if I'd flunked a test I'd been cocky enough to think I'd pass, when I'd done nothing to get ready for it. She just gave me an order.

"Go inside," she said. "I'll take over."

She left me and headed for the car. She only called to the dogs once, each of them by name. They didn't look happy about being interrupted, but they went to her, panting, sweaty, fierce with self-importance. Agnes took hold of Tasha's leash. She made it look easy.

Alfie stood by her in trembling stillness. When he moved away from her, I thought he'd changed his mind about being obedient. But he'd thought of something else. He trotted to a wheel of the Buick and lifted his leg and peed on it.

Alfie peed outside!

I was glad I saw that. I was glad Agnes hadn't turned to see if I surrendered to her command. I did, but I told myself I was ready to go inside anyway. I waited until I saw the window of the driver's side rolling down. The woman was turning her face upward to find out what Agnes had to say. The two dogs flanked her in sits, as good as if someone drew a picture of them with haloes over their heads.

On my way up the steps, I saw Giant George take hold of Dora's paw. She was squirming in his arms, getting upset now. She had realized she needed to express her feeling that no one should be the center of attention but herself. Giant George waved her paw, like she was saluting me herself. I waved back, faking it that I was feeling okay. I wanted Boomer. I knew he'd be worn out from keeping his stance at the window on his sore back legs. He'd need me to rub him before he went to his crate for a nap. I liked how it felt to know my hands would soon be in his fur. My gloves hadn't kept out the cold. I'd tell him I wanted him to warm me, so he wouldn't feel I was rubbing him just because I felt sorry for him for being so old and arthritic. But really I needed some comfort, having crashed from a high I never should have been on. I thought about *control*. I thought, if they're going to throw me out, I hope they get it over with quickly.

When I returned to my room, I stepped on the note some-

one slipped under my door. Of course it was from Agnes. It said,
"If you don't understand what you did today, please come and
talk to me in the dining room. I sincerely hope I wait for you in
vain." Then there was a postscript, after her signature. "PS. If you
think you're right about Alfie, please consider this an invitation
to prove it."

I'd never be told what Agnes said to those people, but I had the
feeling we'd never see them again, and I was right. Giant George
told me later that when he waved Dora's paw to me, he was trying
to distract her from obsessing about getting outdoors and into
the action. She was the one who greeted me as I entered, not that
what she did was a greeting. She tried to slip out before I closed
the door behind me. I had to hold back laughing at her for the
bristling of her fur, her scowl, her sulk. I didn't want her to think
I didn't take her seriously. But it would have felt good to laugh,
long and hard, if only to take the edge off of what it was like for
me to really, really want the people in that car to be hurt by teeth
of dogs.

Twenty-Eight

THE PITTIES WERE a few days away. I was aware of the presence of more volunteers, plus tension, plus a concentrated buzz that felt like preparations for a storm. The lower floor of the Sanctuary was off-limits to everyone such as myself. My dogs were spending their nights in the upper crates and living full-time in the open space of our classroom. For the first time, Boomer wanted the door of his crate closed. He didn't want it latched, just shut, which meant shutting out Josie. She took it personally, but Dora didn't like her crawling in there with him. Boomer didn't like having Dora boss him around. So he copped out, although he probably thought of it as being gentlemanly. He often pretended to be asleep, even when Josie paw-knocked on his door, looking crushed.

We had food up here now, bowls, everything they needed.

Giant George was busy all the time and barely speaking to me. Louise showed up in my class to work on "lie down" with Shadow. Her efforts went nowhere. Cracks had appeared in her calmness; she was too distracted.

Even our mealtime quiet was compromised. For the first time, volunteers in small batches were eating with us, keeping silence while expanding the level of noise. The married man kind of close to my age who reminded me of Romeo turned up often. I kept my distance but overheard him one morning in the hall, talking to staffers. They lowered their voices when they noticed me, but I realized he was an up-up in the Network and so was his wife. By now I'd seen her. I didn't want her to look like a twenty-something version of a perfect Juliet. I was hoping for someone who looked like the daughter of the ugliest witch in *Macbeth*.

Apparently those two had plenty of leisure time and also money. I had picked up the understanding that they were bank-rolling the pitties. If I felt a little splinter of jealousy now and then about that, I made myself think of Othello, and then I pulled the splinter out.

Alfie was letting Tasha into his lie-down space, not only be-cause she was huge and he agreed with her that she could do whatever she wanted. Alfie and Tasha had started looking at each other like they were thinking about becoming boyfriend and girlfriend, which annoyed Shadow. He was awfully sulky, but at least he wasn't toothy like Josie. She kept going over to Alfie and Tasha to nip their faces and chew on their tails; she'd run off be-fore they could swat her. Dora was in a phase of being aloof. She didn't need to learn basic commands. She had them. She was say-ing, I didn't need to be taught anything ever. I'm incredibly cul-tured. I was *born* this way.

I knew I had to do something about Josie and the biting and the don't you dare pat me, Evie. But I didn't know what. Mar-garet had told me to keep a muzzle for her in my pocket. The idea was, Josie was so disgusted by the sight of one, pulling it out of a pocket just a little would give her the chance to rethink her course of action. I was supposed to watch for signs of snapping, not stand around waiting for her problem to somehow take care of itself. Anyway, my pockets were always too full of treats.

Everyone was tense, tense, tense, yet I wasn't complaining

about a thing. I went along in my own private orbit, feeling, at times, almost as buoyant as a bubble. I also felt I should substitute for frazzled Louise. I stepped into the void, filling the need of the dogs to have someone around who could send them vibrations of serenity. I was proud of myself: calm, strong, admirable Evie, star trainee and never mind that I was the only one they had. I was behaving like someone with advanced certificates in the practice of yoga.

And then.

Louise and I were with the dogs, on a morning that was feeling like one long recess. We were supervising a game of "Who can have a toy in their mouth and not destroy it?" In my hand was a cute purple terrycloth bunny, its stuffing intact, although one of its ears was hanging out the side of Tasha's jaws. Louise was trying to get her to drop it, but no one was obeying commands because they knew it was play time. In walked Agnes. She motioned to me to follow her.

Louise came over and took the bunny from me. Josie came over too, letting me know she was interested in going wherever I went. But Louise bent down and scooped her up.

"I'm sorry I still haven't done the assignment you gave me," I told Agnes, imagining she meant to take me to a desk somewhere and tie me to the chair.

It wasn't about that. I followed her toward the dining room. She left me to go in alone. Only one person was there, seated at the table nearest the fireplace. On the table were a box of Kleenex, an open pot of tea smelling fruity and also of chamomile, and two mugs I'd never seen before. The mugs were decorated with, of all things, lifelike pictures of the heads and floppy ears of dachshunds.

Also on the table was an iPad, new-looking, not turned on.

Phyllis. That was the name of the staffer whose voice I'd heard on Mrs. Auberchon's answering machine.

Phyllis, originally Dark Gray, went the notes in my head. Age about seventy, more or less. Reminded me the first time I saw her of Mrs. Treats. Thought she was an alpha but she's not. Isn't around very much. Doesn't work with the dogs. Never seen taking a dog for a walk. Seems to be a manager type. Wears dentures. Has the most wrinkles. Favors long, loose skirts and cardigans and colorful woolen knee socks when not in a sweats outfit. Drinks coffee and tea black. Actually kind of boring.

"Would you like some tea, Evie?"

I sat down across the table from her. Warm as it was, the dining room had the feel of an empty shell, as if the walls could express emotions. The only one it was expressing now was the one of being lonely in all the downtime between meals.

"No thanks," I said.

She poured me a mug of tea anyway, then one for herself. I had never seen a dachshund on something you'd raise to your mouth before. I looked at the long, pointy face, the high-up round eyes, the sheen of intelligence that wasn't just from a glaze put on by a potter. I remembered reading something in the breed book about dachshunds being maybe ten times smarter than the size of their brains. And they're honest, and they're famous as hunters, with a tendency to look at you one-dimensionally, totally stereotyping you, like you're prey they need to go after.

"I used to have a pair of these guys, long before I came to the mountain," Phyllis said chattily. "They lived to an old, old age. I usually keep the cups in my room, but I was in a mood today to bring them out. Did you have a dog when you were a child, Evie?"

"I had . . ."

My voice very nearly stopped coming. Tell the truth? Tell a lie? Something was dachshund-like about her, even though her face was soft and round. I didn't want to feel like her prey.

" . . . books," I answered. "I had dogs in books."

"Ah. Then you have much in common with Mrs. Auberchon."

I let that go. There was nothing to say to such an unreal remark. What did she want with me? Why was I here?

She took a sip of her tea. When she put the cup down, I looked at the way her false teeth were so brightly white. They weren't overwhelmingly artificial-looking, but you could tell they weren't real, like you can tell when someone dyes her hair. Some of us in my former program, when we were let out for walks, supervised, around a few city blocks, played a game of False Teeth, Dyed Hair. You had to exclude hair that was green or blue or some other make-believe shade, on people who thought the days of punk weren't over. Whoever scored the most points could pick the after-dinner DVD on the big TV in what we called the living room, like we were a family. I became good at it. For a while I won every time. This was in my phase of Morgan Freeman movies. I'd be racking up points, not only from people on the sidewalks but from people I spotted in glass-fronted restaurants and shops, and people stuck in traffic too. And everyone else would be groaning and saying, "Oh, please, not *Lean on Me* again. Or not *Clean and Sober* or *Driving Miss Daisy.*"

"Evie," said Phyllis. "There's something you need to be told. We've had an offer for an adoption."

I was sure it would have to be Shadow, now that he had learned "drop it." Even without "lie down," he had the grades to graduate. Shadow! A search-and-rescue program had accepted him! Or a trainer, for one-on-one, like being home-schooled! A massive wave of feeling started building in me right away. He was my first dog. He had peed on my hand when we met. I had told him to get the fuck away from me. I had told him I would murder him if he peed on me again. I had told him how much I hated *Peanuts*. I'd witnessed the return of his voice. I'd counted the number of times he took to change two-ball into one. I worried about him when he was more depressed than Hamlet. But how could I say goodbye to him? I'd have to hide in my room when he left. I was too weak of a trainee. I was too unprofessional.

·I tried to sound professional when I asked, just to make sure, "Which one?"

And Phyllis said, "Eric."

She saw my surprise, my concern. She must have thought I was taking her for an elderly person entering dementia in front of my eyes. It was bad enough that she felt I had "much in common with Mrs. Auberchon," when I'd just finished getting that woman out of my head, from being freaked for hallucinating her. Now she was telling me the name of a dog who didn't exist—at least, not anywhere here.

"His last name will become Fisher," she told me. "That's the name of the family. Eric Fisher."

She waited a moment, letting it sink in. Then she said, "Giant George."

The iPad wasn't right in front of her. She had to reach for it to pull it closer. She turned it. She tapped it. She finger-stroked it. The one who was getting all demented, I realized, was me.

"I'll show you what they look like, Evie. They sent photos. There's one in particular I like very much, of all of them."

I found myself looking at a group picture of a man and a woman and a lot of kids. "A lot" was my first impression, until I counted: three, four, five. They were all pressed closely together. The kids were different ages, from a youngest of seven or so, which I could tell from the missing baby teeth in her smile, to an eldest boy who was maybe a senior in high school. Three girls, two boys. They were in summer-type clothes. They were standing on the deck of a house. I assumed a house was what they were facing, their house. Behind them, past the rails of the deck, was a backyard of a perfect green lawn and what looked like an agility course, but for humans. But of course it was normal play equipment for children. There was also a swimming pool, the raised kind, with a second deck around it. Outdoor chairs were on that deck, little tables, beach umbrellas on poles. On the sunlit surface of the pool was an inflated raft, red as a tomato, with a lump at one end for a pillow. The yard was bordered all around with a fence, against which grew beans, tomatoes, other viny-growing things. There were shade trees too, big ones, thick, healthy, leafy.

"He asked me to be the one to tell you," Phyllis was saying. "He kept putting it off."

"I thought he wanted to go to Alaska," I said. That was all I could think of saying.

The woman and the man had their arms around each other's waists, like a textbook example of longtime-married-people snugness. I could tell they were on good terms with each other in every way. The man was white, hefty, muscular, short-haired, sort of blond. The woman was black, taller than he was, broad-shouldered, straight-backed. On her head was the type of brimmed hat you'd expect to see on a gardener. The youngest boy was black, dark-skinned. The little girl was black, lighter. Neither resembled the man or the woman. The other two girls, of older-middle-school age, were Chinese, which made me think of a Chinese girl in my program. She was gay. She came from a very traditional family. When she tried to not be gay, in order to fit in with them, she ended up with a heroin problem. We became friends for a while, because I was flattered she made a move on me. She liked the way I apologized for being straight. We spent a lot of time talking about how it happens sometimes that you can spend your whole life wondering why you don't fit in with people you're supposed to be part of, like it's all your fault. Or you can go find other people to be part of. Then she disappeared into the outside world.

Phyllis said, "Tell me what you're thinking."

"I'm not thinking anything. I'm looking at the picture."

The eldest boy was dark-haired and white. He didn't resemble the grown-ups either. It wasn't that hard to figure out that this was a family with a history of adoptions.

"You know," Phyllis said, "Eric was only daydreaming about Alaska, because of the husky pups. He was afraid it wouldn't go through with these folks. It's been in the works for quite a while. Are you okay? I'm asking because you'll miss him."

"Of course I'm okay," I said. "I'll miss him, sure, but it's not like he and I are close. I didn't even know his real name."

"He needs to be in school."

"Oh, I know."

"He needs to be part of a family."

"Absolutely," I said.

"He'd rather not have anyone know his past. I hope you don't hold it against him if he didn't open up to you."

"I'm happy for him," I said. "I'd never hold anything against him."

"Would you like a Kleenex, Evie?"

"No thanks."

She gave me one. I made like I was dabbing it under my eyes because I didn't want to waste it, like I was only going through the motions. I wished Josie had followed me here and was sitting in my lap, letting me pat her.

"They're a wonderful family," she said.

"I can tell."

"The man is a stay-at-home dad. The woman, as they say, brings in the dough. She's with a company that's been around for longer than you and I put together. It's an insurance company, and she's a vice president. I believe she runs one of their biggest departments."

"That's very stable," I said. "That's impressive. What about the guy? What did he do before he stayed home?"

"He's retired from having a landscape company. I'm sure you noticed their lawn. It's natural. He's not the type to use chemicals. You see, I had to ask about his choices for treatment. I'd felt it was important to know."

"I *hate* chemicals," I said.

"Would you like to see some photos of the house?"

I shook my head. "When is he leaving?"

"Soon. He won't be part of what's going to be happening with the new arrivals."

She stood up to put more wood on the fire. When her back was turned, I looked at the photo again. Something was bothering me about it. I could see that there was a space for Giant George to fit in with that crowd. I couldn't think of him as Eric, but I could see him with those people. I could see his big shaggy self in swimming trunks, jumping off the pool deck, cannonballing. I could even imagine him getting yelled at by the guy for being lazy about mowing that grass. But something was wrong.

There wasn't a dog in the picture.

If they had a dog, the dog would be with them. It was a family portrait. They were obviously the kind of people who would think of their dog as a member of the family. How could there not be a dog? How could he want to go to a home without a dog?

Phyllis was standing near the fire when I mentioned it.

"They don't have a dog. Is he all right with that?"

She stepped over to me, placing a hand on my shoulder, getting ready to pat me.

"Evie," she said. "He's taking Tasha."

Twenty-Nine

ADOPTION, THE KIND *of people who do it.* People who adopt are not aliens, although it's easy to think they are, in the sense that, first there's everyone who's human, and then there are people who adopt, as if, in evolution, a separate species branched off. Being clever, they were able to adapt. They learned to pass themselves off as normal. They can mingle with the rest of humanity and not draw attention to themselves, like in schools, places of business such as insurance companies, geographical locations such as a desert or a home with a deck and a nice yard and a swimming pool. You can walk by the members of this branch on a sidewalk and not know what's under their skin. It's not like pointing to dogs and saying what breeds they are, or what mixes. It's not like spotting people with dyed hair or false teeth.

However, I think it's a mistake to stand back and be in awe of adopters if you happen to find them out. They want to pass as normal people, so you should respect that. Never fall into the trap of using over-the-top describers for them, such as noble, saintly, superior to normal people, virtuous.

Also, "heart of gold." There is no such thing as an adoptive person who has, in their chest, a heart made of gold. Gold hearts are *lockets.* Just by looking at someone who adopts, you can tell the person has muscles and pumping blood. Also they have flaws. You can't be human and not have flaws. So just because you can't see signs of interior imperfections in pictures of themselves they send via email — well, it doesn't mean they're perfect.

Adoption, problems of. I looked at charts put together by some rescue people for a website geared to people who work in shelters and in fostering. I was searching for testimonials and advice on things like how not to be selfish and emotionally stupid when an animal gets a home. Instead I found the charts. I learned that many adoptions don't go well, especially the ones involving large dogs. Large dogs have the highest rate of return.

Probably, many adopters are idealistic. This can mean overlooking the reality of the many problems large dogs can cause in a household and also in a neighborhood, even when they're housebroken and leash-trained, and did sort of okay in Basic Obedience.

Things are going to be chewed. Things are going to be mangled. It might not always be only dog toys. And that could be the least of it.

Maybe it's naive, or plain bad, to be idealistic about large dogs, or, in fact, any dog of any size.

Awareness. Dogs have heightened awareness in certain situations, like dog ESP. For example, Alfie's having ESP about Tasha. He'd never done his business indoors on the nice woolen welcome mat by the front door, which the staffers are fond of. He'd always been considerate of it. But . . . there he was, expressing himself through his rear end, and not looking sorry or guilty. His mound of shit was saying, I have reached a new level of depression, and it's a whole lot lower than before.

Bonding. Good trainers know that the attachment called bonding must only take place between the dog and the person or persons of the dog's human family.

But what if the trainer has a personal history of things going wrong in the bonding thing that people do with each other? What if the trainer finds out from a dog what bonding means exactly, because the trainer went and felt it for the dog?

Many trainers (I read in several articles) practice a highly disciplined approach to their jobs, because when you come right down to it, realistically, it's just a job. Your level of professionalism is *everything*. Several trainers who share their thoughts on the Internet feel it's helpful to know about aspects of Buddhist thought, such as the one about detachment.

I was interested for about ten minutes in the blog of a trainer who does yoga every day and goes on retreats in American Buddhist places, to meditate with monks. I felt we had something in common, since those things were once goals of mine.

This trainer says you should care for the dogs you work with, because detachment isn't uncaring. But you have to care while being detached. You have to be realistic. "I've wisely learned to do my job without *being* my job," this trainer says. "That's the essence of being a respected professional in the dog-training field."

Control. Do. Not. Lose. It. Ever. And if you do, or *when* you do, hurry up and call yourself back, even though it feels like you went over an edge there's no getting back from. Say to yourself, I'm new, I'm new. Say to yourself, in spite of evidence to the contrary, this training is *working*.

Here comes Tasha.

Dogs, having idealism for. I am so totally ideal, Tasha's saying.

How could I think there's something flawed in being idealistic about dogs?

Dogs, love. The Rottweiler's on me, placing her big head where my heart is. She's listening to the beat of my heart, like maybe she's memorizing me. I put my arms around her. I have zero words.

Thirty

THE VISIT TO Mrs. Walzer in her hospital bed could not have been worse. She looked as if she'd aged by twenty years since the last time Mrs. Auberchon saw her. She was supposed to be getting ready for broken-hip rehab, but she'd made up her mind that she had come to a point in her life where she was better off flat on her back than up on her feet. Her lunch tray was barely touched. Her skin had a terrible pallor, her voice a terrible flatness. They'd cut down her meds as anyone would do with a patient who needed to leave the land of fuzziness and floating like a cloud, but she was making it clear it was the only place she wanted to be. She wanted to have her IV again. She wanted to be fuzzy, to float.

"You don't know what it's like to be old."

That's what Mrs. Walzer had for a response to Mrs. Auberchon's first attempts at conversation. It had the gravity of being true. Mrs. Auberchon was young enough to be a daughter of hers. But still, "old" didn't have to be the most important thing she was. The woman was in fantastic shape in every physical part of her that wasn't a hip that got broken. Think of Boomer! He was her age, more or less, if you measured human years in dog ones. He had a condition that could never be healed. Yet inside himself, his spirit was like a genie in a lamp, as alive as anything, and all you had to do to release it was rub his fur, or just get down beside him and look in his eyes.

But Mrs. Auberchon saw that this was a case of Dora the Scottie all over again. Why couldn't she talk to Mrs. Walzer the way she'd talked to Dora? Why didn't anything she said break through? She just wasn't saying the right things, although they sounded right when she said them. She had pictured herself strolling into that room like a messenger from the outside world, saying, with staunch goodwill and confidence, come back, Mrs. Walzer, come back; there's an empty place where you were, and you have to hurry back and fill it. Plus, you're my only friend.

Of course she couldn't have put things like that, directly — come back, you're my only friend. She didn't compare Mrs. Walzer with dogs except in her own mind. But she thought she did a good job of being caring and concerned, as warm in her tone and manner as sunlight.

And what else did Mrs. Walzer have to say? She told Mrs. Auberchon she didn't want the flowers Mrs. Auberchon bought in the gift shop: a pretty bouquet of perky, bright colors, shiny leaves, and cheer. She rang for a nurse to take it away, and then she explained that falling and breaking her hip had been *a wake-up call.*

A wake-up call! She said this as if she'd come to her senses about something she very much needed to quit, like she was in rehab right now to stop thinking of life as something she had an interest in being part of.

She was the same as a cake in an oven. It was all so simple, she said. She was a cake in an oven and the timer was ticking out, and the most she could hope for was feeling satisfied that she'd done her best with the ingredients she had to work with.

And it wasn't a joke! She was a baker!

"You're not cake batter," Mrs. Auberchon replied.

It was a short visit. That was the end of it. Mrs. Walzer didn't want to talk about the rehab center she was going to be moved to. She didn't want to talk about her faraway children, her grandchildren, the little ones and babies who were her greats. On the bedside table was a stack of get-well cards, untouched, not being looked at. There was a brochure from the rehab place and another about a meeting group for elderly widows. Both had the crispness of having never been touched by the person they were meant to reach.

Mrs. Auberchon had even tried introducing to Mrs. Walzer the subject of *let me confide in you the secret of what I'm going to do in late spring with my nest egg.*

Mrs. Walzer had acted as if she didn't know what a nest egg was, when in fact she'd sat in the kitchen at the inn all those hours taking part in all those conversations that turned corners so suddenly, without warning, from news and gossip into "Oh, Mrs. Auberchon, now when are you going to confide in me what you're planning to do with that nest egg of yours?"

"Oh, you'll be the first to know," was always the answer. Which would be followed by the friend-to-friend grumbling of Mrs. Walzer about how she wished she had a nest egg too. Or she'd rave about admiring Mrs. Auberchon for her self-discipline, her diligence in planning for retirement, old age, still such a long way off for her, unlike some of us others, she'd say. Sometimes she'd say she would miss Mrs. Auberchon very much when the day arrived that she was packing her bags and leaving the inn for . . . wherever. Sometimes she remarked how much she'd prefer being, you know, not in this world anymore, herself, just to spare herself the hardship of saying goodbye. And now she didn't want to discuss the nest egg!

It wasn't only that. Mrs. Walzer didn't ask about the Sanctuary dogs, not even to wonder what they were getting now for treats. She didn't even care about the treats!

On her way out, Mrs. Auberchon happened upon a hospital volunteer with a therapy dog on a leash: a girl pug with a pink bow on her collar.

Of course Mrs. Auberchon stopped to say hello and pat her. Candy was her name. Her puggy little squish of a face was pure sweetness. Her tail was in a soft, beige-white curl at the tip, like the loop of a fiddlehead fern. "I am the best thing about this whole hospital," she was saying, rubbing herself in and out of Mrs. Auberchon's legs like a cat. She was on her way to Pediatrics, her usual hangout, Mrs. Auberchon learned. And in one second, she got the idea that Candy on Mrs. Walzer's bed, in Mrs. Walzer's arms, would be exactly, perfectly right.

The volunteer was calm, soft-spoken, matronly. "Sorry. We already tried," she told Mrs. Auberchon. "We were asked to leave that room almost as soon as we went in there."

That was just unbelievable. "My friend," said Mrs. Auberchon, "likes dogs. In fact she—"

On the face of the volunteer was a look of defeat, as if she'd caught it from Mrs. Walzer, like airborne hospital bacteria.

"Your friend," she said, "told me she's seen sausages that look better than this dog, and she is not a fan of sausages. That was how she put it. Don't worry about Candy, though. She's a pro. She wasn't insulted."

The bus ride back to the inn was gloomy. What about a Sanctuary dog for Mrs. Walzer? Mrs. Auberchon remembered how partial she was to big ones. She was always taking Tasha's side. A real fondness was there. But Tasha was leaving.

Boomer with his golden inner genie? His fur and his personality could be painkillers, better than any drug. Old people and old dogs ought to be with each other; it was a natural fit. But Boomer was too arthritic to leave the mountain. The ride down would be a nightmare. He'd have to be brought bedside in a wheelchair for dogs, which of course the hospital wouldn't have. Alfie? No, he was an indoor pee-er and pooper. He was barely at the point where he was willing to make eye contact with a human, never mind put aside his own issues and be a therapist. Shadow? No. He was too, well, shadowy, plus his face was a sad one, even when he was having a good time. Anyway he was SAR-bound. Search dogs don't belong at a bedside. Dora? She was small but didn't act it. She might be able to draw on her own experience in the infirmary, put it to good use. But if Mrs. Walzer insulted her, she wouldn't be a pro about it. She'd put out her tail and raise hell. As for Josie, she couldn't be considered, not only because of her past. She was definitely on better behavior, but still, she had too much of a reputation as a nipper and an overly zealous yapper.

It was hopeless. No dogs were being trained for therapy. No dogs were coming but the pit bulls. And Mrs. Walzer compared a pug to a sausage!

What could anyone even say about that? There was nothing to be said about that. Mrs. Auberchon couldn't get mad, although she tried. It was too, too alarming. It was on a whole other level from saying she was a cake in a pan. In a way, that was understandable. But a pug was a *dog*.

She walked down the lane with much more caution than usual. A heaviness had come over her. The inn had no guests. No dog was in Solitary to hear her read. No dog was in the infirmary or in Holding. In her room were several books she'd received in the mail that morning. They were not for dogs but for herself. New books for dogs had to wait. All those titles had something to do with pit bulls and fighting. She had homework to do. She didn't want to do it. When she was placing the order, with a rescue group that had an online store, she almost made the decision not to buy anything that came illustrated with photos.

But that would have meant not being prepared for what she was going to be seeing. They were turning Solitary into a private apartment for the eldest dog, who needed to be sequestered completely. The infirmary was about to be full. Holding would be full as well, and all the kennels.

She'd considered asking the staffers if she could voice-contact those dogs without seeing them on camera. She knew they'd say yes. But she didn't ask. She couldn't bear the thought of herself as a coward.

She pushed the door open with the sense that she had never in her life felt such a heaviness before. And as soon as she stepped inside, she knew someone was there.

It was instinct. She could feel an alertness taking her over, partly of fear, but mostly of curiosity, plus the skin prickles coming from her natural annoyance at anything that wasn't as it should be.

The fear part of it was the first to go. She knew how to talk to her inn. It wasn't an intruder. Well, it *was,* but not an intruder who meant to cause harm.

The lobby and the room behind the sliding door were their usual selves, empty. So were the kitchen and her own room. All was as she'd left it. She heard no sounds, not even one creaking or stirring about, but she asked herself, if I can't trust my own feel of this place, what can I trust? The answer was nothing. She didn't need to doubt. She hurried up to the bunkroom.

George!

He was asleep on a bunk in the middle of the room, curled up on his side, his Sanctuary jacket over him like a blanket. He had taken off his boots; he'd left them neatly in the vestibule. The first thing Mrs. Auberchon thought of was how strange it was to see him without a dog. She was aware of a dull thud of disappointment in her chest. She knew she'd better not let it get bigger, so she told herself she was feeling a letdown because George hadn't brought a dog. That was better than saying, "I thought my intruder would be Evie, coming back for a visit to see how I am."

"George," whispered Mrs. Auberchon. "Wake up. It's me. I'm here."

He opened his eyes at once, gazing up at her in sleepy contentment, like a little boy. Maybe he'd been dreaming of his new home. Maybe, in the moment before reality set things right, he took her presence as the presence of his soon-to-be mother.

"Hi," he said.

"I was visiting Mrs. Walzer in the hospital."

"Yeah?"

"Yes. Now I'm back. Congratulations on your new family. I'm going to miss you."

"Yeah?"

"Yes. Of course I'll miss you. Why didn't you come down in the Jeep?"

"I felt like walking."

"Did you come to say goodbye? I wish you'd brought Tasha. Why didn't you bring Tasha with you?"

He sat up and she saw he hadn't come to say goodbye to her. She had the feeling it had never crossed his mind to.

"Tasha's having a bath," he said. "I think they've got four volunteers on it, all new ones, because the old ones won't. I bet they get soaked. I bet, after it's over, they'll never want to clean a big dog again. Did you know they have a pool where I'm going?"

"I didn't know that."

"It's a good thing they do. From now on, that's where she's going. They have a deck around it, so all I have to do when she really stinks is get her up on the deck and push her in. But why I came down is, can I use your computer?"

"My computer?"

"I have to show you something."

Mrs. Auberchon never let anyone in her room. No one but herself touched anything that was hers.

"How about a snack in the kitchen, George?"

"I'm not hungry."

"Should I still call you George? When they sent me the news, they had your real name."

"You can call me George."

"I have popcorn," said Mrs. Auberchon. "I have cocoa. It's just the stuff in envelopes you pour water in, but I'll fix it in a nice big mug for you."

"Please," he said. "It's really important. I wouldn't be here if it wasn't."

She hadn't taken her coat off. She undid the buttons slowly, concentrating hard on each one so it didn't show how much he'd stung her. He was only a boy. He was only another Sanctuary rescue on the way back into the world: another one without a past to be talked about, known. He'd come to her for visits in his early days like a runaway dog. Maybe he'd forgotten that. Did the staffers ever watch movies with him, including terrifying ones, while sitting by him closely, like a grandmother? Of course they didn't! It never would have crossed their minds!

She could not say no to him. She was the Warden. He was, this moment, like a dog put into Solitary. She remembered what he was like when he was younger and new, carrying his loneliness around him like a room just his size. She never laughed at him to his face when he told her how, inside himself, he was a Great Dane. She took him seriously and agreed, patting him.

He waited impatiently while she took off her coat and boots and turned on her machine. He didn't thank her for allowing him in her room. He didn't look at the bookshelf, pointing to titles and reminding her of the ones he'd given her. He didn't mention how much he liked it when he eavesdropped on her, reading about hobbits.

She let him sit in her chair. She stood looking over his shoulder. What appeared on her screen was a website for adoptions of

Siberian huskies, and right away Mrs. Auberchon thought of the sled pups. She'd sat in that chair for hours at a time for their first few Sanctuary weeks, all of them in the infirmary. She didn't remember the details of their rescue. The details didn't matter. She remembered herself talking and talking to sick, scrawny, mewing babies, with George always somewhere close by them. She'd read them Dr. Seuss exclusively: *Yertle the Turtle, Fox in Socks, Dr. Seuss's Sleep Book, Horton Hears a Who!*

And then they were bigger, they were strong, they were going outdoors, and they were gone. Mrs. Auberchon had often imagined them as students in a snow-domed academy of sledding, earnestly working on their degrees, their futures bright, filled with Iditarods.

She said, "What are we doing here, George?"

"You'll see. First I have to lay out some background."

He clicked a box that led to listings of shelters currently holding Siberians. He went to one of them and let her see the notice: "We are no longer accepting dogs due to overcrowding." Then came another with the same thing, and another, another. What was the matter with him? He knew as well as she did that lots of shelters were overcrowded!

A new site came up. A moment later she was looking at a photo of a young male husky in a sitting position in a room with walls made of cinder blocks, painted a pretty shade of blue, like cornflowers. The linoleum floor was new-grass green. Against those colors, the dog was starkly white and black. Attached to his collar was a short length of some kind of flexible metal, which was attached to a bolt in the wall.

One eye of the dog was pale amber. The other eye was pale blue. He didn't look ill. But he didn't look healthy. He was obviously underweight. His muzzle was white, and so was most of his face, up to a meeting place on the forehead with the soft black of his head. The line where white went to black was wavy and gently jagged, like a small splash of sea foam, as if a wave was cresting lightly into a stretch of dark water.

And so the dog was implanted in Mrs. Auberchon's mind with an association of water, not of snow. She had no idea why that happened. She simply had the feeling very strongly that something about this animal was watery and rolling-waves-like. His chest was white to a curving swath of black below his neck: more foam and dark water. His legs were white. His expression was empty of emotion. He was just sitting there, giving no indication that he knew he'd be moved soon, or that he worried he might be sitting there for forever.

Why was she looking at this dog?

"Remember how I named the sled pups before they left?" George suddenly said.

She did. He wasn't supposed to name them. At the Sanctuary they were identified by numbers, per order of the training center that offered to take them. But George had given them names, not that she recalled any of them. She had stuck with the numbers.

Sense was dawning on her, as impossible as it seemed. It couldn't be. Could it?

"I just found him a little while ago," said Giant George. "I was looking for him everywhere. This is Rocky."

"Rocky?"

"Yeah. You forgot. I *told* you."

"Tell me again."

"I was watching the first *Rocky* movie when we found out how those guys needed rescue. He was the smallest when they came in. He was the runt. I should've known this would happen, but I thought he'd work out with the rest of them. He didn't. He ended up getting adopted by some guy on a vacation, on some outdoor Alaska tourist thing. But he didn't work out with the guy, either. This is the fourth place he's been since he left here. I have to get him out."

"George," said Mrs. Auberchon, "don't tell me you're thinking of taking a husky with you, when you already talked that family into Tasha. Even you wouldn't be so crazy."

"I'm not thinking about taking him with me."

"Well, you can't get him sent to the mountain. You know there's a stop on new ones. I expect that'll also go for, you know, a return."

"I expect you're right, Mrs. Auberchon."

Mrs. Auberchon was running out of patience. She wanted to stop looking at this dog. She felt sorry for him, and for George as well, as he was busy, she knew, blaming himself for the unfortunate turn of events. *Unfortunate turn of events*, she was saying to herself, mentally putting up distance between herself and the dog and blue walls and green floor and that attachment thing. She was worn out anyway from seeing Mrs. Walzer. She had half a mind to tell this big brooding boy hunkering in her Warden chair that sometimes, honest to God, enough was enough. Sometimes, in fact, she was *sick and tired of dogs and all their problems.* What about problems of her own? Dogs weren't the only ones with unfortunate turns of events!

George turned in the chair to look up at her.

She smiled at him. She still couldn't really believe he'd be leaving. Once, she suddenly remembered, he'd come down to the inn with a woeful little dog in a sling he'd fixed on himself across his chest from a shoulder. She recognized the sling as a throw cover she'd kept on the big armchair in the lobby. She'd been looking all over for it, and for other items the inn was missing, little things: a pillowcase, a towel, a place mat. She'd blamed it on guests, not that she could do anything about it. He'd grinned at her sweetly when she accused him of stealing from her, as if to say, why shouldn't he? She couldn't get upset, because there was the dog in her throw: a new one, a toy, young, a poodle, full of black curls except for the raw patch of skin on the chest, where the hair had come off and was far from growing back. The missing hair, Mrs. Auberchon remembered, was from self-scratching, the same spot over and over. She remembered there'd been a Sanctuary operation on a house where quite a few dogs had been kept in close quarters by the kind of people who turn up on TV sometimes for being found out as "hoarders." The poodle was the only one of them in good enough shape to be able to keep on living.

On her front paws were tiny booties. "I'm in love with her," George had said, plopping himself and the dog down to watch a movie.

Eventually the poodle was adopted—a fortunate turn of events. Mrs. Auberchon remembered most of all what it was like to hear the word *love* from the mouth of this boy. That's what she decided to hold on to always. Love coming out of this boy. The photo on her screen seemed to soften. She felt a little glow about the husky, like a visit now coming to an end.

"Let's turn it off and have that cocoa, George," she said. "You'll need it for the walk back. Maybe when the pit bulls are settled in, I'll speak to them up there about bringing him, if he's still available. I'll keep tabs on him. I promise."

"I don't want you to just keep tabs on him," George said.

It wasn't that he was looking at her hopefully. He was looking at her as if he knew something, which he was giving her the chance of figuring out for herself.

Uh-oh, thought Mrs. Auberchon.

She was already shaking her head in a *no* when he put it to her.

"You have to take Rocky for the inn, Mrs. Auberchon," he said. "He'll fit in. He'll be *great* here."

"Get out of my chair, George. You know I couldn't—"

He didn't let her finish. He lifted a hand toward the screen, flat-palmed, as if he were patting the photo. "I called them," he said. "They have a fee, or a donation, as they call it. You have to pay it before they'll do a release. But it's only, like, a couple hundred. I told them you'll get in touch with your credit card number, so, yeah, we can go have hot chocolate. You can use the phone in the kitchen. But don't ask about transport. They don't have it. We can set it up separately."

"Stop!" cried Mrs. Auberchon. "If I wanted a dog for the inn, I'd already have one! I don't want a dog!"

"I figured you'd say that," he said calmly. "So now it's out of the way. I just have to ask you one more thing."

"What!" cried Mrs. Auberchon.

"If you don't feel like living with a Rocky, I'll understand. But pick something that's right for him. Don't change his name to George. You'll want to. You'll totally, totally want to, after I'm gone."

Thirty-One

AGAIN A SUMMONS from Phyllis. But this time I wasn't meeting with her in the dining room. Boomer led me through the kitchen and up a flight of stairs to a hallway similar to mine, not that I was calling my part of the Sanctuary "mine." I was just calling it a place where I'd sort of grown used to living.

Behind the kitchen was the room that belonged to Giant George. The door had always been closed before, but I knew it was his. This was the only place where the air smelled like a guy. I'd picked up whiffs of him often on my trips to the kitchen. He wasn't there now. I only looked inside long enough to see that it was somewhere someone was moving out of. I was working on having a positive attitude about his new non-Sanctuary life, as in, yay for him and also Tasha. But so far I was only at: this sucks.

Then there I was, at the living quarters of the staffers. It was silent up here, but not stuffy, not unwelcoming. All the doors were shut except one at the front of the hall. Boomer dropped to a sprawl in front of it and immediately lidded his old eyes for a nap. I had to step over him.

I found myself in sort of an office, centered by a table exactly like the ones in the dining room, with four chairs around it.

Phyllis looked up at me and gestured for me to sit beside her. She smiled as if she knew the first thing I'd think of was the possibility of facing all four of them at once, and I'd be standing there by myself, getting judged for I didn't know what exactly—but of course, whatever it was for, it wouldn't make me look good.

"It's just the two of us," she said.

She was dressed in a new sweatsuit, deep maroon, with a pale blue turtleneck underneath. I picked up the scent of a catalog order, fresh from being opened. I liked the feeling of having something personal in common with her, even if it was only the fact that we both bought clothes without going into a store.

The room was a small one, made smaller by one whole wall being lined with filing cabinets, metal gray, looking ancient. They must have once been filled with ski-lodge data. She saw me looking at them, then at the maps tacked onto the opposite wall, half a dozen of them: the United States divided into six parts. Each was dotted with pushpins, mostly silver ones. Here and there the several red ones really stood out.

"Red means a rescue that didn't go well," she said in a quiet way. "The files are all about dogs. Years and years of them. But you must know I didn't send for you to talk about our maps and files."

A long silence now took place. Understandably, I almost didn't want to know why she'd sent for me. I figured out that whatever it was, I wasn't going to like it. I looked at the way her face was so worn, so heavily lined. She wasn't the eldest of the staffers, just the most wrinkled. I wondered if a dog, licking human skin, would be able to tell the difference between wrinkles and smoothness, like the difference between a soft cotton chew toy and a corduroy one. I had noticed Tasha with a new stuffed animal of the thickest corduroy that probably ever existed, and for the first time, she wasn't interested in tearing it apart. She only mouthed it lightly and seemed to cherish it, although the toy was in the shape of a cat. Dogs respect tough, wrinkled outer layers, and I've totally learned to do the same, I was thinking. But that was only to postpone the effect on me of "rescue that didn't go well." All along, I'd taken it for granted that every rescue operation worked out like a movie or television show loaded with suspense and danger, but in the end, everyone is cheering. I saw that I couldn't base all rescues on my own experience getting Dapple. I remembered the operation that took place remotely on my first Sanctuary night. I remembered Giant George in the shadows of my room, when I thought he was planning to sneak into bed with me, and he was telling me no one got shot—that is, no one got shot with a bullet that actually hit.

I had to admire Phyllis for being patient with me. Technically she wasn't one of my teachers, but I was getting the sense that she was actually a type of *mega-teacher,* which you could also call "alpha teacher," using *alpha* in its positive, Dora-like way, not that I'm saying Phyllis was queenly, or that she had the personality of a diva. She was letting the silence that had fallen between us grow as deep and wide as I needed it to. She was letting me make my own decision about learning something I couldn't have discovered on my own. It's not as if you can do an Internet search on "attempted rescues of dogs that ended badly." If I wanted to continue believing it was all happy outcomes, and never mind the red pushpins, I could do so, and she wouldn't judge me badly, she was saying to me, without coming right out and saying so.

Well, that's a mega for you. That's teaching taking place in silence—just like what happened when the other three staffers silently looked at Shadow to see if he'd decide to follow a command to lie down. He never did. I totally, totally didn't have to know about unhappy outcomes.

I said to Phyllis, "When rescues don't go well, what happens?"

She didn't look at me as if mentally patting me for making the right choice. She just answered the question.

"Sometimes, weapons are involved."

"Like with the guns the night the pitties were taken?"

"Yes. Sometimes owners of dogs who need to be taken inter-rupt an operation, as carefully planned as it was. To the own-ers, the rescuers aren't rescuers. They're intruders. They're law-breakers, coming to their property to rob them. In many states, of course, it's not a serious crime to be abusive to animals."

"But it's a serious crime to save them?"

"Yes."

"Did anyone in the Network ever go to prison, like in the cases with the red pins?"

"No prison. We have excellent lawyers."

"Did anyone ever get shot?"

"Yes."

"Did anyone who shot at a rescuer ever get arrested?"

"No."

"Did any rescuer ever *die?*"

She shook her head, then said, "Not yet." She didn't sound dra-matic about it. She simply stated it matter-of-factly.

I said, "Do new people keep joining the Network, even though they know that?"

"Yes."

"When Sanctuary trainees finish their programs, do they auto-matically get into the Network, or do you have to apply?"

"You can get into it automatically," she said.

I paused to let that sink in. I noticed she hadn't said something like, "Everyone can get in automatically except for you, Evie." My pausing was due to the reality of having never before in my life imagined myself as a person with a profession, or a *calling,* in which someone might be aiming a gun in my direction, and the someone, to begin with, was a known, very guilty abuser of dogs.

Maybe Phyllis was mind-reading me. Or maybe she felt she'd grown to know me pretty well.

"You don't have to do the high-risk rescues as a Network person," she said. "Those are in the same league as things a SWAT team would handle, say, in a regular police department, not that our rescuers are ever armed. But you get the idea. You can basically be a trainer who helps out with transports, if you like."

At that, I was, oh my God she just said I can be a trainer. Oh my God I actually have a future. Oh my God she really said *I can be a trainer.* I wished Boomer would wake up so he could sense what this meant, and maybe give me a paw like he was congratulating me. On he slept, unaware. But I didn't let on to Phyllis that inside myself I was massively sighing with relief, and I was also feeling the thing that was called, in my former program, *validation,* which happened when a counselor suddenly said to you one day, in front of a group, without warning, "I validate your commitment to staying off drugs, because I truly believe you'll make it," and everyone clapped and did Homer Simpson–type cries of whoo-hoo, whoo-hoo! I was never the person receiving the validation thing—but then, I'd left before I was meant to. I'd left on *a crazy impulse for a crazy new thing I didn't know anything about, which was as bad as getting into another drug, probably a worse one.*

I remembered that people who'd been validated often compared it to being in a karate class, or some other martial art, and one day you're surprised to find out you're being graduated to a higher level of belt.

They had that right. And I thought, red, and looked again at the pins on the map.

"I just also want to know," I said to Phyllis, "do the red pins mean that someone needs to go back and try again? Like, send the SWAT team back in?"

She smiled at me. "You're an optimist," she said.

No one had ever called me that before! I was willing to think of more questions to keep the momentum of *wonderful things to say to Evie* going, but Phyllis was clicking into a different manner, businesslike, the same way I'd noticed the change in dogs as they come out of sniffs or tussles with one another and settle down to something serious, like chewing on a plastic bone, or ripping apart some toy.

She was dachshund-like again, yet I didn't feel I was about to be chewed or ripped apart or metaphorically pursued as prey. I'd noticed the absence of tea. There weren't mugs with the heads of dachshunds. There wasn't a box of Kleenex. Nothing was on the table but a single sheet of paper, folded in half.

She unfolded it and showed it to me. On it was a number, written as words. The number was forty-two. Was it supposed to have a Sanctuary meaning I didn't know about? Was it something I should have known about but didn't? Maybe it was the number of dogs at the moment in situations they needed to be taken from soon. Maybe there'd be pushpins going onto the maps to indicate rescues waiting to happen. I thought that was an excellent guess.

"Evie," she said, "forty-two is the number of times people in your life you haven't stayed in touch with got in touch with us instead. To tell you the truth, it became a problem."

Oh *no*. I hadn't seen that coming. I turned to look at Boomer. This time I felt I might be able to message him to come in and stand beside me, so I could hold on to his fur. Or maybe I'd get lucky and he'd be having ESP with me in a dream, and he'd figure out on his own that I needed him. But he was still too deeply asleep.

Then I realized that one thing I knew for sure about this staffer was that she wasn't careless with words. She was a very meticulous person with how she said things. She hadn't said forty-two was the number of times *so far*. She hadn't said "it *is* a problem."

So she was talking about something that somehow had been resolved. It seemed to me there wasn't anything else to be said about it. I made a move to get up and go back downstairs to the dogs. I was planning ahead to how I'd just say no to peeking into

Giant George's room again. I couldn't believe he was leaving. With *Tasha*.

And Phyllis stopped me from getting away, before I was even up on my feet. She closed her hand over mine, not roughly, but firmly. She was playing the part of a good trainer—a mega one, in fact. She was preventing bad behavior before it happened.

"We're sure you have a good reason for everything you do," she said. "We decided we'd be able to help. It took a little ingenuity, but we want you to know we're taking care of it."

"Taking care of it?"

"Yes. That's what we do. After all, we're sisters."

I *hated* that. I just hated it when women go around saying to other women we're all sisters. I could see where it was useful in, like, maybe the nineteen-seventies and even sixties, in a completely political way. I took a poli sci course on American feminism when I needed credits in things that weren't in my major. I loved it. For example, not that I cared about basketball, I was extremely burned up when I found out that girls playing basketball in the old days could only go half-court, unless you were a *rover*. And girls playing softball, which also I didn't care about, used to wear white, ironed blouses, and they only played seven innings and couldn't steal or overrun a base; you had to step on it ladylike or you'd be out. Rovers and ironed blouses and overstepping were the slogan words of that class, from the first day. Everyone in it was female. The professor was just a little older than we were. She was also a coach of rugby. That was why we started with sports. She even brought in a side saddle so we could see what it was like for women who weren't allowed to have the back of a horse between their legs. When she said to us, "We're all sisters," *she had a reason*.

I was willing and glad to call myself a student of Phyllis in all her mega-self, but I was drawing the line at calling us sisters.

Suddenly, someone was in the doorway: Giant George, preppie-looking, in a button-down shirt and khakis. He appeared to have spent at least an hour on personal grooming. He gave off such strong smells of after-shave and deodorant, Boomer started twitching his nose, like he was smelling some stranger in a dream.

"Here it is," Giant George told Phyllis. "You didn't break it. It just needed a charge."

I recognized her iPad. He set it down on the table.

"Can I stay for a minute?"

"Thank you, Eric, but no," said Phyllis.

"But I have to say bye to Evie. She's been avoiding me, and here she is."

My back went up at that, like he was picking a fight. "I have not been avoiding you," I told him.

"You have."

"I have not. But fine, I'll say it. Goodbye. Goodbye and have a great new life."

"I *will*," he said. He looked like he was ready to say something else I didn't feel like hearing. I waved to him in a handkerchief flutter of my fingers, so traditional with girls. In my feminism class, we'd also studied social gestures.

"You'd better keep in touch with me," he said. "In case you're wondering what I'll do, if you don't, I'll never talk to Tasha about you. I'll never show her pictures of you. Rottweilers don't have that big of a brain. She'll forget you."

I was very mature about not raising my voice. I wasn't doing a reactionary thing about Tasha. I was thinking of Boomer, glad to be asleep. I didn't want to startle him. I asked, extremely calmly, "What pictures?"

Giant George grinned at me with the whole of his squeaky-clean face. He really looked innocent when he said, "Oh, you know. I have some stuff of you."

I wanted to kick him. I wanted to scream at him while kicking him. Of course I'd realized what he was talking about. Those little videos. Every one of which made me look like an idiot. Every one of which he'd promised to delete.

Validating myself into a whole new level of professionalism and decorum, I did not lose my temper. I didn't even tell him under my breath he was an asshole. His grin turned bigger, more toothy, as if his face were a pumpkin someone just carved.

"If you keep in touch with me, Evie, I swear I'll never post them anywhere. If you don't believe me, keep checking YouTube. I'll never show them to anyone but Tasha, and she already knows what you're like."

Zip it, Evie, and keep it that way, I was telling myself.

And he backed out fast and stepped over Boomer and ran off, charging down the stairs in a noisy, huge way, like a Newfie.

Meanwhile Phyllis had tuned us out completely. She had something going on with her iPad. When she had it ready for me to look at, I saw a box of a graph, color-coded. It was the type with bars, or maybe I should call them columns, on a background of horizontal lines. There were four. The colors were yellow, green, orange, blue. At the top of the graph was my name and the word "Messages." At the bottom was an explanation. Yellow was for "Members of Family." Green was for "Persons Connected with Prior Place of Residence." Orange was for "Friends from College, etc." Blue was for "Gentleman Calling Himself Her Boyfriend."

Yellow was the highest. Green was pretty close to it. Orange was kind of tiny. Blue was way bigger than orange, and a little over half of green. I started trying to do the arithmetic to figure out how the number of forty-two played out here. But it wasn't a chart of calls coming into the Sanctuary about me. It was a chart of messages that were given as responses. They were *outgoing* ones.

It took Phyllis a lot of explanation and patience to make me understand what they'd done. She could have saved herself time if she'd simply started with the fact of Evie, believe it or not, we've got your back. But it had to be staffer talk. She didn't ask me if I wanted to see anything they'd already sent out about me. I would have said no. I kept interrupting the explanation with lit-tle bursts of questions such as, are you kidding me? She found it funny. They didn't kid.

Eventually I understood that they—well, Phyllis, for she was the prime mover behind it—had gathered phone numbers and email addresses of "everyone from your past we just couldn't al-low to keep contacting us, asking for you, Evie."

The first outgoing piece of information, she told me, was a statement made to seem official, like a description of a Sanctu-ary policy. This statement was offered with an apology, as in, "We deeply apologize for the worry and stress we caused by neglect-ing to tell Evie, before her arrival here, of our policy concerning trainees and communication with outsiders. It's a rule that may seem unnecessary and perhaps harsh; however, trainees greatly benefit. Our trainees are encouraged to be in contact with fam-ily and friends only in cases of emergency. I assure you, Evie has been, in every way, emergency-free. If you would like, some of us on the staff would be happy to update you with news of Evie as she makes her way through our program."

The policy statement was the ingenuity part.

"You mean you lied," I said.

She didn't feel it was lying. She felt it was *taking care.* I wasn't surprised to learn that Agnes, the notes writer, handled email re-ports on me. She had also written the statement. Louise and Mar-garet divided the phone calls. Phyllis kept the tallies and ran the graph. It was the same type of graph she liked to make as a handy visual aid for things about dogs and the volunteers. She really en-joyed it, she said. She liked to feel that things were in good shape.

So they had my back. But I saw a flaw in the arrangement. What if someone felt like making a trip? A trip, say, to here?

I said, "What if someone says they want to come and see me?"

"Are you interested in having visitors?"

"I'm not."

She pointed to the blue bar. "What about this one?"

"That one especially," I said. "And please take off the word gentleman. Also take off boyfriend. Don't ask. Okay?"

"What should we call him?"

I didn't want them to call him anything. "I want you to stop with him," I said. "Tell him Evie sends her best wishes for a long and prosperous life, one she doesn't want to ever hear about again."

"In that case, I suppose I'd better handle him myself."

"Thanks."

"We'd already thought of the question of visitors, actually. I forgot to mention it. It's in the statement."

"Did you say you have a rule against anyone coming up here who's not a dog or a dog person?"

"We didn't put it quite like that," she said, smiling. "We said we're cloistered. Naturally, we'd expect people to understand what that means."

More ingenuity! Cloistered! I was speechless with admiration for the very idea. I *loved* that. I couldn't think of a thing to say without gushing about it. So I didn't say anything. I figured it was more of "taking care." Then I sat there giggling like a child, imagining how that went over.

"I wonder," I finally said, "if anyone asked you if I became, you know, religious or something."

She bowed and raised her head in a yes, keeping up her seriousness. "There were several, shall we say, eyebrows raised. But we sent out assurances we're very liberal, and your involvement here is only as a trainee."

"Like your religion is dogs," I said, keeping it real.

"Something like that, yes. Now I have two questions for you. The first is, except for the gentleman, that is, the blue one, would you like us to continue with this, and if you do, would you like to be copied from now on with the emails?"

I nodded, then shook my head.

"Evie," she said, "wouldn't you like to know about things being said about you?"

"I wouldn't," I said. "Was that the second question?"

"It wasn't. This isn't either, but how long have you ignored your messages from home?"

"First you have to tell me what you mean by home."

"You know what I mean."

"Kind of since I arrived here," I said.

"That's what we thought. You don't have to explain. This isn't the second question, but do you feel you trust us?"

I didn't hesitate. I didn't even think about it. Maybe it had something to do with validation and saying I have a future. I'd entered that room as tense and nervous as Hank, before he started jumping, even though I didn't have his fear of being hit in a physical way, and I didn't have his problem of obsessive pacing. I was actually beginning to feel as comfortable in my own skin as Boomer was, wearing all his fur.

I said, "I can trust you. Even Agnes, who's probably writing about me like I've got four legs and a tail."

Phyllis didn't laugh at that. "The outgoing messages about you are brief," she said. "They're news items. Simple information only."

"Like saying I'm quiet at mealtimes? Like, I can follow rules?"

"Not in those words exactly," she said.

Then it was my turn to point to a column. I pointed to the green one. I said, "I know you know what my prior place of residence was."

"And I," she said, "know you know that."

"I'm guessing people who know told you things, and you didn't, like, do some kind of a background check on me. Am I right?"

"You are."

"Okay then. What's the second question?"

She turned off the iPad. But she was still all business.

"Evie," she said, "what are you going to do about getting through to that greyhound?"

The truth was, I didn't know. But I didn't get the chance to admit it. Suddenly, below, the dogs started barking, all of them at once. Boomer woke up and immediately let out a deep woof, as if he already knew what was happening. Then came the alarm of Shadow's howl. Phyllis stood up. She looked at her watch and *oh my God the pitties are here.*

Thirty-Two

THE VILLAGE VET still reminded me of the smooth-faced older guy in the English countryside of James Herriot. He could have waited in the infirmary for the new arrivals, but he positioned himself in the yard at the top of a little slope, where he could see them as they came off the transport. He wore an orange down vest over his doctorly lab coat, so he looked like he was playing a double part, not only as the chief attending medical guy but as a traffic manager or school-zone crossing guard. On either side of him were the two leading volunteers, Romeo and Juliet, in dark, funeral-type coats. They looked grim and pale, as if they were actors who hadn't put their makeup and costumes on, and didn't want to, even though it was show time.

Also with them were two very young veterinary assistants, trying not to look cold, for they were only in their white coats, so new they were whiter than the snow. These two were students, a boy and a girl. I could tell by their expressions I was not the only one who was witnessing a delivery such as this one for the first time. I was at the windows with Alfie, Boomer, Josie, Shadow.

My job was to watch them like their nanny, keep them quiet. I knew they'd be anxious and agitated, so I grabbed a jar of peanut butter from the kitchen. One thing I'd learned was that there's nothing in the world like peanut butter when it comes to inviting dogs to do what you want them to. I was also using it as a training aid to get Josie to quit snapping. It was sort of starting to work.

If you want a dog to stop biting your fingers, stick them in peanut butter. This can be called, in the language of dog training, "not biting the hand that's Skippied." Or it can be Peter Pan or a health-food brand, or a generic one. Whatever you have.

I had the jar nearby, on top of one of the crates. The dogs knew it was there. They didn't care. I didn't need it. After the outbursts of barking and howling when the truck first appeared, they were stricken, each of them as an individual, then together as a group, with a need to enter a zone of silence. The hush that came over them was almost an actual thing I could see and touch. It was the presence of something solemn coming up to their surfaces, taking them over. Somehow they knew what their job was, without being told, not that you can say to dogs, "Even though I'm keeping you indoors, I want you to be the honor guard for this event."

Alfie was tall enough to rest his chin on a windowsill. I dragged over a crate and put Josie on top of it. I dragged over another one and did the same with Dora. I didn't want Boomer up on his back legs, so I brought in two chairs from the dining room, placed them seat-to-seat, like a bench, and helped him get up on it, which wasn't easy. I didn't mind the burning strain of every lower-back muscle in my body. I'd forgotten to shift my own weight to my legs, as is necessary in moving anyone who feels bigger than you. As for Shadow, he was okay standing up, paws on a sill.

Soon the window glass fogged with breath of dogs. I used the sleeve of the sweatshirt I was wearing to keep wiping the fog away.

In the road behind the truck were Giant George and Tasha. He had her on a short leash. They were the outdoors contingent of our honor guard. I knew Giant George had wanted to help with the delivery. He'd been told instead to stay off to the side. His job was to make himself and Tasha ready for their departure. Now and then, Tasha looked over to the windows. I could tell, from the look on her face when she turned back to Giant George, that she had figured out she was his dog now.

He held her leash at a slack. She stood beside him somberly, at perfect attention. I was never going to see her again. Maybe, I was thinking, inside her, like an extra bodily organ, like a tiny secondary heart, beating and pumping, there was a part of me.

I wished the staffers were outdoors to see how she was behaving. It would have given them their one bright moment. They were inside, below, as the internal reception committee.

This was an all-volunteer operation. When the unloading began, the vet and his students would join them, and so would Romeo and Juliet. Juliet's coat wasn't buttoned. The wind blew at the flaps, revealing a Sanctuary volunteer's work smock. I was sure Romeo wore one too. So I'd been wrong to think they'd just stand around and let everyone respect them for being up-ups who were paying the bill for all this.

The line of volunteers went from the side of the truck to the back. Their formation was that of an old-time fire brigade. They were so bundled up, it was impossible to tell which were men and which were women. All of them wore long, heavy gloves. Not winter gloves, but protective ones. Some wore aprons over their jackets, like the kind you'd see on welders or in an X-ray department.

The truck was a reconditioned large-animal carrier, of a size to fit, I think, at least four cows or horses. The inside was full of wall-attached cages, with a floor lined with straw. That was the first thing to notice when the door slid open. Two men of about thirty, in overalls and jean jackets, had hopped down from the cab. They went inside.

I noticed that the volunteers at the front of the line had dog-travel crates with them, at their feet. The first volunteer handed up a crate to a transport guy. Before he opened the first cage, he held out his hand to the other guy, who passed him a muzzle. It was the basket kind, which looks sort of like the cup of a lacrosse stick. And materializing in there was a third guy, in the same overalls and jacket. They'd had someone riding with the dogs. I should have known that.

The cage with the dog they were muzzling was blocked by their bodies. A moment later, two of them were passing down the crate to a pair of volunteers. It was heavy; they staggered with it. I caught a glimpse of muzzle behind the bars of the crate. Then it was on the move and the process was repeated for a total of six times. They were taking the most unsocialized ones out first. I'd find that out later. *Most unsocialized.* That was what the staffers decided to say so they didn't have to say "dangerous."

All along was the strangeness of a strange, strange silence. When the door first opened, there came out, into the sunny mountain air, a blast of frenzied, high-volume barking and whining, along with sounds you could only call screeches. These were unlike anything I'd heard from a Sanctuary dog.

It seemed to me that the entire carrier was rocking on its axles from the noise. But suddenly it was the same as what happened with my dogs when they'd finished making a racket, here inside. But it was only the same in terms of coming on fast and settling deeply. The hush in the cages did not have a solemnity. It was not the quiet, dignified calm of dogs who were doing their jobs as watchers, as witnesses. It was eerie. It was unnatural. It was like a landing of aliens, as if the carrier were a spaceship that touched down on the first American hilltop they'd spotted, and this particular species, while known for such traits as exuberance and vast amounts of personal power, had cloaked themselves with muteness, worse than Shadow's because it really might never go away.

And inside that silence was a terrible tension, a deep and disturbing unease. I couldn't help feeling almost desperate for my ears to pick up any sounds out there that were the normal sounds of dogs being dogs. I even wanted the screeching again. That silence *hurt*.

A little one was taken out of a cage: a square-headed pup, maybe six or seven months, passing to the cradle of a volunteer's arms. Another pup came, another. The silence was even worse when it was coming from babies. My dogs were absolutely still. The only movements, in this space of our own sanctuary, came when Shadow left the window to rest his legs, then raised himself back up.

I wondered what Hank would be doing if he were here. He could tap into two different parts of himself. Maybe he'd be acting all retriever, the ghosts of ancestors behind him with their genius at waiting alertly, patiently, for a signal before bursting to life and going to fetch whatever needed fetching, on land or in water. Maybe he'd want a signal from me that he should rush to the carrier and retrieve a pittie on his own—a small one, alive, our new class pet. Or maybe he'd know in his soul that he was more of a pittie than a Lab. He'd know he was looking at members of his own tribe. He'd be upset. Maybe he'd go back to pacing.

And Dapple? I don't think she would have felt a connection to the arriving dogs as dogs. She would have been too busy being scared. That would be the main thing she'd pick up on, like she could only tune in to one feeling. She wouldn't know that pit bulls are famous for courage.

I'd read that they were the mascots of the U.S. Armed Forces in the First World War. I had looked at posters online. Posters of pit bulls used to be everywhere. I saw pictures of pit bulls wrapped in American flags, pit bulls wearing navy caps, pit bulls shiny and smiling energetically, proudly, draped in parade-like buntings. Looking at their faces, I had a little glow. It was the first time in my life I had any idea what people are talking about when they talk about patriotism. I wasn't just looking for something historically uplifting about pit bulls to balance what I'd read about fighting. I looked at the dogs on those posters, and I was *jelly.*

A volunteer now at the head of the line held a blanket in her arms. A guy from inside held a pittie he'd just taken from a cage. Another guy sat down on the edge of the truck, his legs hanging out the door. They had reached the stage in the delivery where they were bringing out the ones who needed special handling.

The guy who was sitting received the dog into his lap as tenderly as if the dog had just been born. I saw a beautiful white and brown face, almost half of each, from forehead to chin, like the running together of the symbols for yin and yang. The eyelids were partly down. I saw what could have been fight marks near both eyes. I saw a limpness in the body overall. I saw a normal pittie stand-up folded ear, and then an ear I thought was somehow, I didn't know how, folded the wrong way. I tried to think of it as folded, even though it was so jagged. I will never forget the beat of my heart that didn't happen when I realized half of the ear wasn't there.

You cannot look at the partly missing ear of a pit bull and tell yourself that maybe there was a good explanation, like maybe it was an accident. Or maybe the dog was born that way. I thought I was so safe, seeing the newcomers at a distance. I thought I was prepared. Then came a mental flash of Tasha the day she roughed up that terrycloth bunny. She'd looked so sweet and funny and also bad with the purple ear in her mouth. I tried to set up an equation of the two things, in an algebraic way. I used to like algebra in school. I remembered how thrilled I was to find out there's such a thing as math that had letters of the alphabet.

I was hoping that the purple bunny in my head would cancel out the partly missing ear of the yin-yang dog, which also would have meant not thinking about how, in real life, with a real animal, *it had hurt.*

Into the blanket went the yin-yang dog. That volunteer was

big — a Rottweiler of a person. The way the dog was carried was the same way a child would be carried by a firefighter out of a hell — into safety, peace, a sanctuary. Maybe the dog knew what *rescued* meant. Maybe she didn't.

The next volunteer also had a blanket. The next dog was tawny and nervous. I could see the trembling. It was worse than Dapple's. That was when I stopped watching, although there were still quite a few to come out. In another mental flash, I remembered the notes on Tasha, the part that said she was almost adopted by people involved in dogfighting. I remembered how those two words put together were actually only words to me.

I was standing by the crate Josie was sitting on top of when I turned my head from the window. I didn't realize, until I looked at her, that I had a hand on her. I was patting her. She was letting me.

Dora didn't like that at all. She moaned for my attention. Boomer wanted to get down from the chairs and return to his crate. Shadow came over to me, rubbing himself against my leg. And Alfie? He stayed at the window, the only one keeping it up, his tail out, his eyes wide open, his body intact, unscarred. He was so unlike his usual "fuck you" self, it seemed a greyhound who looked like him had replaced him. I looked at the angle of his head. I thought maybe he was staring at Tasha and thinking sad, lovelorn thoughts. He wasn't. He kept staying there watching the carrier until the last one was out and the door was closing.

Meanwhile Shadow scored points with Dora and Josie by getting the jar of peanut butter to fall off the crate I'd put it on. Naturally it was a plastic jar. The three of them lunged for it as it rolled on the floor, as if they were pretending they had hands to open the lid.

But they were working off the stress; it was a good thing. Boomer changed his mind about a nap and got involved too. Some of the label came off from being drooled on and pawed.

Shadow grabbed it. It felt wonderful to see that bit of paper hanging sideways out of his mouth, like a vintage poster of a movie star with a cigarette, like he was James Dean or Marlon Brando. I couldn't believe I was saying to them, "You guys are so normal. You guys are so *lucky*."

I had them line up to wait their turns to lick my fingers, starting with Boomer. Dora was next. We were going by age. After Dora had her turn, she backed out of line and went to the other side of Shadow, like maybe I'd think I hadn't gotten to her yet. She sat there tipping her head up in complete innocence. We'd never done it like this before, in a line. I didn't fall for it. But I almost did. I just had to deal with the possibility she might be smarter than I was.

When I brought the jar to Alfie at the window, he ignored me. I put it near his nose. He didn't even want to sniff it. Peanut butter was his favorite thing.

He was still witnessing. I wondered if he'd been transported on a carrier like that one. I wondered where he'd been picked up, where he'd been dropped off. I wondered how many places he'd been before he came here, how many places he was sent away from with all his stillness and bad attitude and lack of participation and, fuck you, I'll poop indoors whenever I feel like it.

I thought of my own notes on him, and how I'd imagined his past. And what I wanted for his future.

Then it was naptime.

Everyone but Alfie went into shutdowns. Boomer didn't make it into his crate. He dropped to the floor and shut his eyes and started snoring. Josie placed herself against him.

I sat down against the wall, and Dora came to my lap. Shadow lay with his head on my legs. Below us were multiples of sounds, of movement, of talking, muffled, faraway as I grew drowsier. I had one hand in Dora's fur, the other on Shadow's head. My breath came and went in Dora's rhythms. I wondered what it would be like for the pitties to wake up tomorrow morning and not understand right away where they were. I knew their confusion would make them afraid, maybe even panicky, and I wished I could tell them I knew a little bit about that sort of thing, from being small and going back and forth between houses. Sometimes they moved me in the night, because maybe the days of who was supposed to have me were mixed up, or someone decided to go out for a late supper, or cocktails somewhere, and they traded having me in phone calls I was too deep in sleep to eavesdrop on. I had tried for a while never to go to sleep. That didn't work out at all. It also didn't work out when I put up a campaign to have the two different bedrooms of mine, in those two different houses, redecorated to be identical, so I'd never feel like an alien in my own beds, crash-landing into almost awakeness, and wondering, oh no, where am I?

How was I going to talk to those dogs? What could I say to those dogs?

I remembered an article I'd read about people involved in dog-fighting. I learned that when they're training a dog to be a fighter, they don't call it "training." They call it "conditioning." They feel proud about putting it that way: conditioning bodies to *achieve a maximum of potential,* like, hey, pit bulls want to fight each other because that's who they are, and all we're doing is *helping.* Some dogs, I had read, are conditioned by being placed on treadmills. Some are attached to heavy objects they are required to try to pull. Some are taken out running on long leashes or ropes or chains, while the person doing the conditioning is not running with them but riding in a car, with one door slightly open. I wondered if any of the pitties below me had any of those experiences.

Alfie came over and curled up at my side. I let him lick the peanut butter right out of the jar. I held the jar like I was feeding a baby with a bottle. Then I sleep-drifted. It occurred to me that, no matter where in the Sanctuary I happened to fall asleep, I would always know, all the time, where I was.

I didn't hear Giant George come inside. Tasha wasn't with him. But I'd already said goodbye to her, even though dogs don't know that word.

I knew that a volunteer was going to give George and Tasha a ride to somewhere a couple of hours away, then someone else would give them another ride, and so on, until they got to where they were meant to be. All the drivers and the vehicles involved were part of the Network, which made sense. You can't take a Rottweiler on, say, a bus.

Giant George was looking down at me. I held a finger to my lips to tell him *hush;* please don't wake these dogs. He squatted down and motioned for me to hold out the hand that wasn't on Shadow. Into my hand came the keys to the Jeep, on a plain silver ring.

Shadow opened his eyes and saw who was there. He didn't know about the leaving. He had an expression of, oh, it's only you, no big deal. He went right back to sleep. It had been a hard day.

"I'm not driving that thing," I whispered. "Take these back."

He laughed at me. Then he whispered to me that he wanted to have my socks, the ones on my feet. I'd been wearing that pair for I didn't know how many days. They were white crew socks. Over them I had on my L. L. Bean slippers. It took me a moment to understand. When I did, I nodded to him, strange as it was, to give him the okay about taking off the slippers, then the socks, since I certainly couldn't do so myself.

He was gentle about it. He put the socks in a pocket of his Sanctuary jacket. I was pleased to see he was taking it with him.

He whispered, "Should I wait to give her these until we're there? Or should I give them to her on the road?"

"Give her one on the road," I answered. "And the other when you're there."

"Okay," he said. "I hope I don't worry about you too much."

"Don't. Why would you?"

"Well, I'm leaving you on your own with, you know, them."

"You mean the staffers?"

"Yeah."

"I'm all right with them," I said. "I'm getting used to them."

"But doesn't it make you a little nervous, or something, that they're so *good,* and it's like, you have to be good when you're around them, like totally watch yourself?"

"They're not that good, George. I mean, they're great about the dogs, but basically, they're just people. They're just old."

"Don't you ever wonder about them?"

"Kind of. Maybe. Not really, though. I'm too busy. I'm at school here, remember? Me, student. Them, teachers. That's it."

He gave me a shrug. I had the feeling he was about to go into some sort of debriefing with me, some Sanctuary-staffers-insider thing from a voice of experience, as a runner in a relay hands the next one a stick, or whatever object is in play. But instead, he just came closer to me, to my face. The kiss he placed on my cheek was as slobbery as a dog's. Then he was gone.

I wouldn't find out until later that there was no such thing as a Sanctuary jacket. He'd had one of the staffers sew the decal on a jacket they'd bought for him through an online outlet for winter gear.

Dora sleep-stirred in my lap. I couldn't tell what was happening with her by the sound of her sigh or the tone of the little yip she let out. Maybe she was dreaming about being alone in that apartment. But maybe she wasn't. Maybe she'd forgotten all about it. Maybe Josie had forgotten her past. Maybe Shadow too, with his new vocabulary meaning for *outside.* He was still having trouble with the command to lie down, unless he commanded himself to, but maybe that was okay. I thought about how that moment, somewhere in America, someone was buying a cup of coffee, or talking on a phone, or having daytime sex, and ahead of them was a future in which they found themselves trapped in a partly burned-down building, or in the wreckage of a plane or rubble from a bomb or snow from an avalanche, and here would come this puzzle of a dog with his deep, wise eyes to save them, and they would not care less what his grades were in Basic Obedience, or even if he forgot his manners and peed on their hand.

You're going to be heroic, Shadow, I messaged him in his sleepland.

Someone will adopt you, Dora, I messaged her, and she sounded another little yip. I just hope, I added, whoever they are, they have really high IQs.

I looked over at Boomer and Josie. I couldn't think of Boomer doing anything except butlering. Josie was so peaceful beside him. I couldn't send thoughts her way about believing she'd be adopted too. I didn't believe it, even though little dogs are supposed to be so much easier to place than big ones. But what if she'd be better off here?

It was the first time the thought occurred to me. What if Josie was feeling she didn't want to leave?

On that awful Skype interview with the maybe-adopter who said Josie didn't fit her moron idea of identity, Josie ended up with hurt feelings and also some hopelessness. I was sure she was sorry she lost control of herself and bit Giant George in the interview before that one. I was sure she'd felt terrible about it. What if she'd prefer to stop with the interviews, and forget the whole thing of find another family, another home? What if she'd found them already?

Boomer had to tell her he didn't want her in his crate with him, but that was only when Dora was around. He never invited Dora in there for a sleepover or even a little cuddle. So naturally Dora was not about to let Josie have something she'd been denied herself. Josie never, ever snapped at Dora. But she was dying to, and

Boomer was too much of a golden to be able to tolerate the friction. What if Josie knew that? What if Josie was really connected
to Boomer? Everyone knew what it was like to see those two look
at each other.

Boomer was lonely! All along, while doing his job, he was
lonely! He was too much of a professional to let on!

What if, pressed against his fur for a nap, Josie dreamed of becoming a sort of under-butler, trotting about with Boomer while
he worked? And taking over herself on the days his arthritis was
too much for him?

Josie, I messaged her, you have to stop snapping. There cannot
be people coming here who need to be greeted and instead get
the feel of your teeth.

Boomer, I messaged, hang on. Trust me.

And what about Alfie?

Just then Agnes appeared, coming toward me. She entered the
sweet normal silence of these sleeping dogs without changing it
by even a tiny ripple. She'd come to give me the news that the
pitties were settled. I don't know how she didn't look exhausted.
She looked like she'd just woken up. I saw no sign in her face or
body of the ordeal she'd been through so far today. You'd think
the new dogs had arrived in great shape, from homes where people loved them, as if they'd come to a grooming salon, like all
they needed was a little freshening up.

She whispered to me her feeling that the volunteers were *superb*.
I liked the way her mouth moved with that word. I had made a
resolution to get to know those people better. I'd promised myself,
Evie, get going on *cruising the unmarried guy volunteers*.

Then she thanked me for taking care of the dogs who were my
students. I would have to continue being in charge of them. The
pitties were going to be sequestered indefinitely. Was I all right
with that? I was. I tried to remember the last time I had a reason
to say, "I'm all right." I didn't remember. It didn't matter.

Once again I waited for her to bring up the subject of did I do my assignment of the notes on myself? If she mentioned it, I was ready to answer with a "sort of." Or I could say I'd forgotten, and thanks for the reminder.

But she said, "I'm sorry we had to delay the agility course, Evie. We know you weren't happy we postponed having it."

"We can have it now," I pointed out. "Next week, maybe."

"Actually, we can't. We'll be busier than we'd thought with the new ones. And there are more than we expected. We need to wait much longer."

"We need a fence," I said.

"We'll have to wait for that too."

She smiled and drew herself away as silently as light. It was practically spring! We still couldn't have agility? The ground was almost unfrozen. I could smell winter leaving. The dogs had been smelling it a thousand times more.

Into my head rushed the arguments I could make to get this thing under way. Included in the arguments were the pitties. What if they went outdoors to a cheerful, exciting new playground? What if the yin-yang dog could start erasing the past by learning to jump through a hoop? What if the pups could course-train while still babies? They could compete in agility tournaments and win trophies! We should start immediately!

Alfie opened his eyes and stared at me as if I'd spoken my thoughts and he understood what I was saying. He wasn't forgetting his vigil. No one could undo what he knew about those dogs, just from watching the way they were carried. I was thinking about tournaments? I was thinking about *trophies?*

Teacher, you're so fucking idealistic, he was telling me.

Go back to sleep, I answered. Would you please go back to sleep and dream of pooping outdoors like a normal dog?

I tipped my head to look out the window, at the air above. I thought about obedience. The sky was so blue. The clouds were

so white. I saw many of them, floating serenely, all of them small.
And in front of my eyes, not the eyes of someone hallucinating,
I saw that one cloud had started forming a letter of the alphabet.
Then another one did, another, another. It was skywriting, with-
out a plane. All the letters were in capitals. One cloud turned into
a comma.

Okay, I'd wait for agility. I sighed so hard when I saw what the
letters spelled out, my breath went all the way to my legs, stirring
Shadow, who wiggled in his sleep as if a breeze had come in.

The letters said: SURRENDER, EVIE.

I jumped up. I made it outside before Tasha and Giant George
disappeared. I had the feeling Giant George was hoping I'd do
exactly what I was doing, but he'd also prepared himself to be
disappointed. I didn't care that it was cold and I wasn't wearing a
jacket, and my feet were in slippers, without socks. I squatted beside Tasha and let her lick my face. I touched two fingers to her
polka dots. I whispered to her that I loved her.

Then up on my feet, I said to Giant George, "You suck for taking her."

"I know," he said.

"But I love it that you're taking her," I said.

"Yeah. I know. Can I ask you a question? I was going to text
you, like tomorrow or something. But now I don't have to."

"Is it about keeping in touch with you?"

"No. I already figure you will. Anyway, I'm not someone you
want to have in a chart on an iPad."

He was so hobbity, and so sure of himself, I had to laugh at
him. Tasha stared up at us with her tongue hanging out and her
eyes all sparkly. Her tail was in a steady, smooth back-and-forth
of a wag. Maybe she wasn't his dog only. Maybe she was mine
too. Maybe we could share her, like in a long-distance relationship.

I was starting to picture Tasha's face in a Skype on my laptop when Giant George decided to tell me one more thing. He'd waited until I stopped laughing. His look became serious, and I could see he was suddenly nervous. Then he drew a deep breath and blurted, "I just want to know, Evie, like if I told you I was kind of like a puppy, when it comes to certain experiences, you'd be interested in that. Like, maybe, if I didn't want to be a puppy about it anymore, you're the one I wish I could . . . well, you know. Do you know? I mean, do you know what I'm talking about?"

It wasn't just the cold that was making his face turn pink like a quick-flashing sunburn. I slipped one hand into his. I stood on tiptoes and kissed him on the cheek, on one of his flushes. My lips against his skin were just like my fingers on Tasha.

"I'm too old for you," I said. "Go to high school. Go to the prom. But I'll tell you, if I were your age, and you weren't about to leave, you know what we'd be doing right now? We'd be in my room, honest to God. We'd be *naked*."

"We wouldn't. I'd be busy with the new dogs."

"If we didn't have the new dogs," I said.

"Yeah? You think so?"

"Totally," I said.

For a moment, I was afraid he might mention the fact that I sort of had a history of not being dependable about telling the truth. I actually expected him to bring up "Sure, I know how to walk on snowshoes." But he didn't. He cheered up. He stopped looking at me like I was someone who might be willing to break his heart, because I was a grown-up and he wasn't.

"Don't think I'm going to any prom," he said. "I'm not that type of kid."

"You are."

"I'm not."

"You *are*. You just don't know it yet."

Tasha was getting bored. She head-butted Giant George on the leg. She seemed to know that the car pulling up was the one she needed to get into. She seemed to know that no one in that car would open a door later on and push her out and drive away.

I hugged Giant George, and he hugged back, tightly, cushioning me with his Sanctuary jacket. Then I hurried inside so I didn't have to see them go. Josie and Alfie met me at the door. When I leaned to pat them, Josie let me touch her for about half a minute before she went to Boomer. But Alfie went into a sit in front of me, his head tipped to one side, like he was trying to figure out what tears were. He stayed that way until Shadow came over and jumped me for some attention. I didn't remind him that jumps on humans are bad. I ruffled his ears and said he was good. He wanted me to keep going with that, but Dora woke up and decided to try climbing the side of my leg. I sat down and let her into my lap, and I messaged to Alfie, as he curled himself up by a window, I will die before I ever give up on you, you beautiful, beautiful dog.

Thirty-Three

<hr/>

APPRECIATION. THERE'S a mall off the highway. A pet-sup-plies store moved in. For their opening day, they held a Pet Ap-preciation event, where people with pets could show up and re-ceive free stuff, and take part in raffles and various games and contests. There was also a buffet of dog food and treats the store sold, plus an indoor agility course.

I wanted to be there as soon as I overheard some volunteers talking about it. They were arranging to carpool in a minivan one of them owned, so they could attend together, with their own dogs, who could officially be called "pets," because that's what they were.

I thought about bringing Dora. As the eldest, not counting Boomer, she'd be the logical choice. But first was the problem of getting there. I asked the volunteers if they had room in the van for two more. But they said they didn't. They were suddenly in a hurry to walk away from me, like I was inviting myself and a Sanctuary dog to a place where we'd be non-pet aliens — like there's a circle around dogs who belong to someone, and there's a border patrol on the whole perimeter to keep the rest of us out.

So that was a big never-mind. I had to be glad my dogs couldn't know what they were missing. I gave them all treats, as random acts of appreciation. I really wanted them to know that word.

And because I was in the right mood for it, I told Agnes I appreciated getting news about Dapple and Hank. I'd been worried the staffers would exclude me from knowing about them, maybe as a lesson on what it means to keep in touch with someone. I had found two sheets of printouts waiting for me at my usual place in the dining room. One was a photo of Hank in his new life as Basil. The picture had been taken with a background of that herb garden. Some of those basil plants were as big as small bushes. Some were deeply purple. I could tell, from the look of the light, that Hank was in a desert. So I had to acknowledge the reality that anyone who grew plants like those in a desert would be okay for Hank. He was in a sit. His face was relaxed. It seemed to me the photographer had caught him in the moment he realized, for the first time, after looking around, he was somewhere without trees. The only wood around was part of cacti, which he'd never think of as actually being woody. Hi, Hank, I messaged to the photo. I was willing to be uncritical of the fact that his new people had posed him wearing a cowboy hat. It wasn't on his head. It was a white one, perhaps purchased in a boutique that sells accessories for animals. Or it might have been a cowboy hat for humans. It was on the back of his neck, secured by a loop of fabric that was even more purple than the herbs. He didn't seem to mind the hat. He seemed to think it was cool.

The other sheet was also a photo. Dapple. She was lying in a curl on a cushion on a dog bed that looked like a laundry basket missing one side. It was an up-close shot. Nothing indicated where she was or what type of room it was. I looked at her spots. I looked at her expression. She seemed to be at ease, in a zone of quiet. I told the photo I thought she looked like an ideal of someone put into Witness Protection by protectors she could count on.

Under the photo was a handwritten note from Agnes. "Was

found to be pregnant, a condition which no longer applies. Will be ready for adoption after healing."

I appreciated getting the news in the hush of the dining room. A feeling of relief came over me, a sort of calmness after a storm. I was glad the staffers were all around me. Our silence was the right way to have a connection to that dog, even though she didn't know we were holding her close to us, even though she wasn't here.

Belonging (backward and twisted). The pitties are in isolation. Sometimes we hear them barking. They don't sound like they're in pain, or hungry, or upset. They're not complaining in any way. All the barks come with question marks, and it's the same question over and over. Where am I? Where *am* I?

Louise told me, in her same quiet, gentle voice, that sometimes abused rescued dogs go through a rough period of confusion and inner conflict, because as glad as they are to be free from what was happening to them, they lost their known place of belonging. Just because their attachment to their abusers was terrible for them — well, it was still an attachment.

Oh, I was saying to myself. It's like detox. They're sort of in *detox*.

She also told me that, now and then, rescued dogs will try to bolt from the rescuers and head back to the only place they ever felt they belonged, and never mind what's in store for them if they make it. Because sometimes you don't call it abuse when it's happening to you, even if you're doing it to yourself. You just call it "my life."

Belonging (normal). I haven't been sleeping well. Boomer and Shadow and Josie and Dora and Alfie, downstairs just below me in the night, keep breaking into my sleep with all sorts of noise, including those weird yippy sounds dogs make when barking in their dreams. And the voices of the pitties rise up to me, muffled, uneasy, still strange. I open my eyes to moonlight. It really does sound as if an alien invasion is taking place, like I'm the only one on earth who knows about it. I'm saying, "This is so cool."

A little while ago I needed a break from dogs. I was running a little low on patience. But when I decided to head back to my room for a while, I called it going *home for a quick time-out.* I didn't correct myself. I don't think I'd started calling it home just from being so frazzled. It just felt normal.

Companion. Busy as she was with the new ones, Agnes with all that height of hers remained true to her terrier qualities, not that I was comparing myself to a rat or other small, annoying animal terriers were long ago bred to go after. She wasn't letting go of how I'd lost control of Tasha and Alfie so they could charge the car of Dapple's owners. I could tell from the way she kept looking at me that she was silently nagging me about it, and finally I found a note from her slipped under my door, with the suggestion that I should go online and look at videos of people walking their dogs. She was sure I'd find some and pick up some tips.

I did both of those things, and then I wanted to see if there's a difference between a leash attached to a harness and a leash attached to a collar. There had to be differences that are maybe profound, like neck walking would be such and such, and torso walking would be totally something else. But in just a couple of minutes I forgot the assignment I'd given myself. I wondered, can you tell if a person walking a dog is out for a walk with a companion? Or is the person walking the dog because, if you have one, someone has to take care of that chore?

You can tell the difference! Anyone looking at a human out walking with a dog would know if the human was saying to the dog, "You and I are in this together, fair and square, because that's companionship." Or if the human was saying, "Dog, you're my chore."

It's not just about walking. I sat still with myself for what felt like a long time, trying to work out the question of how it's possible to be a trainer and also a companion, at the same time, like they're two things that can actually fit together.

Then I had to decide not to make a theory about it. It's not as if I have to write a paper on the subject. It's not like I'm in graduate school. So I'm just doing it: I'm just going to be both a companion and a trainer.

Doing. All of that led to me back to Alfie. I turned off my laptop and found him by a window. He was standing with his back to it, just standing there.

I said hi. I told him I thought he was attractive. I told him that if he were a guy, I'd totally fall for him, even though he's so skinny. Then I placed my hands on each side of his head, as if forming a cup or little bowl. I was harnessing him, sort of. I needed him to feel extremely invited to give eye contact with me another try. I said, "If you think you're only a chore to me, Alfie, you're the stupidest dog there ever was."

I was just going with being non-alpha and trying out the teacher-companion thing. But I think he knew what I meant. Of course he figured out that the only way he could stop being in contact with me was to close his eyes. Which he did.

Now what? I could feel the other dogs watching me. Was this some kind of a showdown? I couldn't keep holding his head much longer. Where were the staffers? Why wasn't a staffer around to help me out?

I remembered something. The other day when I was brushing Josie, I wanted to see what would happen if I blew on her face, just lightly, not like blowing up a balloon or exhaling to put a flame out. I'd seen a list of "Things Dogs Don't Like" on the web page of a longtime dog person. It was alphabetical. Blowing on their faces was near the top. I didn't recall anything else, just that. So I blew on Josie, and she got mad and jerked up, and went for a bite of my nose. I was able to turn in time to avoid it.

Alfie was so lazy, I knew he'd show his teeth but wouldn't use them. He understood very quickly that the only way to make me stop blowing on him was he had to keep looking at me. Well, this is what we're doing, I messaged him. We're *making contact.*

And I was asking him, want to run, just to run?

Dogs, decision making. I didn't think Alfie would decide to go back to the place where he used to belong. I think he loved being rescued, and ever since, he'd been living in a nowhere place in his head, like the land between sleeping and waking. So I was also telling him, it's up to him if he wants to live his life as a zombie or not. But it was up to me whether or not to keep blowing on him.

Then I stopped. I went to the door, opened it. What's it going to be, Dog? Want to run for no reason?

I could feel the vibrations of the other dogs: an excited tension, like they were joining together in a pack. They knew perfectly well what was happening. They knew the open door was not for them. Maybe they were tapping into an ancient leftover thing of being wolves, way deep in themselves — but as they grouped up near Alfie, Boomer and Josie and Dora and Shadow didn't resemble wolves in any way. They looked at each other like, want to place some bets? Like, will he, or won't he?

Clean, strong hilltop air was rushing in. Alfie liked it. I saw him tip his head and drop his jaw, as if he wanted to swallow some wind.

Dora forgot she was queenly and almost elderly. She started jumping around and yapping at him. Josie joined right in. If the two of them had been wearing little skirts and holding pompoms, their cheerleaderness would have been complete. Boomer nosed Alfie's bum, as if nudging him. Shadow gave me a look like he was telling me not to worry if Alfie left. He would find him.

And the greyhound took off so fast, I didn't have time to give him a countdown. Boomer and Shadow put their paws up on sills, to be lookouts. I scooped up Josie, so she could look too.

Her little body was trembling in my arms, while Dora kept hopping about and making air kicks, now and then yapping at me so I could turn to tell her she was *perfect*.

I was the only one going into a panic of terror that Alfie might head for the road, but he went tearing around the back. He decided to circle the building, and soon we heard the barking of pitties. They were watching out the kennel windows! They sounded like they were asking a question, but it was totally along the lines of, WTF? Like, is that creature actually a *dog?*

And here came the staffers, four, like the points of a compass. They were in time to welcome the runner home.

Everyone was barking. Everyone was pawing high-fives, and I was sending out a message to Alfie: I hope you took a moment to poop while you were out there, like a normal dog. But if he didn't, that's all right. One thing at a time. This is rehab. One thing at a time.

Dogs, disgusting. I cannot believe what dogs will do in the event that one of them throws up. I should have known Alfie would be attracted to grass. Grass doesn't grow on racetracks! So one minute he's streaking back inside, as gorgeous and sleek as a comet, and the next, he is puking, and there's an awful lot of it, and it's green. You would think he'd brought his friends a picnic. I was horrified. But at least they were sharing nicely.

Dogs, yay. I could not believe I was letting Alfie lick my face and he didn't swill mouthwash or even get a drink of water. He was telling me he thinks I'm the stupidest person ever for taking so long to do the simple thing of opening a door so he could take off and do his thing. Like he was never a zombie! Like this was the first time he had the chance to go out a Sanctuary door!

He was saying, by the way, this is the first time in my life I felt like slopping my tongue all over the face of a human. His eyes were so shiny.

Evie, appearance of, plus manners of behavior and also per-

sonal history. I have to stop driving myself crazy with that assign-ment from Agnes about writing the notes on myself. I must have started a hundred times in a hundred different ways, including many long paragraphs that sound like glowing references writ-ten by someone who believes I have no flaws, or only very minor ones, which are actually sort of admirable.

Also I took the opposite approach of "flaws only," plus a well-argued (I'd thought) opinion paragraph on "Can a Person Who Had a Relationship with Cocaine Be Trusted as a Trainer of Abused Rescued Dogs?" The conclusion I worked out was, ab-solutely not. Then I tried to describe myself physically, and also my clothes, my L. L. Bean slippers, my backpack, et cetera, and that went nowhere, because I emerged in those lines as a short, slight-of-build human who should only be near dogs if posing with one for a catalog. And when I made the effort to list some words about my manners and behavior, and be honest about it, I found myself going for "agreeable," "consistently mature," and even "sophisticated."

Give it up, I was telling myself.

Evie, future of. In the last part of the story about the student monk who questioned his teacher, then swept the patio, then started learning how to blow in a leaf to make a beautiful sound, he's still a student. One day, he goes into a panic about the rest of his life. He's young, but he knows it's not a permanent condition. He also knows he has lots of options, even though, in his state of mind, he can't be rational about, like, making a list of what they are. So he finds himself at the windows of his monastery, look-ing out toward the hugeness of all the rest of the world, and he thinks, with tender, intense emotion, of everyone he was close to in the life he'd left behind, even the ones who did very shitty things to him, which he's still working on, in terms of forgiveness and getting over all the stuff in your background you just abso-lutely have to get over.

He grows agitated, restless. He can't sit still for meditation time, and when other monks complain, he has to be told to find a corner of his own somewhere, bothering no one but himself. Finally his old teacher comes over to him and wants to know what's going on. When he hears the words "I don't know if my future is where I am now," what does the old monk do? He throws back his head and laughs and laughs and laughs. Baffled, the student points out that this would be a good time for him to receive some guidance, and the old monk nods in agreement, and asks, "Why isn't your future the leaf you should find to practice on, because the one in your hand, take a look, is coming all apart?"

Evie, notes on. Oh my God, haiku! Of course I had to make the title seventeen syllables too. I'm calling it, "Everything Important About Evie, Human Female, Twenty-Four." Note to self: prepare Agnes for the fact that she's getting the assignment at last, but not in the way she expected. I don't want her to flunk me.

> *Came in as a stray.*
> *Is not completely hopeless.*
> *Please allow to stay.*

Thirty-Four

TWO HOURS AGO, Mrs. Auberchon had returned to the inn from seeing Mrs. Walzer and stopping in the village at the little branch of the national bank where she kept her nest egg.

This time she hadn't approached Mrs. Walzer's room with an image of herself as a sort of rescuer, sweeping in from the outside world full of hope. She hadn't planned a flutter of things to say that sounded like sentences on a greeting card. The only things she'd thought to talk about were how the pit bulls had arrived at last, and how *a young Siberian husky she didn't want was being forced on her.* But she never had the chance to talk at all, except to a duty nurse. Mrs. Walzer had requested a little something to help her sleep. She'd been sleeping badly. Her therapy to get her up on her feet again had been delayed.

Sleeping was what she was doing. Mrs. Auberchon called her name softly several times, but it was the same as speaking to just the bed or the pillow. The room was in shadowy daytime darkness.

Mrs. Auberchon asked the nurse if any of Mrs. Walzer's children or grandchildren had come to see her. The nurse put on a sympathetic expression: oh, you know, they live far away; they have busy lives, jobs; they know she's well cared for here; they call all the time. One of Mrs. Walzer's daughters had told this nurse on the phone that the family as a whole had decided to wait to travel here until their mother/grandmother was up and around and at home. They wanted to give her something to look forward to, like an incentive for getting herself healed and out of the hospital.

Absence was an incentive? Someone thought this way?

"They're a very close family," the nurse declared.

"I see," said Mrs. Auberchon. She went back to Mrs. Walzer's bedside and looked at her white hair on the white pillow, her loose and fragile skin all mottled with age spots, her slightly open old-woman's mouth, her chest rising and falling in the long, slow spaces between sedated, old-person's breathing. If she were this woman's daughter, she thought, she would have done some traveling. She would have guessed that in the room where this woman lay, the invisible presence of loneliness was the biggest thing there was.

Mrs. Auberchon could feel it. She could almost smell it. This woman had been a baker her entire life! She was a baker still! A baker should not be day-sleeping on pills in a room that smelled of being lonely!

And yet, not once in all the time she knew Mrs. Walzer did Mrs. Auberchon call her a "close friend," not even to herself. She thought about how, every time Mrs. Walzer had said something that broke Mrs. Auberchon's rules of their conversations, she, Mrs. Auberchon, would turn away, embarrassed by showing good manners, as anyone might do, she now felt, when sitting at a table with someone who sneezed without covering her mouth, or let out a belch, or outright farted.

Breaking the rules meant getting personal and also bringing up any time of Mrs. Auberchon's life that wasn't now — and yes, it was just that way, like someone disturbing her by sneezing, belching, farting.

And where would Mrs. Auberchon look away to? To her own future. Her own years in front of her as an old, white-haired woman, not here, not in the inn. Wasn't Mrs. Walzer all along just someone to come and keep her company on treat-making days? It wasn't as if the inn had neighbors. You cannot be a good inn-keeper by socializing with guests, which anyway she had none of right now. And it wasn't as if she'd become friends with the Sanctuary staffers. She certainly wasn't one of them. All these years, they'd remained a little exotic to her, like rare breeds of dogs.

She was sure that when Phyllis and Margaret and Louise and Agnes found out she planned to fix up that nearly derelict eyesore of a lodge, they'd throw all of their combined weight, which actually wasn't much, against her. Well, let them. She felt they still thought of her as a rescue who keeps on needing to be rescued. And look what they'd have to deal with! Soon she'd be rescuing them! Well, sort of.

She knew very little of their pasts. She knew almost nothing about nuns, so she couldn't be certain if they were unusual. They'd never confided a thing to her of where they'd come from or why they'd broken away from whatever they used to be part of. "Broken away" was her own phrase for how to think of them. Something about them, all four of them, made her think of dogs who looked around in their lives one day and made up their minds they had to get away from whoever it was who was being too much of an alpha with them.

Or maybe they were sick and tired of being kept in a place that was simply too small. Or maybe they'd even found themselves, in a way, as confined and attached as Shadow. They were always so partial to Sanctuary dogs who'd been rescued from being tied all the time in a yard. Those were always their favorites, and that was a fact.

Anyway, Mrs. Auberchon didn't care what they thought of her. She was going to do what she wanted. In her mind, the lodge was deteriorating more with every passing hour. Having gone in her thoughts from shabby to derelict, it was now on a path toward ruin. She wouldn't use the words "fix it up." She would say, she decided, *I am going to make sure it gets saved like my own self.*

Not that any of this was personal! She was being, she reminded herself, completely practical, realistic, and forward-looking, unlike the nuns.

It felt wonderful to be mad at the nuns all over again. They turned blind eyes to passing hours! They knew she had a nest egg, and they could have asked her for help! They were, in their own way, stupid! They couldn't even look after their own website! The website had deteriorated too! They were terrible at being in touch with the outside world!

Plus, they were purely and simply old and getting older by the minute.

And so Mrs. Auberchon, huffed up as a protection against the heavy, smothering feel of the invisible loneliness, told sleep-deaf Mrs. Walzer goodbye. Off she went for a visit to the bank, which she knew would be a good one. And here she was, in her room. She'd gone straight to her computer. The pitties were still in the stage of being settled in — that is, the ones who didn't need to be in the infirmary, which was full. They were calling it isolation, but there were almost as many humans as dogs. The jail and the holding area were kennels now. Volunteers were night-shifting, and the only ones allowed access were those who knew what they were doing with rescued fighters. It was sort of like an emergency ward, she knew. She was not an ER type of worker. No one needed the presence of a voice, talking and reading. Not yet.

But she had plenty to do. She had just finished looking at a Siberian husky website with tips for coping with shedding, mouthiness, and about one hundred other problems described by people who had those dogs in their lives. Before that, she looked at opinions people had about whether or not a Siberian husky could be successful as a therapy dog. You don't have to be a "close friend" of someone who needs a therapy dog to go ahead and bring them one.

Yes, Siberians make terrific therapy dogs, some people said.

Absolutely, completely no way, said others.

But you might as well ask the same question of a human. What type of human should be a therapist? A small one? A thin-haired one? One who didn't have eyes of different colors? One whose name wasn't Rocky?

She had taken a break from reading about pit bulls and fighting, which she could only do for short periods at a time. She wished she could feel all right about being Warden to the pitties without all this homework. She had tried to convince herself it wasn't necessary. But she knew it was. She hadn't yet opened the books she'd bought that came with photographs. She was putting that off, especially the one with a sticker on the front saying, "Contains graphic images that may be upsetting."

Tacked to the wall beside her bookshelf was a list she had made.

> *Rocky is not allowed to get up on inn furniture.*
> *Rocky is not allowed to sleep on my bed.*
> *Rocky is not allowed to lick skin except hands.*
> *Rocky is not allowed to sit begging while humans eat.*
> *Rocky is not allowed to eat human food.*
> *Rocky is not allowed upstairs in the bunkroom.*
> *Rocky is not allowed to dig holes in the yard.*
> *Rocky is not allowed to bark for no reason.*
> *Rocky is not allowed to mingle freely with guests.*

She was just about to start a search for pictures and video clips about Siberia itself, for some background, when she realized that someone was knocking on the front door.

Already? She had told that man she wanted tips on hiring professional renovation people for an old structure needing lots of work. He might have thought she meant the inn, which also would have meant she was exaggerating the need; but that didn't matter. He'd promised to ask around and have someone get in touch with her.

Mrs. Auberchon loved going into the bank, since the arrival of the new manager. She never stopped feeling pleased with herself for the way he came out of his glassed-in box of an office to greet her as a preferred customer, as he put it. He was not a native of the village but a friendly, sort of bulky and slow-moving man about her age, a little balding on top of his head, which he didn't try covering up like some men did, which meant he didn't have the personality flaw of being vain. He was as good at greeting her as Boomer. In fact, today she realized that a golden retriever was exactly the type of dog he'd reminded her of all along—a golden retriever in a suit that never fit quite right, who had gone through, as Mrs. Auberchon knew from Mrs. Walzer, an extremely ugly divorce, in which he was the innocent, blameless party. Mrs. Walzer kept her money in that bank, too. But her personal estimation of the manager was that he was as bland as store-bought white bread, and lacked social graces, and needed to be put on a diet.

Today when she asked to have a statement of her balance, he took care of it himself. He told her he was delighted that she was planning to put her nest egg into action. He was expressing this feeling, he said, as a fellow human being, not as a banker.

It seemed to Mrs. Auberchon that the low-voice conversation they fell into was a compensation for not getting to talk to Mrs. Walzer. The bank was in a hush. There were no other customers. The tellers were doing other things behind the counter, such as reading paperbacks and filing their nails. But should she worry? Did it seem she was wearing a sign that said, "I need to have a conversation"? Did the manager think she was *lonely*? Had she spoken to him like sneezing and belching and farting? Oh no!

Did she give off a sense of herself as a woman who'd like to pat him like she'd pat a golden?

He called her Mrs. Auberchon, as everyone did, as he let the conversation go on. Was her nest egg from a lifetime of saving, or was it, say, a piece of luck, like winning a lottery?

No, no, she'd never had luck, she admitted; it was half the sale of a house. A house right here in the village? Yes. A house right here in the village that she had owned half of because someone else had the right to the other half, as in, not that he was prying, please stop him *immediately* if she thought he was prying, a case of a divorce? And she'd stood there trying to think of a way to return to the subject of please can you help me find structural-renovation people? But she saw they'd gone too far beyond it. He'd already committed himself to helping with that. Yes, she'd had to say, a divorce, a long time ago. But she still went around as a Mrs.? Yes, she acknowledged, she did. Well, did the person who received the other half of the nest egg still live right here in the village?

Oh, no, she confided, no, not at all. That person had only been interested in rushing away to a new life with his new . . .

That was when she stopped talking, feeling herself prickling from her head to her feet, chafing and prickling as if she'd broken out in an awful rash on the entire inside layer of her skin. What was she *doing*? It was a bank! She didn't know anything about this man! She was such a fool! She almost hadn't been able to cut the conversation off!

It chafed and prickled even more to realize that if she'd stayed there talking even one more minute, she might have found herself so totally out of control, she'd be blurting things out that she'd regret so horribly, she couldn't even think about it.

She'd hurried out and had the luck of spotting a taxi. If it weren't for reading about pit bulls and fighting and then Siberian huskies, she couldn't imagine what she would have done with herself when she was back inside the inn. Would she have gone into a tizzy, spinning about in herself as if she contained a little tornado? Would she have thought of that bottle she'd poured down the drain the same day she saw the true condition of the lodge? Would she have wanted to do something about getting one to replace it, not to be poured down the sink?

And then it was pit bulls and husky shedding and other problems and yes or no about being a therapy dog, and someone was at the front door, and what if he'd already contacted a renovation person who'd jumped into his car, or probably truck, and was coming over? She wasn't ready for that yet! She wanted to be in charge of her own project! She would have to send him away, but what if it was *him?* What if he was on a lunch break from the bank and drove out like an alpha to be prying and pushy? She was willing to be open to the possibility of future conversations between herself and the manager, but she'd had enough for one day! If he hadn't noticed that she'd had enough, he was someone she should never speak to again, except on bank business, if she ever went in there again!

Mrs. Auberchon caught her breath with difficulty and tried to be calm as she made her way out of her room and through the kitchen and the lobby. Yet she was shaky. She wouldn't give him a piece of her mind for failing to know she'd had enough of him for now, but she was good and ready to tell him he'd made a mistake, which looked bad enough to jeopardize any further give and take between them, perhaps permanently. She would send him away like a Sanctuary dog who'd come scratching at the door. Not like Boomer. Maybe he wasn't really a golden inside. She'd have to treat him more like Tasha, overbearing, pushy Tasha, who didn't know the meaning of no, who'd slobber around and give less than a damn about anything that didn't look like it would fill her own needs.

Mrs. Auberchon remembered that Tasha had chewed up the

food processor. She remembered that she hadn't reported it. Why hadn't she reported it? Because Mrs. Walzer had a soft spot for that dog; that was why. Mrs. Walzer never recognized what a selfish, insensitive creature that Rottweiler was.

Mrs. Auberchon opened the door.

"Hi," said Evie.

The Jeep was parked just behind her, running in idle. The window on the passenger's side was rolled halfway down. Poking her head out the open space was Dora the Scottie, nose up, sniffing, enjoying a breeze that was blowing through the inn's front yard, smelling not of winter but of almost-spring. She gave her head a turn toward Mrs. Auberchon in the doorway. She recognized the Warden and sent a slightly unpleasant look her way, as if she hadn't decided whether or not to hate her guts for making her get up from her cushion in the infirmary. But she was willing to put that aside for now, she was saying, as it was lovely to be out on whatever adventure this was.

"I sort of have a problem," said Evie.

Well, there she was, in her expensive jacket. Her hair had grown longer. It was parted in the middle, pushed behind her ears. She looked tidy and alert and fresh from a shower. Mrs. Auberchon's first reaction was one of such huge relief, she very nearly threw out her arms to hug her for not being the bank manager. Then she had the sense that something was not all right, in a major way — something below the surface. She didn't know why her instincts were telling her that whatever problem Evie would talk to her about, it wasn't the same problem as the one that was bothering her.

Mrs. Auberchon reminded herself that Evie was, well, complicated.

"Come in, come in," she said. "But first turn off the Jeep. And bring in Dora. It's still pretty cold out. I don't have any treats, but I'm sure I'll find something she'll like."

Evie was shaking her head. She didn't come down here to come in. Mrs. Auberchon sighed.

"All right, what's the matter?"

"It's been a while since I drove. I sort of don't have a license. But I made it down the hill. Do you see I made it down?"

"I'm aware of that."

"I still can't believe it. Do you know where the mall is?"

Mrs. Auberchon did. There was only one, outside the village off the highway. It was the type of mall that's all enclosed: an atrium, a food court, stores with wide rectangles of front openness. She used to go out there on the bus to kill time when the inn had no guests. That was a long time ago, before she was the Warden. But she might have stopped going anyway. She hadn't liked how it felt to wander around by herself, trying to seem like she was someone temporarily separated from her friends. "I told the staffers I'd drive Dora to the mall," said Evie. "Remember when you had to drive for the new muffler because Giant George was only about ten or eleven?"

"He's fifteen," said Mrs. Auberchon.

"You know what I mean. This is the same thing, except I'm not a kid, so the reason I don't have a license isn't the same as his reason. I can't get pulled over. Or have an accident. Please don't ask me why. I'm not saying I expect something bad to happen. I think I'd drive great. I'm just saying, it's a really good idea for me not to drive anywhere, like, in public. In a just-in-case way."

"But I only got home a little while ago," said Mrs. Auberchon. "Why don't you come in and . . ."

Wait a minute here. Why would Dora need to go to the mall? She had a vivid mental flash of the Scottie sitting with Evie in some corner of the Sanctuary and saying to her, actually saying, like any girl old enough to hang around at a mall, "I want to hang around at the mall today, but obviously, being a dog, I can't get there on my own."

"Evie," said Mrs. Auberchon, "what are you talking about with the mall?"

"I'm talking about Dora and maybe adopters."

"At the mall?"

"Yes. I'm talking about . . . this."

Evie pulled a sheet of paper from a jacket pocket and unfolded it. She handed it to Mrs. Auberchon. It was an announcement of an Adopt-a-Pet-Day being held at the mall in the atrium, in a section, Mrs. Auberchon saw, that wasn't near the food court.

"They're having cats too, but I think she'll be okay with cats," said Evie. "I mean, we'll find out. And she needs a new collar. The pet store moved in a little while ago, one of those chain things. It's like a Walmart for animals. Usually I wouldn't go near it, but they're the ones sponsoring this. It's the first one, so I think we should be supportive. We can run in for a collar. It needs to be pink."

Mrs. Auberchon looked at the collar Dora was wearing. It was a standard Sanctuary fabric one, a hand-me-down. Nothing was wrong with it. Then she met Dora's eyes with her own, straight on. She thought of *left alone in an apartment for an unknown amount of time.* She thought of *obstruction from a non-food substance.* She wondered if there was such a thing as a dog being bigger than a presence of loneliness so large, it couldn't be measured.

Then she thought of Dora turning deaf ears to Beatrix Potter and scorning Mrs. Tiggy-winkle. She decided to forgive her.

"I don't like to drive, you know," she said to Evie, as a last defense. "I only keep a license because I don't want to be the kind of person who doesn't have one."

"Did you get into an accident or something, and then you gave it up?"

"No. My record is perfectly clean."

"Then you're better off than I am, Mrs. Auberchon."

"Oh, I don't know about that."

"But you can't tell them up there I'm asking you what I'm asking you. I didn't lie when I said I could drive the Jeep. I just didn't give them information I thought they didn't need to have. We need to get going, okay?"

What *was* it? A look was in Evie's eyes Mrs. Auberchon hadn't seen before. Somehow the bright excitement seemed a little too much like a gloss, hiding something that wasn't all the way hidden. Mrs. Auberchon wondered if perhaps she'd drunk too much coffee that morning. Or maybe she was on some kind of a drug—an upper type, the opposite of the stuff that was coursing through the system of Mrs. Walzer. She almost asked, as if questioning someone about pills, or whatever, was the most normal thing in the world. But that wasn't it. She was nervous, yes. She was . . . shaken. Something had rattled her. She was upset in herself in a deep place. Mrs. Auberchon realized she knew this just as she knew what was going on with a dog, just by looking at the dog on her screen. She thought of Hank and his pacing. Evie was pacing, without moving.

Again Mrs. Auberchon suggested coming inside. Again, no. It was ridiculous to stand here talking in the doorway, but at least it wasn't like the conversation in the bank. A calmness was inside Mrs. Auberchon. She was letting it grow larger, to try to absorb the vibrations coming at her from Evie. She wanted to know what was wrong. She wanted whatever was wrong to go away.

Suddenly Evie started speaking quickly, in a rush, as if she'd pressed a button to fast-forward herself. Her voice was almost yapping as she went on and on about her plans for Adopt-a-Pet Day and how she'd handle the potential adopters of Dora. Mrs. Auberchon was not to worry about how it would go! She, Evie, wasn't expecting someone to fall for Dora and then they pick her up and bring her home! She was being realistic, and she'd also be incredibly careful! She'd take names, and put anyone who signed up for Dora through a total, total background check. Plus a pink collar! Did Mrs. Auberchon agree that Dora would look fabulous in a pink collar?

Mrs. Auberchon spoke softly when Evie paused for breath. "I suppose she would. I agree. Pink would suit her. How about coming inside?"

Evie ignored that and exclaimed, "I hope they have bright pink ones, really hot ones. She's so not a pastel kind of dog. She'll probably want one with jewels, but I'm drawing the line. It's not like she'd understand what fake means. I mean, you can't explain rhinestones to a dog. Could you imagine that? Telling a dog what *rhinestones* are?"

"Evie, stop," said Mrs. Auberchon softly. "Tell me what's the matter really."

Evie blinked at her, a little stunned. "What?"

"Tell me what happened. Something happened."

Maybe it was the directness that got through to Evie, or maybe it was the tone. Mrs. Auberchon had never spoken to her in her Warden's voice before. She looked past Evie to the Jeep. Dora was still in the window, watching silently. Her Scottie face was taut with concern. Mrs. Auberchon smiled at her and wiggled her fingers in a wave. She kept her eyes on Dora for a long moment, so that Evie would have the chance to get herself together and take care of whatever it was that needed to be cared for.

A slump came over her. She blinked rapidly, as if fighting tears, although her eyes were dry. Her face went as soft as if melting with . . . surrender. She was just like dogs in Solitary who figured out that they'd never get out of there on their own.

"I saw some of the pitties," said Evie. "I mean, I saw them from the windows, from a distance, when they were coming off the truck. But this was up close. I went down there. It was early, practically not even dawn. I knew where the keys were, in the kitchen."

Mrs. Auberchon tried to imagine what Evie's eyes had seen. She did not know what to say. Then she said, "They told you not to."

"I know. But I was thinking, I'm going to have them in class. So I thought we should meet. I was only down there a little while. A volunteer threw me out."

"They don't want those dogs to get agitated with people who don't have experience," said Mrs. Auberchon.

"They didn't get agitated. Mostly, they were asleep."

"Did you look in the infirmary?"

"Just a quick peek."

Evie didn't need to say anything else about that. Her expression said everything. Mrs. Auberchon wondered if this was the way she herself looked through those horror movies she'd watched with Giant George, even though the pitties were real. A few beats of her heart went by in a speeded-up way, like she'd caught a bit of Evie's anxiety.

"I think it'll be a while before any of those dogs are ready for a training class," said Mrs. Auberchon.

"I could see that. In the kennels, some of them woke up, like they sensed me. They looked afraid of me, and sad too, and all empty, even the puppies. But it wasn't, like, me. It wasn't even afraid and sad and empty, not really, like anyone would be if just one awful thing happened and you need to get over it. It was more, they were having their usual expressions. It's like, they were telling me they don't know there's such a thing as being a dog who doesn't feel that way all the time, or *ever*. I guess it kind of got to me."

Mrs. Auberchon remembered Evie's page of writing about aliens and the monk who had a vision of Buddha. She felt a powerful aching for her. It was a little like a stomach cramp moving up toward her chest. She wondered if the heat it seemed to be generating was menopausal. Lately she'd kept herself on the lookout for hot flashes, which Mrs. Walzer described to her one treats-making day, in great detail. But she knew it wasn't that.

Everyone new to rescues, Mrs. Auberchon reminded herself, had to deal with the same thing that was happening to Evie. *It got to me.* Sometimes the "got to me" went deep, too deep, like something that could never be undone. She had to pick the right words to say in response. She had to think of just the right thing.

But Evie was telling her something else. She said, "You know what I read in an article online, when I was looking up dogfighting? A reporter doing an investigation went undercover with some hard-core fight guys, and he found out that, sometimes, they have vets who do surgeries to cut a dog's vocal cords, so the dog doesn't bark in a fight, especially in places where the fights are illegal for real, like places where the guys would actually get busted. They train dogs anyway not to bark, but with the surgery, it's guaranteed. They can put on fights in their garages and no one would hear, even if they live next door to a police station or something, or some animal-rights person. Do you know what that is, Mrs. Auberchon? That is . . . That is . . ."

Evie paused as if she would never find a way to say what she thought that was. Then she said, "What if some of our pitties had that done to them? What if, if they don't bark, it's not like when Shadow didn't? How can anyone handle that?"

Mrs. Auberchon saw her chance to take care of things. "Evie," she said, "I never heard of that happening, but maybe it's because I have a book on pit bulls and fighting and I didn't get around to it yet. But one thing I know is, if dogs came into the Sanctuary without vocal cords to bark with, the sisters would *do* something. They'd figure out, oh, maybe a sign language class. There has to be such a thing as dog sign language. Let's think about that. Let's talk about that when we're going to the—"

Evie interrupted her with a sudden sharpness. If she were a

dog, she'd be teeth-showing, snarling. Her voice was a little shrill, and sounded cold and harsh. Maybe she said what she said because she needed to use the word hate.

She was glaring at Mrs. Auberchon as if Mrs. Auberchon herself had done terrible things to an animal. "The sisters? You mean, the staffers? Of course you do. I hate it when people call people that, when they're not. I just *hate* it. Phyllis did it too. She told me one day they're all sisters. Probably, the other three told me the same thing, one way or another, but I don't remember exactly. I just tried to ignore it. But you know what? We're not on the mountain. We're down here, so could you please not call them sisters?"

"All right," said Mrs. Auberchon patiently. "I'll say ex-sisters. Or ex-nuns. The *ex* can apply, more or less. They haven't lived in a convent or dressed in habits for at least as many years as you've been on this earth. So in a way, I'm agreeing with you."

To Mrs. Auberchon's amazement, Evie's mouth opened wide, in a big, jaw-dropping O.

Uh-oh, thought Mrs. Auberchon, as she realized what was happening. I'm not helping. I'm making this worse.

And Evie said, "I'm killing Giant George. I'm finding his address and I'm taking a plane and I'm killing him. I'll drown him in that backyard pool for not *telling* me. I mean, they're nuns? How was I supposed to know they're nuns?"

"Ex," Mrs. Auberchon said. Personally, she didn't care who told what to whom, or didn't. And she wasn't going to make even one tiny comment about Giant George, or how every volunteer knew about the staffers, or how every other trainee who lasted more than a week had known about them too, usually by figuring it out on their own, plus putting together clues right in front of their eyes. Even guests of the inn who made the trek up the mountain for short visits were able to see what was what, especially if they were making donations and were invited to a meal in the hush of the dining room, or they'd had experiences with sisters in their own lives, and could tell right away. In fact, most people were not surprised at all when they found out.

And it was never a big deal. But Evie, Mrs. Auberchon knew, was not most people, and now she was all over the place inside herself, like a dog in Solitary who's just been let out — like Tasha, in fact, in her early Sanctuary days, all trouble and complications. Even if she'd only been in there ten minutes for an extremely necessary time-out, alone with herself, she'd come out glaring and mad at all humans and even madder at herself, for she always knew why she'd been in there to begin with. She'd rocket about in the hall and abruptly go into a sit and hang her head miserably, then she'd rocket about again, over and over and over, shrieking out barks as she ran, panting and whining in her sits. No one could go near her physically. Emotionally, she was also unreachable. She didn't care if she crashed into walls, had her legs slide out from under her, panted herself nearly breathless. To calm her down, while everyone on the mountain went into spasms of worry, Mrs. Auberchon had to sit at her computer with an extra feeling of confidence. In the right way, she had to speak the right words, special Tasha words, arrived at through trial and error: treats, eat, food, biscuit, jerky, chicken.

"I just remembered," Evie was saying, "how Phyllis told me something about who they are, and I laughed. It was a thing when she was talking to me in sort of a meeting we had, never mind about what. She told me they're in a cloister, and I was, that is the funniest thing I ever heard. I thought she was making up a story."

"It's not important," said Mrs. Auberchon. "It doesn't matter."

"It does. They think I'm an idiot. They think I'm borderline brain-dead."

"They don't think any such thing. Let's go back to talking about my driving."

"No thanks. I think Dora and I should go back up the mountain."

"I disagree."

Mrs. Auberchon stepped closer to Evie and patted her on the arm. When she used to watch those movies with Giant George, and she saw some horrible thing she didn't have time to close her eyes for, he put the movie on pause, and thought of a way to distract her. He'd tell her a story of a Sanctuary dog, or highlights of a rescue, or gossip he'd heard about a volunteer. She'd just remembered this. The important thing was to talk about another subject, which had to be interesting, or the distraction wouldn't work.

She took a deep breath. She could not believe she was deciding to comfort Evie by telling her the worst thing she'd ever wanted to do. She didn't take the time to get Evie ready for it. She plunged right in, so she wouldn't have the chance to change her mind. She had never told this to anyone before. But that was no reason not to tell it now. She felt the best thing to do was stay in her Warden's voice, but this time, she'd use it as if reading a book.

She said, "The reason I don't like driving is that one morning, when I was very upset, I wanted to run over my husband. Or my ex-husband, I should say."

"You were *married?*"

Mrs. Auberchon did not let on that she was sighing inside herself because that was the first thing Evie thought of saying. "It was a long time ago," she answered. "I used to have a car, but I sold it."

"Oh my God," said Evie. "What happened?"

"I was backing out of our driveway. He was near the end of it. He'd gone out to pick up the newspaper, and he was bending to pick it up. I could have called it an accident, you see. No one would know I knew exactly where he was. Ever since, I'm always a little afraid that whenever I have to drive, I'll remember that."

"Like having a flashback?"

"Yes."

"You must have been mad at him."

"I was."

"You must have had a reason."

"I did."

"Did you stop the car at the last minute, or was he still a ways away?"

"It wasn't a long driveway. It was the last minute."

"Wow," said Evie. "You were almost a murderer."

"I never put it like that. But I suppose so, yes."

Evie was looking at Mrs. Auberchon closely, straight on. A brightness had come into her eyes, and it was like seeing someone return to life. Her body was letting go of being so tense. She didn't seem to think that being taken into Mrs. Auberchon's confidence was unusual. She looked like she felt it was natural, as if people told her their worst things all the time, just blurting them out, without warning. And after the worst thing, what else was there to do but carry on with what you were supposed to be doing?

It was working! The distraction was working! Evie was snapping back to herself!

In the Jeep, Dora had decided that enough was enough with all this waiting. She chose that moment to let out loud, energetic yips, as if saying, Hello? Have you forgotten the most important one here is *me*?

Evie laughed at her, and the laughing was the opposite of harsh and shrill and cold. She cried, "Hey, you little dog! Zip it!"

That made Dora go fully into her queenly Scottie self. She shook her head from side to side and furrowed up her whole face and yapped louder. Then she lowered her head and stared at the ground, eyeing it as somewhere she'd jump to. But the window wasn't rolled down enough for her to wiggle out.

"She's such an alpha," Evie said to Mrs. Auberchon. "But I

think she's having a flashback of when she was trapped by herself in that apartment. Do you think the pitties are having flashbacks right now? I bet they are. I bet their brains are *hurting*, just from *memories*. Probably they're afraid to fall asleep because of everything they know they'll be dreaming about."

"Let's have a break from the pit bulls, Evie. And let's have a break from flashbacks. I would like very much to drive today without thinking about running someone over."

Meanwhile, Dora was upright on the driver's seat, yapping her head off, her paws on the top rim of the window glass. She seemed to believe she'd be able to push it hard enough to widen the opening.

"I think she needs to pee," said Evie. "So okay, we can have some breaks. I guess we'd better stop talking."

"I'll get my coat," said Mrs. Auberchon. "And my purse."

She hurried to her room. She'd thrown her coat on her bed. She grabbed it, grabbed her purse. Then she went to her computer to turn it off. In her absence, it switched to her screen saver. She'd forgotten she set it up with a new image. Looking at her was Rocky, attached to a wall, waiting for he didn't know what, with the beautiful watery suggestions in his fur, like waves and sea foam. She didn't have a date of arrival. Just, soon. She didn't know if someone in the Network would deliver him to the inn, or if she'd have to use the Jeep to get him at a pickup point. Would he need a new collar? He probably would. And a food bowl! A water bowl! And oh my God, food and treats! She hadn't even thought of these things! And chew toys! A dog bed! A brush! A leash!

She put on her coat. She put her purse on her arm. She turned to leave, but turned back, and went to the wall where she'd hung up her list. She yanked it down so hard, the tack that held it popped out and fell to the floor. She had to find it and pick it up. You cannot have tacks lying around a room a dog will enter.

She found it. She put it in a drawer and balled up the list and tossed it at her wastebasket. She missed the shot. But she'd have to leave it for later. Outside, Dora was terrier-barking and Evie was calling to her, impatiently, bark-like, at the top of her lungs.

"Mrs. Auberchon, hurry up! Come!"

Acknowledgments

In the thirty-five years I've been writing and publishing novels, I've been lucky in many ways to work with excellent editors and publishing teams, but I have to say that with *Mountaintop*, my past experiences were practice for the best one I've ever had. My team at Houghton Mifflin Harcourt blends solid professionalism with plain old human caring, warmth, passion, and commitment.

My editor, Jenna Johnson, entered the world of my novel not as an overbearing visitor or outside consultant (I've had those types), but as a partner who came to live there for a while, bringing her keen intelligence, insightfulness, wit, and natural ability to make a writer end up saying *I'm better than I was before she edited me.* And I'm hugely grateful that everyone behind my book, in production, promotion, sales, and social media, made me glad for their energy and attentiveness, and a belief in *Mountaintop* that has been, to me, probably because I live in coastal Maine, a tide that came in when the book was in manuscript, and has shown no sign of ever going out. Thank you especially Stephanie Kim, Hannah Harlow, Chelsea Newbould, Nina Barnett, Chrissy Kurpeski, Lisa Glover, Liz Anderson, and Carla Gray. To my copy editor, Margaret Wimberger, with whom I spent many happy hours absorbed in repairs and grammar-geek stuff, I have only one comment: I can't wait to do it again next time.

I've dedicated *Mountaintop* to my agent, Joy Harris, and I hope it covers at least some of my gratefulness for everything she's done as the engine powering it forward. From the moment she finished reading the first draft and called to say "I love it," I've felt her strength and conviction as forces I've come to rely on, even take for granted. One way or another, her presence is with me all the time.

When I was first gathering myself to write what I was only so far calling "a novel with dogs," I had the accidental good fortune to connect with a longtime rescuer who belongs to a secret group involved in kidnapping chronically abused dogs, often at great risk, when there are no legal, neighborly, or other possibilities. My gratitude is deep for the education I was able to receive, even though, like my main character Evie in her trainer-trainee learning, I often wished I was not finding out what I was finding out about real-life details of maltreatment of animals. But I don't think I'm writing fiction when I say I believe that for every abuser, there are many, many more rescuers.

It's impossible to list all the help I received from trainers, rescuers, shelter people, and adopters who shared their stories with me and trusted me to get them right. Over and over, no matter the specifics of the harm or the rescue, one thing came clear to me, with the beautiful shine of truth: a dog who has suffered at the hands of humans is always willing to give another human a chance. I'm deeply grateful to all the dog-people who made me less alone as I was writing this book, especially the two rescue groups my own dogs came from: Memphis Area Golden Retriever Rescue (MAGRR), who brilliantly and passionately run a program for Tennessee–to–New England adoptions, and Puppy Love, Inc., on Bailey Island here in Maine, founded and expertly run in partnership with rescuers in Louisiana and elsewhere in the South, with a mission to save dogs in high-kill shelters.

As I type the words "high-kill shelters," my youngest dog, Maxine, a wire-haired terrier/retriever mix, is sleeping on her favorite blanket on the floor of my writing room. She is here because a volunteer rescuer removed her from a cage that was the only home she'd known. The rescue occurred not even one hour before she was scheduled, at the age of seven months, to be euthanized, because there are more homeless dogs in the world than people who think to adopt one, even though there are way more people than dogs. So, to Maxine's rescuer, and all rescuers, and everyone involved in rehabilitating and loving animals hurt by humans, *thanks.*